Scraping the bottom of the barrel . . .

She approached her booth from the rear but was able to see her pickle barrel, which stood to the side of the shelves of jars and spices. Her green tarp was still in place over those items, but the barrel lid was definitely up. Piper stopped, suddenly afraid to see what might have happened to her precious container. Trash dumped into it? Worse?

Ben caught up with her and paused, following her gaze. He continued a few steps more. Piper watched his face as he made his way to the front of the barrel. His mouth worked soundlessly, then she heard, "Good God."

"What?" Piper lurched forward to see for herself.

Two legs, partly covered in tasseled socks and barely edged with a tartan kilt, hung over the rim of her pickle barrel—the same kilt and socks she remembered seeing the day before on Alan Rosemont. The legs were attached to a torso about Rosemont's size that was pitched forward into the barrel, deep into Piper's pickling brine. A bagpipe lay on the ground nearby, deflated and looking as dead as the body in the barrel . . .

To Lorraine + Al,

Happy reading

The
Pickled Piper

Fondly,

MARY ELLEN HUGHES

Mary Ellen Hughes

BERKLEY PRIME CRIME, NEW YORK

THE BERKLEY PUBLISHING GROUP
Published by the Penguin Group
Penguin Group (USA) LLC
375 Hudson Street, New York, New York 10014

USA • Canada • UK • Ireland • Australia • New Zealand • India • South Africa • China

penguin.com

A Penguin Random House Company

THE PICKLED PIPER

A Berkley Prime Crime Book / published by arrangement with the author

For information, address: The Berkley Publishing Group,
a division of Penguin Group (USA) LLC,
375 Hudson Street, New York, New York 10014.

ISBN: 978-0-425-26245-0

PUBLISHING HISTORY
Berkley Prime Crime mass-market edition / May 2014

PRINTED IN THE UNITED STATES OF AMERICA

10 9 8 7 6 5 4 3 2 1

Cover illustration by Chris O'Leary.
Cover design by Sarah Oberrender.
Interior text design by Laura K. Corless.

For my sister, Barbara Gawronski, who's always been an inspiration.

Acknowledgments

Top thanks definitely go to my endlessly supportive husband, Terry, who, when I wondered what to write about next, said "pickles." Though I'd laughed, that seed of an idea took root (a dill seed?), and before long Piper, Aunt Judy, Uncle Frank, and the many people of Cloverdale, New York, came to life, and a new series was born. They and I are highly indebted to him.

I'm very grateful to my agent, Kim Lionetti, for her encouragement and efforts on my behalf, and to my editor, Faith Black, along with the other hardworking people at Berkley Prime Crime, who sanded and polished this book with their talents and skills to its final stage.

Many thanks, once again, to my long-standing and ever-patient critique group—Ray Flynt, Lynda Sasscer Hill, Debbi Mack, Sherriel Mattingly, and Marcia Talley—who did their meticulous first readings and either cheered or steered me back on track with their tough love whenever I strayed.

Finally, gratitude is due to the many fine cooks who, over

Acknowledgments

the years, developed the intricacies of pickling and preserving. Without them our meals would be so much less tasty, and the idea for a mystery mixed with a dash of vinegar and spice might never have taken root.

1

~~~~~

Piper's phone chirped just as she picked up a six-pack of sweet gherkins. She groaned and carefully set the carton back down in the rear of her Chevy hatchback to pull out her phone. A second groan escaped when she saw the name of the caller on her display. She answered anyway.

"Yes, Scott?"

"Piper! You won't believe the amazing meal I just had."

"You called from Tibet to tell me about your dinner?"

"But you like food! You're always talking about your pickling stuff."

"Not on calls from halfway round the world. Why don't you e-mail me about it? Send me the recipe if you want. I can't really talk now, Scott. I'm in the middle of setting up at the fair."

"You're still in Cloverdale?"

Piper drew a deep breath and tucked a strand of brown hair firmly behind her ear. Scott Littleton, her onetime fiancé, had a definite blind spot for retaining things she told him. "Yes, Scott, I'm still in Cloverdale because I moved here, remember? I physically transferred all my belongings from Albany to Cloverdale. I signed a lease on a building, moved in, and opened up a shop in Cloverdale."

"Yes, but I didn't know you were really going to stay there."

"Well, now you know." Did he realize they weren't actually engaged anymore? Sometimes Piper wondered. An orange Toyota pulled up next to her. "I've got to go. Have a good breakfast tomorrow." Or would it be today? Piper had a hard time keeping all the time zones Scott was traveling through straight. She closed her phone as an arm reached out from the Toyota and waved.

"I hope none of my jars cracked," Amy Carlyle called. "I really worried about them as I bounced over some of these ruts."

"We'll find out!" Piper picked up her gherkins once more, and Amy climbed out to grab a box from her own car. Or rather, her father's car, on loan. Amy had recently returned home after studying at culinary school and currently worked two jobs—one at the A La Carte restaurant, and one at Piper's shop—while living at home and saving assiduously for a hoped-for restaurant of her own. Piper felt extremely lucky to have her.

As they lugged their loads across the open space to the vendors' booths, Piper took in the colorful sight of the fairgrounds set up at the edge of town and breathed deeply of the fresh, late-August morning air. A feeling she couldn't quite label burbled up inside her. A good feeling, so good it almost made her cry. Piper felt that she, like Amy, had come home, even though Cloverdale hadn't strictly been her home. She'd spent only summers there at Aunt Judy and Uncle Frank's farm from the time she could walk and talk. The thing was, those summers were the happiest times of her life. It just took her too many years to realize that.

"Nate will fetch the other box from my car," Amy said. "I called him on my way over."

"Great. Uncle Frank picked up a bunch from the shop earlier, which helps tremendously." Piper had temporarily closed her newly opened shop, Piper's Picklings, to participate in the fair, aware that most of her customers would be there anyway so she might as well join them. Besides, it would be terrific fun, except, of course, for all the work of lugging over heavy jars of her hand-pickled vegetables and boxes of uniquely blended pickling spices.

She reached her booth along with Amy and set down her carton with a relieved sigh. Next up was unloading and arranging. "How do you want them lined up?" Amy asked.

"Alphabetically. I'm not going to worry about keeping vegetables with vegetables and fruits with fruits, or anything else. Just plain old A to Z."

"Works for me!" Amy quickly found a jar of pickled apples and got started. Soon she had pickled artichoke hearts, beans, beets, and corn in place. Piper started at the other end, lining up pickled zucchini, watermelon, and tomatoes.

As she worked, Piper remembered how years ago in Aunt Judy's kitchen, she'd been amazed to see how just about any vegetable or fruit could be pickled. Not just in the familiar cucumber pickle brine, but each in its own

3

wonderful concoction of spices. Piper had traditional cucumber pickles for the fair, of course, and had set up an old-fashioned barrel of dill pickles floating in filled-to-the-brim brine, an eye-catching display that had already garnered many compliments.

Piper's new shop actually focused on pickling spices. But she liked to have jars of all these delightful, sweet, tangy, spicy foods to demonstrate to customers who were new to the idea of pickling just what they could do with her spice blends. Many bought a jar or two to take home and soon came back to purchase the spices for making their own—as well as recipe books and canning tools. That was always so satisfying to Piper, winning over a new convert.

"There's nothing like biting into your own custom-made, crisp cucumber dill in December," Aunt Judy often said, and Piper heartily agreed.

"Oh, there's Nate," Amy said. Piper looked up to see Nate Purdy winding his way through the crowded fairgrounds carrying one more carton of Piper's jars. Amy waved to catch his attention. "Over here!"

Piper saw Nate's face light up as he caught sight of Amy, who looked particularly pretty in a green top and jeans that showed off her trim figure. She'd pulled her red curls up and off her neck, taming them, at least for the time being, with a green hair tie.

Piper had heard all about the two meeting just weeks ago during Amy's bus ride home from culinary school. Nate had been traveling with his guitar to a gig in upstate New York and halfway there had learned it was canceled. Left with a ticket to nowhere, Nate decided on the spot to disembark at Cloverdale, which not-too-coincidentally happened to be exactly where Amy was getting off. Before long, he managed to land a nightly gig at A La Carte, the restaurant where Amy also worked.

Seeing the lights dance in both their eyes as Nate drew nearer made Piper smile but also brought on a bit of wistfulness. She and Scott had once been like them, though it now seemed eons ago. The end of their long relationship had been one of the prods that spurred Piper toward this new start in life, though Scott apparently believed he had simply put their engagement on a temporary hiatus.

"A few months, that's all I need," he'd said, claiming the many years working toward his law degree followed by the long hours on the job as a prosecutor at the State Attorney's office in Albany hadn't allowed him to really "find himself."

Since not too long before that, Scott's main obsession had been finding the perfect sushi bar within walking distance of Albany City Hall, Piper at first didn't take him seriously. When he announced he'd sold his retractable-hardtop convertible Volvo C70 to help finance a trip to Tibet, however, she had to believe him.

Scott took off, but instead of sitting and waiting hopefully for him to find his way back, Piper decided it was time to live life for herself. She quit her unfulfilling job in the state tax office and promptly packed up for Cloverdale. The decision, though wrenching at the time, turned out to be the best thing she could have done. Though she did, once in a while, miss—

"Here you go!" Nate plopped down the heavy carton of jars, snapping Piper back to the present.

"Thanks so much, Nate," she said. "That looks like the last of the bunch."

"Glad to help." Nate pushed strands of his dark blond hair off his face, looking much too young to be on his own, scraping together a living in the uncertain world of musical performance. Did he have family to fall back on? If so, where were they? Piper was naturally curious but didn't want to pry. The important thing was that Nate was a likable as well as talented person who seemed very pleased to find himself in Cloverdale.

"Did you get the job?" Amy asked. Her face fell when Nate shook his head.

"They gave it to the old guy."

"What job?" Piper asked over her shoulder while setting a jar of pickled squash on the shelf.

"Master of ceremonies for the fair talent show," Amy said, crestfallen. "It was perfect for Nate. He could have opened the show with one of his own songs and kept everything lively by performing between acts. He would have been great!"

"And who got it instead?"

"Alan Rosemont." Amy spoke the name in a tone Piper might have used for finding mold on a tomato.

"Is he the man who owns the antique shop?" Piper vaguely remembered seeing a man of about fifty through the cluttered windows of Cloverdale Country Antiques, a shop she hadn't yet been into.

"That's him. And he's been master of ceremonies for the fair talent show since caveman days. He tells these same, lame jokes year after year, and his idea of musical entertainment is playing the bagpipes!"

"I wouldn't mind so much," Nate said, "if he was any

6

good playing them. But it's pretty bad when you can actually tell a bagpiper's missing notes."

"He uses any excuse at all to wear his Scottish outfit," Amy added, "which gets a bit silly, if you ask me." She shivered dramatically. "That bagpipe is so awful!"

Piper had never attended the Cloverdale Fair during her summers with Aunt Judy and Uncle Frank, usually having headed home to get ready for school by the time the fair began, so she couldn't say if this assessment of Rosemont's talents was correct or colored by Nate's having lost out to him. Suddenly, to Piper's pleasant surprise, thoughts of Aunt Judy miraculously brought her into view.

"Hellooo!" Piper's plumpish, white-haired aunt called from a spot near the ceramics booth. Her arms were wrapped around a cardboard carton of her own.

"I'm taking my jams to the judging tent," Aunt Judy said, indicating her load with a head tilt.

"Let me give you a hand." Nate sprang forward to help, and Aunt Judy made mild noises of protest while gratefully yielding her heavy box.

"I'll stop by later," she called over her shoulder as the two took off.

"He's so thoughtful," Amy said, smiling.

Piper agreed but turned briskly back to work. The crowd was growing and her booth was still a disorganized mess. Amy pitched in, needing little direction, and demonstrating to Piper once again how lucky she was to have her. With only part-time employment as assistant chef at A La Carte available, an opportunity for excellent training Amy wasn't about to pass up, she'd grabbed Piper's offer of a few hours'

work at her shop, especially since Piper was happy to schedule the time around Amy's restaurant hours.

Amy's presence at the shop allowed Piper precious time
off, but she was particularly helpful with Piper's pickling
efforts. Amy could slice up pounds of vegetables like
nobody's business and could more than handle the cooking
end. She'd even created a new recipe for pickled orange
slices that Piper was delighted with and gave Amy full
credit for, naming that blend of spices after her. All in all,
Amy was a treasure of an employee for whom Piper
thanked her lucky stars daily.

"Are there really pickles in that great big barrel?" A
grandfatherly man stood with two young children on the
other side of Piper's counter. He wore a hopeful, happy
grin.

"Absolutely," Piper assured him. "Crispy dills, floating
in brine. And you can pick your own." Each of the children
had paper-wrapped hot dogs in their hands, as did their
grandfather, who was by this time nearly drooling as he
gazed at the pickle barrel. He slapped down his money,
and Piper lifted the barrel lid to let the three pull out the
dills of their choice with their own set of handy tongs.

Piper had actually pickled the cukes in crocks lined up
in her basement. For the fair she'd transferred them to this
specially ordered, ceramic-lined barrel with an old-timey
wooden finish on the outside. The barrel had been expensive, but it was proving to be worth every penny for drawing people to her booth. Piper hoped to use it for many
fairs to come.

Grandpop and grandkids wandered off to the sound of
crisp chomps and pleased *mmms*.

"I'll bet they'll be back again," Amy said. "Or at least send us everyone they run into."

"Hope so," Piper said, then grinned. "Or I'll be eating a lot of dill pickles in the coming months."

"Not such a bad thing," Amy said. "But I wouldn't worry about leftovers. I'd worry about running out."

"Ah, the optimism of youth!" Piper said, laughing as she turned back to arranging her jars.

"I'm nearly twenty-one!" Amy protested, handing Piper two jars of okra. "And you're not exactly decrepit."

"No." Piper grinned. "Not exactly. But the nine or so years I have on you just might give me a slightly more realistic view of things." Like the realization that spending your life catering to someone else's dreams can be a huge waste of time.

"Well, I don't care how old I get, I'll never stop believing that just about anything can work out if you want it badly enough."

Piper smiled noncommittally and took a third jar from Amy's hands. She privately hoped, however, that when—not if—Amy learned otherwise, it wouldn't be too painful.

2

~~~~~

The fair was in full swing, with crowds of families milling about between rides, livestock exhibits, and vendors, some holding bags of their purchases.

Piper's booth, to her delight, was drawing brisk sales, both from her pickle barrel and one other surprising item—her pickled watermelon. On an impulse, she'd set a couple of jars on the front counter, next to the brochures she'd printed up to introduce her shop. The jars piqued plenty of interest, and Piper soon found herself explaining to many a customer that these were in fact pickles made from watermelon rinds, and that the sweet, tangy flavor came from the combination of vinegar, brown sugar, sliced lemon, cinnamon, allspice, and cloves. Usually before she'd run through the entire list of ingredients, hands would dip into pockets or purses to buy, and Amy would be reaching for replacements from the back.

Next in line of popularity were Piper's boxes and packets of spices, which were eye-catching to anyone interested in preserving their own delicious bounty of garden produce. Piper had just bagged up one such purchase when a male to her right said in a deep, rolling voice, "Hi there, sugarplum." A salt-and-pepper-haired man with a slight paunch stood on the other side of the counter, his thumbs hooked into the belt of his black uniform.

"Hi, Daddy," Amy said. She leaned over to plant an affectionate kiss on Sheriff Carlyle's cheek. "But please," she begged in a low voice, "don't call me sugarplum in public."

"Hello, Amy." Piper hadn't noticed the man next to the sheriff until he spoke. Younger, dark-haired, and an inch or two taller than the sheriff, he wore what Piper at first took to be a deputy's uniform until she spotted the badge on the sleeve that said "Auxiliary Officer." He was gazing at Amy with near puppy-dog eagerness.

"Hi, Ben," Amy said much more casually, as though greeting an often-seen older cousin. "I see you're helping Dad for the weekend." She turned to Piper. "You know my dad, but have you met Ben Schaeffer?"

"No, I haven't. How do you do?" Piper extended a hand to the man who wrenched his gaze away from Amy with obvious effort. "What is an auxiliary officer?" she asked after his quick handshake.

"It's a new volunteer program," Sheriff Carlyle explained. "Ben, here, is our top man. The volunteers fill in a few hours a week as an extra set of eyes and ears for the department."

"Do you make arrests?"

"Oh no," Ben assured her. He had pulled himself up a little straighter and tucked his shirt in a bit tighter. "But we'll definitely issue warnings to speeders if we catch them on radar."

"The auxiliary officers operate the radar guns from our squad cars," Sheriff Carlyle informed her. "Just seeing the cars parked along the highway works to slow down most traffic. They also pitch in on things like directing traffic. It really helps free up my deputies."

"Sounds like a great program."

Both the sheriff and Ben voiced agreement, but Piper noticed Ben's gaze had turned back to Amy. Amy, however, was looking over his shoulder into the crowd.

"Here comes your Aunt Judy," she said, "and Nate!"

The faces of both men darkened perceptively before they turned. Piper didn't believe for a moment it was because of Aunt Judy, who was just about the best-loved person in Cloverdale. So the negativity must have been meant for Nate.

"You should see Alice Kippler's peach pies!" Aunt Judy exclaimed as she came near. "Absolutely beautiful. They'll win a prize for sure. Oh, hello, Sheriff Carlyle. And Ben! How nice to see you both."

The sheriff and Ben greeted Aunt Judy warmly but barely managed a nod for Nate. Nate seemed blissfully unaware, having quickly circled around to Amy. The sheriff continued to respond amiably to Aunt Judy's chatter, but Piper saw Ben watching Amy and Nate, and the look on his face, though showing dislike of Nate, included enough pain to make Piper's own heart ache for him.

The man was obviously crazy about Amy, yet Amy

seemed oblivious. Each nod of her head toward the young musician, each laugh at Nate's jokes or touch of his arm made the auxiliary officer wince. Piper saw the sheriff glance Ben's way then take in Amy and Nate with a shake of his head. Sheriff Carlyle at least was aware of Ben's feelings, even if his daughter was not. And he clearly didn't care much for her leanings toward Nate.

Later on, during the late afternoon lull, Piper found a chance to talk to Amy about what she had observed. Amy would be taking off soon for her job at A La Carte and was checking for any last-minute things she could do.

"So, Ben Schaeffer," Piper said, plowing right in. "I guess you've known him a long time?"

"Ben?" Amy pulled a handful of brochures from their under-counter box and started refilling the wire "Take One" holders. "Oh, sure. I've known him, like, forever. He's my friend Megan's older brother."

"Ah, Megan Schaeffer. I should have connected the name. How much older?"

"Gee, let me think. He was graduating from college when we were sixteen, I remember. So he must be . . . twenty-seven!"

"You sound surprised."

"I am. Twenty-seven isn't that old. But Ben always seemed like one of the grown-ups when I was just a kid showing up at Megan's to play. And he spends so much time with my dad. I suppose that makes me think of him as part of Dad's generation. But he's only twenty-seven. Wow!" Amy shook her head.

"What does he do when he's not volunteering for the sheriff's department?"

"Ben has his own insurance office. It's over on Beech Street near the bank."

"Very enterprising." And possibly very dull and mundane to someone like Amy, who clearly leaned toward the more creative things in life. Her father, however, might see it very differently, caring more for the financial stability of anyone showing interest in his daughter. Something he clearly wasn't seeing in Nate Purdy.

Amy's thoughts had clearly left Ben for Nate, too, though in a much more upbeat way. She checked her watch, saying, "Nate should be here any minute to ride with me over to A La Carte."

"He's performing tonight?"

"No, they canceled tonight, figuring a low turnout because of the fair. But he needs to pick up his guitar to practice some new material." She scanned the crowd, frowning as she didn't see him. "He really could have used the talent show gig, you know. A La Carte doesn't pay all that much. But Alan Rosemont has the fair organizers under his thumb, just like he has most everyone else around here."

The name started ringing more bells for Piper. "Is Rosemont on the town council?"

"Uh-huh. And you'd think he was elected mayor by the number of times he manages to get his way on council decisions. Dad's been aggravated more than once because of his penny-pinching on things that affect his department."

"Tina Carson, the woman who just opened the coffee shop down the street from me, also had problems with him,

I remember now. Rosemont felt that part of town had enough eateries and wanted to block approval for her permit."

"I'm not surprised. But she got to open her shop after all."

"Right, after a major struggle."

"Oh, there's Nate!" Amy reached down to grab her purse from under the counter.

Piper looked over to see Nate winding his way through the crowd. He was perhaps thirty feet away when she heard someone call out sharply, "Purdy!" Nate stopped and looked to his left. Piper followed his gaze to see a large man of about fifty dressed in a Scottish kilt and tasseled socks closing in on the musician. She caught her breath as she observed the dark look on the man's face and his clenched hands. Several people in his path scattered out of the way.

"Who is that?" Piper asked, though from the costume she thought she could guess.

"Oh Lord. It's Alan Rosemont. What does he want?"

"Trouble, it looks like."

Rosemont's face was florid as he shouted at Nate, shaking a fist. "I want you to keep away from my shop from now on!" he said. "You cost me a major sale, putting your worthless two cents in when nobody asked you. You wouldn't know a samurai sword from a Swiss Army knife."

Nate's face flushed. "I know enough to tell what's genuine and what's not."

"Oh yeah? And you've been handling antiques for how long?" Rosemont asked with a sneer. He had now closed in on Nate, but still shouted. "You're nothing but a deadbeat

15

troublemaker, Purdy, poking your nose into other people's business. We don't need your kind here."

"My kind?" Nate drew in a deep breath before asking, "You mean someone who hates to see a tourist being suckered? Or do you mean someone who actually knows a thing or two about music and might run a decent talent show?"

"Oh, so you're mad you didn't get the MC spot? Too bad. You can't just show up out of nowhere and take things over, you know. It doesn't work that way, buddy. The job goes to the best man, around here."

Piper watched with growing concern. If she didn't know better she would have sworn she saw steam begin to rise from Nate's head. The area around the two had cleared as people stepped back but stayed near enough to watch.

"Nate," Amy said in a low, worried voice, "let it be."

But Nate, despite a visible struggle, apparently couldn't. "Don't worry, Rosemont, you'll probably always keep your MC spot. But only because you've bullied your way into it. Not because you're any good."

Rosemont's already florid face turned purple. "Why you little—" he cried, swinging hard at Nate, who easily sidestepped the clumsily thrown right.

"Fight! Fight!" a high-pitched voice pealed from the crowd.

"Nate! No!" Amy cried.

Nate turned toward Amy. Rosemont was bouncing on his feet, both fists raised and ready, but looking somewhat worried—and in his kilt, sagging as it was under a significant paunch, just a bit ridiculous.

Nate glanced from Rosemont back to Amy, then stalked

away toward Piper's booth, clearly simmering. "Let's go," he said to Amy, who grabbed her purse and dashed out from behind the counter. The two took off, and the crowd, disappointed, began to disperse. When Piper looked back, Alan Rosemont was nowhere to be seen.

"A grown man making such a scene in public," Aunt Judy said, shaking her head and bouncing her short white curls. She'd joined Piper at the booth not long after Amy and Nate hurriedly left, holding her dog, Jack, on a leash. Jack, a black-and-white mixed breed, had shown up at their farm several weeks ago, fur matted and emaciated, and had stayed ever since.

"I asked Frank to bring Jack along when he came to the fair," her aunt explained, looking fondly at the pet, who actually seemed to be smiling back. "I hated to leave him alone all day. We'll take turns looking after him, today." She leaned down to ruffle Jack's now-shiny fur and pat his plumped-up side. "I know he'll behave because he's such a good dog, aren't you?" Jack wagged his fluffy tail and yipped apparent agreement.

"As far as Alan's concerned," Aunt Judy said, "I'm sure that losing a sale is annoying. But why broadcast it to the world? And is it really that important who gets to direct a talent show?"

"That part does sound a bit middle school," Piper agreed, "though for Nate the added income was important. I doubt that was Rosemont's concern, which makes me wonder what's truly behind his anger." Piper's thoughts flashed to

Ben Schaeffer. "He wouldn't have an interest in Amy, would he?"

"Amy's half his age and then some!" Aunt Judy protested, then added, "Not that that always means anything. But no, dear. I don't think so. Alan has been seeing Brenda Franklin fairly steadily. At least where age is concerned, she's more his type."

"At *least* agewise? Sounds like you have reservations on the rest of that relationship."

"Well, it's not for me to say, is it? It's just, oh, Alan Rosemont is a man who likes to have his own way. I suppose that's what riled him up about Nate, the fact that anyone would challenge him on anything whatsoever."

"Amy said he's led the talent show since caveman days."

Aunt Judy smiled. "Not quite. He's only been here in Cloverdale for—let me see—ten years?"

"That's all?"

"Yes, I'm sure that's right. He took over Bob MacAulay's hardware store space to open his antique shop when Bob decided to close up and retire to Florida. That was ten years ago."

"He certainly seems to have developed plenty of influence in Cloverdale in that amount of time. I mean, he's got a powerful position on the town council, and he's obviously forged strong connections with the decision makers of the fair."

"That he has." Aunt Judy's brows pulled together with concern.

Piper looked off in the direction that Nate had gone with Amy. How badly might it impact that young musician, she wondered, that he had managed to cross someone like

Alan Rosemont? But then she shook her head. It was, after all, just one argument between them. In a day or two, everyone involved would forget about their differences and move on.

Or so she hoped.

3

~~~~~~

"Why don't you take a break, Piper?" Aunt Judy suggested. "I'll be glad to watch the booth for you; that is, if you trust me to handle it?"

Piper laughed. "Since you're the one who taught me everything I know about pickling, I don't think you'd have any trouble. But if you're sure you don't mind, I'd love to find a quiet place to sit down. Just for a few minutes."

"Then go. Scoot!" Aunt Judy made sweeping motions with her hands. "Jack can lie here in the shade and people watch. You'll like that, won't you, Jack?" Currently crunching on the dog biscuit Aunt Judy had slipped him, Jack seemed just fine with the arrangement. A thoughtful look crossed Aunt Judy's face. "There's a nice, shady bench behind the youth group's concession stand. You could grab something cool to drink there and relax."

"Sounds good."

"Oh, and would you mind giving Will Burchett a message for me while you're there?"

"Sure. Who's Will Burchett?"

"Will bought the Christmas tree farm from the Andersons two years ago. He's running the barbecue grill at the stand today, to help out with the fund-raising. Tell him if he runs low on onions for the barbecue, I threw a couple of bags in the truck. He can just call Frank or me if he needs them."

"Okay. See you in a bit."

"Take your time," her aunt called out as Piper took off in the direction of the food concessions and the youth group stand. She didn't have to search hard, as the aroma of spicy barbecue soon wafted her way, allowing her to follow her nose.

She waited her turn at the counter, watching as a busy group of teens filled orders for hungry fairgoers, looking like they were having a great time while raising money for their organization. They scuttled back and forth between the front counter and a smoke-spewing grill at the rear, manned by someone in a blue T-shirt who Piper assumed was Will Burchett.

When she got her tall cup of lemonade, Piper went around to the back to deliver her aunt's message. She'd been expecting someone about Uncle Frank's age, but the closer she got, the more off the mark she realized she'd been.

"Will Burchett?" she asked of the tall man whose back was to her. The T-shirt topped trim khaki shorts, and the arms wielding the cooking tongs were muscular and tanned. A huge, sauce-stained apron was tied at his back.

"Be right with you," a baritone voice answered as Burchett flipped two meaty ribs and slathered them with thick red sauce. He set his tongs down and turned around.

Piper gazed up at the bluest eyes she'd ever seen, set into an even-featured face. But what she liked most was the solid, open expression on that face, a kind of what-you-see-is-what-you-get, no-games look. She smiled.

"Judy Lamb asked me to tell you she has plenty of onions on hand, and you can call her or my Uncle Frank whenever you need them."

"Great! You're their niece?"

Piper held out her hand. "Piper Lamb. I have a pickling booth across that way."

Burchett grabbed a towel to wipe his hands before shaking hers. "Nice to meet you." He kept on shaking. "Your aunt mentioned you, and I meant to stop by your shop sometime. But things have been kind of busy at the tree farm."

"Yes, I can imagine there's a lot to do." Piper thought she should probably pull her hand back, but it felt really nice enveloped in his large one.

"Mr. Burchett? Two more burgers?"

"Coming up, Shawn." Burchett released Piper's hand and slapped two beef patties on his grill.

"I'll get out of your way," Piper said, stepping back reluctantly.

"Ah, right. Sorry. Got to keep up with this. But, hey, thank your aunt for me. And I, ah, I'll stop by at your shop sometime and say hello."

"That'd be great. Nice meeting you, Will."

Piper backed away, holding her drink, then remembered

the shady bench that was supposed to be nearby. She found it and sat, taking a sip from her lemonade and thinking what a nice guy Will Burchett seemed to be, volunteering his time for a good cause as he was. She hoped he really would come by her shop.

S hortly before eight the next morning, Piper was sipping the last of her coffee in the apartment over her shop, when she heard familiar beeps out back. She ran to her bedroom window and threw it open.

"Morning, Uncle Frank!"

"Good morning, peanut." Uncle Frank had called Piper "peanut" as long as she could remember, and though she'd eventually grown taller than her aunt and stood within an inch or two of her burly uncle, she was happy to still be called that—but only by Uncle Frank. He leaned out of the cab of his freshly washed tan Ford pickup.

"Can I take any more heavy stuff out to the fair for you?"

"Sure! I'll be right down." Piper dashed down to the shop to unlock her back door, then ran about gathering up jars of the pickled vegetables she'd decided to take— definitely more pickled watermelon—and packing them carefully into divided cardboard boxes. Uncle Frank walked in, pulling off a green John Deere cap and smoothing down the few remaining strands of his gray hair.

"I have to swing by the garage to pick up a tractor part," he said, "but I'll get these to you by the time the fair opens up."

"That'll be fine. Oh, I got a call from Mom and Dad

last night. They arrived in Bulgaria. Said to give you and Aunt Judy their love."

"Bulgaria. Well, well." Uncle Frank gave a low chuckle. "That brother of mine does get around, doesn't he?"

Piper smiled. Although her father and his brother had grown up together and even resembled each other physically, they couldn't have chosen any more widely divergent paths in life. Uncle Frank considered a drive to Albany a major excursion, whereas Piper's father had been twice around the world with his archeological pursuits.

"We both like to dig in the dirt," Uncle Frank often joked. "Only difference is the things I come up with are a bit fresher and they're edible. But the things he digs up he can write about. I don't know anybody'd want to read about my beets or carrots."

"Maybe not, but I can't pickle an old candlestick, can I?" Piper would respond.

Uncle Frank's organic farm provided most of the fruits and vegetables that Piper preserved with her pickling spices. And Aunt Judy grew in her garden several of the herbs that Piper dried and either used or packaged for sale. They were the perfect team, as far as Piper was concerned, and she was daily grateful that her Uncle Frank had chosen farming rather than anything he could write about.

"Just these two boxes should do it," she said. Uncle Frank reached for the larger of the two and headed out. Piper followed close behind with the second, unsurprised—once she stepped out—to see Jack occupying the passenger seat of her uncle's truck. Jack yipped an excited greeting, and as soon as Piper deposited her load in the back of the cab she reached over to rub his ears and receive a few juicy licks.

Uncle Frank climbed into the driver's seat. "Thanks a bunch," Piper said, giving her uncle a kiss on his leathery cheek. He started his engine and pulled off, a well-tanned arm waving out the window as the truck disappeared around the corner.

As she watched him go, Piper thought of all the summers she'd spent with Aunt Judy and Uncle Frank. Though Piper knew her parents loved her dearly, she had realized long ago—and gamely accepted—that they loved archeology even more. Each summer, therefore, they flew off to far-flung corners of the world to pursue their passion, parts that were usually less than congenial for children, and therefore Piper was sent to Cloverdale. Not that—once Piper fully understood what they were up to—she ever really wanted to go along with them. Her parents had their passion and Piper had hers. It had just taken her longer to discover it.

Was it simply coincidental, she wondered, that Scott, another important person in her life, had discovered he was happiest when he was hundreds of miles away from her? Such thoughts were best pondered on another day, Piper decided, so she shook herself to get moving and on her way.

Minutes later, Piper was locking up when she remembered that Tina Carson had asked her to drop off more of her pear chutney at the coffee shop. Apparently it was a big hit with her customers. Piper ran back into the shop for the jars, thinking she could stop on her way. But when she pulled up in front of Tina's shop, a "Closed" sign hung inside the door, and the shop's interior was dark.

Bummer. Especially since the lettering on the door

proclaimed the opening hour to be eight A.M., and it was twenty minutes past that. Piper got out of the car and peered into the shop, hoping to see signs of life. She rapped but spotted no movement in the darkened interior. Tina, she decided, must have seen her business, like A La Carte's, drop off and felt it wasn't worth opening during fair days. Piper would have to get the chutney to her some other time.

As she continued down Beech Street she noticed much lighter traffic than usual. Most of the bigger draws at the fair, such as the midway rides, didn't open until ten, which probably explained it. If the majority of Cloverdale residents had shifted their activities from town to fairgrounds, they apparently had also decided to sleep in a little that day.

When Piper pulled into the vendors' parking area, there was only a scattering of other cars. She had come early to do a bit of tidying and rearranging at her booth, since spreading a protective tarp over her wares the night before was about all she could manage. Piper had also sold out of pickles from her pickle barrel, proving Amy's optimism to be spot-on, so she'd brought a fresh batch of dills to restock it. She lifted up the hatch on her white Chevy to unload them.

"Morning, Miss Lamb."

Piper looked over to see Ben Schaeffer walking toward her, dressed in khakis and a plaid shirt rather than his auxiliary officer uniform. Piper's first thought was that Ben Schaeffer, who was only three years younger, had just addressed her as if she were his former kindergarten teacher.

"Call me Piper, please," she said. "You're here early, Ben. Are you on duty?"

He shook his head. "Not officially. But I thought I'd check around. You know, make sure nobody's dumping trash where they shouldn't. Things like that."

"That's conscientious of you." Piper reached for one of the large plastic bags of dill pickles.

"Help you with that?"

Piper smiled, resisting the elderly-woman-aided-by-Boy-Scout feeling that Ben seemed to automatically stir. "Thank you," she said, and handed one of the bags to Ben, then grabbed the second, larger one herself. They took off toward the vendor booths.

"The fair seems to have slowed things down in town," she said, conversationally. "Have you closed your place? Amy said you have an insurance office."

"Amy mentioned that?" Ben's eyes lit up and a spot of red appeared on each cheek.

"Well, yes. When I asked her, specifically." No use getting the man's hopes up.

"Oh." Ben cleared his throat. "Well, I'll be heading in to the office later on to do some paperwork. But I don't expect new clients to pop in during fair days."

"No, people's minds are definitely on more fun things right now. Not to imply, well, you know. Insurance, obviously, is serious. Not something you think of when you're in the mood to get away from it all."

Piper was afraid she may have dug herself into a hole, but all Ben said was, "Right."

Piper mentally ran over what insurance she already owned, expecting a sales pitch to soon follow, but as they drew closer to the stage where the talent show would take place she was distracted by the condition of the area. Papers were strewn about the stage, chairs were disarranged, and a pot of artificial flowers lay tipped over, its papery roots half out of the container.

"Look at that!" Ben cried, disgusted. "Did they have to leave things in such a mess after rehearsals?"

"I thought Aunt Judy said rehearsals were held at the high school," Piper said. Then she saw something up ahead that drove thoughts of rehearsals out of her head. "Something's wrong," she said, quickening her pace.

"You're darned right something's wrong. When people can't take the trouble to pick up after themselves—"

"No, I mean something's wrong at my booth." Piper had seen what looked like the lid of her pickle barrel standing upright, though from the distance she couldn't be sure. She took off at a run, struggling to hold on to the bag of pickles that bounced and slipped in her arms. She was sure she'd firmly clamped down her barrel lid the night before. After seeing the disarray around the stage, her fear was that vandals had been at work. What would she find at her booth?

She approached her booth from the rear but was able to see her pickle barrel, which stood to the side of the shelves of jars and spices. Her green tarp was still in place over those items, but the barrel lid was definitely up. Piper stopped, suddenly afraid to see what might have happened to her precious container. Trash dumped into it? Worse?

Ben caught up with her and paused, following her gaze. He continued a few steps more. Piper watched his face as he made his way to the front of the barrel. His mouth worked soundlessly, then she heard, "Good God."

"What?" Piper lurched forward to see for herself.

Two legs, partly covered in tasseled socks and barely edged with a tartan kilt, hung over the rim of her pickle barrel—the same kilt and socks she remembered seeing the day before on Alan Rosemont. The legs were attached to a torso about Rosemont's size that was pitched forward into the barrel, deep into Piper's pickling brine. A bagpipe lay on the ground nearby, deflated and looking as dead as the body in the barrel.

Ben Schaeffer fumbled for his cell phone, clearing his voice several times as he pressed its buttons. "Sheriff? Schaeffer, here. I'm at the fair. We have, uh, a situation, here. I think it may be a homicide."

Piper blanked out on the rest of Ben's report as her mind struggled with the awful scene in front of her. Her thoughts swirled until, at Ben's final words, her attention suddenly snapped back.

"Yes, sir. And, Sheriff, if you don't mind me saying? You might want to send someone to check on the whereabouts of Nate Purdy."

4

Piper watched the bustling activities of the sheriff's department from behind the crime scene tape, where she'd been politely but firmly moved after a brief questioning. A large area around her booth had been cordoned off, although the rest of the fair, after some discussion with frazzled fair officials, was allowed to carry on. From her position, all Piper could see were crime scene technicians moving about and department vehicles with flashing red lights.

Not that she really wanted to see Alan Rosemont's body—for it had been identified as his—any closer than she already had. But much of her shop's merchandise remained in the midst of that barely fathomable scene, and though she couldn't move any of her jars or pickling spices out of harm's way, remaining within watching distance made her feel she was somehow keeping them safe. Which, at the same time, made her feel horrible. A man was dead and she was worrying about her pickles? The only rationalization she could come up with was that she knew her pickles much better than the man.

"So, someone did Pinky in?" A voice behind her made her turn.

"Pinky?"

"Yeah, you know, Rosemont." The speaker was a denim-clad, grizzled man whose earthy aroma signaled he'd wandered over from the livestock barn. "We all called him Pinky. Not to his face, though."

"Why?"

"Because he would have punched you out if you did. The man had a temper."

"No, I mean why Pinky."

"Oh." The man scratched at his day's growth of beard. "Well, first it was Rosey, from his name, you know? But then that library business turned it into Pinky."

"Sorry to sound so out of it—I'm fairly new around here—but what library business?" Piper asked.

Her companion seemed more than happy to fill her in. "A few months ago, the library needed a new paint job, and the town council had to approve it. Councilman Rosemont, there, didn't want to put a lot of money into things like that. From what I heard he was looking into installing new, fancy streetlights on the block where his antique shop is. So he cut the cost of redoing the library by buying a paint called Azalea Bloom, some color that they were practically giving away. Once it was on, we could see why. It made the library look like a great big bottle of Pepto-

Bismol." The man chuckled for a moment, then added, "Lyella Pfiefle was fit to be tied."

"Lyella—?"

"The head librarian."

"Oh."

"So Rosey became Pinky."

"Ah." Piper couldn't help a lip twitch or two, first from picturing the library, then from imagining that in-your-face, belligerent man being called Pinky and how he would have reacted if he'd ever learned of it. A movement near her booth caught her eye, sobering her. They'd started setting up privacy shields around the crime scene.

Her informative companion moved on, to be replaced by clumps of other curious spectators. The sun, having had to fight its way through an overcast sky, had yet to burn off the early morning chill, and Piper rubbed at her arms and thought about scaring up a cup of coffee. As she glanced around, she spotted a woman charging her way: Charlotte Hosch, owner of Charlotte's Chocolates and Confections, whose booth was next to Piper's. The confectioner's flying hair and steely expression gave Piper an uh-oh feeling, and she braced herself.

"No one can get anywhere near my booth," Charlotte shouted once she got within whites-of-her-eyes distance.

Unsure what Charlotte expected her to do about that, Piper said, "I'm sorry, Charlotte."

"You're sorry? What happened at your booth is ruining my business! How could you let that man drown in your pickle barrel?"

"I didn't *let* anything happen, Charlotte."

"Don't you lock your things up like the rest of us do? You can't just leave traps of that sort for people to fall into."

Piper took a deep breath. Charlotte could probably guess that pickle barrels didn't come with locks—combination, padlock, or otherwise. And Piper didn't feel the need to explain, as she had to Sheriff Carlyle, that she'd firmly clamped her barrel lid closed before leaving the night before. Besides which, Piper was pretty sure Alan Rosemont didn't die because he'd decided to go diving in her pickle brine. Before being shuffled away from the crime scene, she'd overheard comments about head trauma, which told her he most certainly had been dead before he ended up where he did. If whoever killed Rosemont hadn't deposited him in her barrel, his body would likely have been found lying somewhere nearby, and this entire area would still have been blocked off.

But Charlotte Hosch was a fellow businesswoman whose shop was within walking distance of Piper's Picklings. It was best to stay at least on speaking terms with someone she'd likely have to deal with for years to come.

"I don't think it will be much longer, Charlotte. You don't sell much candy before lunchtime, anyway, do you?"

Charlotte huffed but pursed her lips. Piper pressed on. "You know, once the crew there finishes up, they're going to be famished. I'd get your fudge ready and extra bags of those fruit and nut mixes you have lined up if I were you."

Piper could see Charlotte's mind clicking as she calculated what she had on hand and what she could expect to unload. For a woman surrounded daily by highly fattening foods, Charlotte kept herself amazingly slim, and Piper expected a lot of that came from the energy she used getting upset with everything and anything around her. She'd heard comments from others, though, about the number of calories Charlotte probably burned up counting her money. Either way, the confectioner's anger seemed to be deflected away from Piper for the moment, though she had a parting volley.

"Nothing like this ever happened around here before you showed up with your pickling shop."

And a nice day to you, too, Charlotte!

As Charlotte tramped off, a voice from behind said, "Awful woman, isn't she?"

Piper turned to see Tina Carson, proprietor of the coffee shop. "Not the easiest to get along with," Piper agreed.

She looked more closely at Tina. When she'd first met the woman several weeks ago, Piper had judged her to be in her late forties, with a pretty face and wavy brown hair offsetting the twenty or so extra pounds on her frame. Tina usually wore a cheery smile, but that morning dark shadows under her eyes gave her a somber look.

"Are you okay?" Piper asked.

Tina shrugged. "Just a headache. I'll be better once the aspirin kicks in."

"I hope so. Was that why you were closed this morning? I stopped by with those jars of chutney you asked for."

"Oh, I'm sorry I missed you! I probably could have opened up, even with this dumb headache, but business has been sluggish because of the fair and I figured I'd take the day off. But then I heard sirens heading out here. Nobody on the street seemed to know what was going on, so I came to find out for myself."

Piper gestured grimly toward the crime scene, still bustling with technicians. "Alan Rosemont was killed here last night."

"Oh my gosh!" Tina's hand flew to her mouth. "The poor man. I'm really sorry to hear that, even though he's the one who caused me all that hassle about regulations and inspections when I was trying to set up my shop."

"He caused a lot of people a lot of problems," put in a large man who'd just walked up. He took a bite from the cone of cotton candy he held. "But someone got even with him, and not just by doing him in but by how they left him."

"What do you mean?" Tina asked.

"Didn't she tell you?" the man asked, indicating Piper. "Rosemont's body was dumped in her pickle barrel!"

Piper grimaced, wishing fervently, first of all, that it hadn't happened, but next that that particular information could somehow have been kept quiet. Impossible, of course, but—

"Tina!" Piper cried, realizing that the coffee shop owner had turned white as a turnip. Tina started sinking down, and Piper grabbed on to her. "Give her some room, please," Piper begged, waving people back and bracing Tina as she eased to a sitting position on the ground. "Does anyone have water?"

A nearby woman passed over a bottle, and Piper twisted the cap off. Tina took a sip, then followed it soon with a longer gulp, and Piper was relieved to see color gradually return to her face.

"Should I call someone from first aid?" the man asked.

"No!" Tina cried, waving. "I'm fine. I'm fine."

"Maybe you should let them check you out," Piper said. But Tina had struggled to her feet. "I'm okay, really."

The woman who'd handed over her water bottle said, "Pete and I were just about to leave. Why don't we drive you home?"

"I think that's a great idea," Piper said.

Tina, after some hesitation, nodded agreement, and after a few more sips of water and apologies for the trouble, she took off with the couple.

Piper felt terrible for springing the news about Alan Rosemont on Tina as she had, though, of course, she'd had no idea Tina would react so strongly. She made a mental note to be much more careful in the future.

Aunt Judy came bustling up. "Oh, thank goodness. I was just making my way over here when I saw the commotion. I worried it might be you." She gave Piper a hug. "What a terrible thing to happen," she said, looking toward Piper's covered-up booth. "Are you okay?"

"Not too bad," Piper said. "Better than some, I suppose."

"That poor man," Judy said. "Who could have done such a thing? He wasn't the easiest person to get along with, but still . . ."

Her aunt's question reminded Piper of Ben Schaeffer's advice to the sheriff, that he check the whereabouts of Nate Purdy. Surely that hadn't been taken seriously, had it?

Just then Amy ran up, her red hair loose and flying. "I just heard! How awful! And your poor pickle barrel! Will you ever be able to use it again?"

That was something Piper didn't want to think about yet. "Amy, have you spoken to Nate lately?" she asked.

"Nate? Not since he took off from A La Carte yesterday with his guitar. Why?"

At that point, Sheriff Carlyle came up, his face all

seriousness. "Amy, where have you been? I've been trying to reach you."

Amy looked puzzled but pulled her cell phone out to check it. "I guess I forgot to turn it on. Why? What did you want? I told you I was stopping at Megan's on my way here."

The sheriff looked relieved. "That's right. I forgot. Look, we're trying to find Nate Purdy. He's not at his place. Do you know where he is?"

"Nate?" Amy searched her father's face. "Why are you . . . ?" She glanced toward the booth. "Daddy! You can't be thinking—!"

"We just need to talk to him, honey. Now, do you know where he is?"

Just then, Aunt Judy made a soft "Oh!" sound, and Piper turned to follow her stare. Nate strolled at a distance, hands in his pockets and looking as if he didn't have a care. Then he stopped, apparently spotting the gathered crowd and official vehicles and several pairs of eyes on him.

"There he is!" Ben Schaeffer shouted. Two deputies took off to intercept the startled-looking musician.

"Daddy, you can't do this!"

"Honey, this is police business. Please go home. I mean now!"

"No, Daddy! This is all wrong!" But Amy's pleas fell on empty air as her father left to join his deputies.

She turned to Piper. "This can't be happening!"

"It must be just routine, Amy." But as all three watched Nate being led to a waiting squad car, Piper began to share some of Amy's worries, especially as Ben Schaeffer walked closely beside Sheriff Carlyle, speaking steadily in his ear. She knew Ben's bias against Nate, and she'd picked up the sheriff's leanings toward Ben as a suitor for his daughter. The question was, how much trouble did that spell for Nate?

"Daddy won't tell me a thing!" Amy cried, looking distraught as she entered Piper's Picklings that afternoon.

Piper sat at her shop table behind a large bowl. She'd begun putting together a batch of mixed pickling spices, lining up large-mouthed jars of spices on her table along with measuring cups and spoons. The blend of aromas arising from cloves, ginger, dill seeds, nutmeg, and more was wonderful, making it one of her favorite parts of the job. But that afternoon she'd tackled it mainly to keep her mind off what she'd seen that morning.

The sheriff's men had promised to let her know when her booth and all its contents would be released, so she'd reluctantly given up her vigil of staring at the privacy shields and headed back to the shop. But Amy's distress took precedence over spice blending at the moment, so Piper set her scoop down.

"My guess is that he can't tell you anything. That your father would be way out of line if he did."

"I know, I know. That's what he always says. But this is Nate!" Amy started pacing the length of Piper's worktable. After two or three brisk passes, she looked down. "Want me to crush those cinnamon sticks?"

"Sure!" Besides being a help, Piper hoped it might work

off some of Amy's frustration. She pushed a mortar and pestle Amy's way, then got up and switched on the shop radio, searching for soothing music. The classical music station came up with the goods.

They worked together silently for a while, Piper measuring and Amy pulverizing—at first with such energy that Piper feared her cinnamon sticks might not be just crushed but liquefied. But gradually her assistant's white-knuckled grip on the pestle loosened and Amy's voice calmed.

"Daddy probably took Nate in simply to check him off the list," she said as much to herself as to Piper. "Nate had that argument with Rosemont—did you know a lot of people called him Pinky?" she asked, looking up. Piper nodded, and she went on. "But Nate wasn't the only one to ever fight with that man. Not by a long shot. He just happened to be one of the latest, and unfortunately it was out in public. It's fresh on everyone's minds, so of course Nate's the first person they think of. They'll talk to him and find he was at his place all night. He was practicing his guitar, for goodness' sake! The whole neighborhood can probably verify it."

"That's great. That'll put an end to it." Piper added a cup of mustard seeds to her bowl.

The radio station had moved on to Gilbert and Sullivan's light music. Piper smiled and hummed along for a measure or two, then scooped out a tablespoon of nutmeg. Amy added her cinnamon to the mix, and Piper stirred. She was ready to portion out her batch of mixed pickling spices into jars.

Piper got the funnel, and Amy pulled out labels from one of the drawers. They worked carefully in companionable silence, Piper filling and Amy pasting labels, until Piper happened to glance up. Erin Healy was hurrying toward her shop. Erin, she knew, had been Amy's friend since kindergarten, and with her dark hair and large brown eyes was a contrast to her friend in looks as well as temperament, being generally quieter and more reserved. At the moment, however, "reserved" was not the word Piper would have applied to her, especially as she burst through the shop's door.

"Amy, did you know your father's been questioning Nate!"

"I know," Amy cried, jumping up from her chair, all her hard-won calm disappearing in a moment. "I hate it, and I can't wait till it's over and done with!"

"But did you also know Nate's getting a lawyer?"

"What! Why? How can he get a lawyer? He can barely afford food."

"All I know is he was seen going into Darryl Huggard's office."

"Oh Lord." Amy sank down in her chair, her shoulders drooping.

"Who's Darryl Huggard?" Piper asked.

"Only the worst lawyer anyone could have to represent him," Amy said with a dramatic eye roll. "But he's cheap, which is why Nate probably picked him. Why should he need a lawyer at all?"

At that moment, Nate himself walked in, looking grim.

"Nate!" Amy bounced up and hugged him. "Are you

okay? What happened?" She pulled back, looking at his face. "And why are you talking to Darryl Huggard?"

Nate gave a half smile. He looked at Piper, who'd stayed behind her table. "Sorry to bring all this into your shop. It's just, I wanted to see Amy. To explain."

Erin had eased away, giving her friends space, but Nate put a friendly hand on her shoulder and drew her back. Piper remembered that Erin was on the bus the day Amy and Nate met and had fully endorsed their budding romance. Nate probably remembered, and appreciated, that, too.

"I'm glad you came, Nate," Piper said. "Now, please tell us what's going on."

Nate ran his fingers through his hair. "Things have been happening so fast I can barely wrap my head around it. But I seem to be a 'person of interest.' Maybe front and center."

"But why?" Amy asked. "You were home all night, weren't you?"

"Yes, I was." Nate looked steadily at her. "I absolutely was from nine o'clock on. But I was alone. Nobody can back me up."

That's not good, Piper thought, but she kept silent.

"Around maybe eight or so, I needed to replace a string on my guitar," Nate said. "I went out to the music store, but it was closed. Ninety percent of the stores in town seem to be closed because of the fair. So I didn't see anybody I know, went back to my apartment, watched some TV, and turned in early. Nobody heard me practicing because I *couldn't* practice. But I was home the rest of the night, and that's the truth."

He slumped into the chair opposite Piper. "That's why I went to talk to Huggard. I'm sure I'll be called back for further questioning or worse. He wants a retainer, and I don't have it right now. But I'll scrape one up."

"Nate, this is awful." Amy said it quietly, fully grasping the pickle Nate was in. "We know you didn't kill Alan Rosemont. Why should you have to prove you didn't?"

"It hasn't come to that, yet," Erin pointed out softly. "Maybe they'll find evidence that will point to someone else."

"And maybe they won't look as hard if they think they already have their man," Amy said worriedly, and Piper feared she had a point. Then Amy said something that totally caught her by surprise.

"Piper," she said. Amy leaned earnestly her way. "I'll bet you could come up with something that would help Nate. Would you try?"

5

〰️

"Amy wants me to look into Alan Rosemont's murder." Piper sat at Aunt Judy and Uncle Frank's kitchen table, having been urged to come for dinner. After the day Piper had just experienced, her aunt hadn't needed to press hard. Gracie, Aunt Judy's plump gray cat and another of a string of rescued strays, leaped up onto Piper's lap and offered an ear to be scratched.

Aunt Judy glanced over her shoulder from the stove where she was testing the doneness of her boiling potatoes with a fork. "Why you?"

Piper sighed. "She seems to think that because I was once engaged to a criminal lawyer, I have some kind of special, insider-type knowledge."

Aunt Judy smiled knowingly.

"I know," Piper said. "If only it were that easy." She

43

shifted Gracie to a more comfortable position. "Although Scott did talk an awful lot about what they did on the investigating end of their cases."

"Well, there you go. You're all set."

Piper laughed. "I wish. Though I really would like to do something to help. Nate seems so alone, except for the few friends he's made here in Cloverdale."

"He seems like a nice young man."

"I like him, too. Unfortunately, not everyone does. Alan Rosemont, for one, obviously really, really disliked him."

"Well, Alan . . ." Aunt Judy set down her testing fork and took a peek at the roast in her oven.

"I don't suppose it would hurt to just poke around a bit," Piper said. "It sounds like Alan Rosemont ruffled enough feathers to make more than one person want to do away with him." She shifted Gracie to the floor, then stood to take plates from her aunt to set the table. "I've already heard about the terrible paint job on the library that Rosemont was responsible for."

Uncle Frank walked into the kitchen, chuckling. "Lyella Pfiefle was fit to be tied," he said, leaning over to give Piper a peck on the cheek.

"Don't laugh, Frank," Aunt Judy scolded. "How would you like one of your barns to end up looking like that?"

"I wouldn't like it one bit. But I wouldn't run around clucking like a wet hen for weeks on end about it."

"She surely didn't fuss that long. Here, pull that roast out of the oven for me and set it on the carving board, will you?" Uncle Frank grabbed the oven mitts, and Aunt Judy waited until her roast was safely settled before adding, "But Lyella was upset, that's for sure. Alan had Dennis

Isley do the painting when Lyella was away for a library convention. It must have been a terrible shock for her when she got back. People said she marched into Alan's antique shop and chewed him out royally. He ended up pushing her out and locking his door."

"Maybe I should find out where Lyella Pfiefle was around the time Alan Rosemont was murdered?"

"Amy's asked Piper to find out who might have wanted to kill Alan other than Nate Purdy," Aunt Judy explained to her husband. "Oh," she said, snapping her fingers. "I forgot my wax beans. The ones I put up with honey and ginger. I want you to try them, Piper."

She disappeared into her pantry, and Uncle Frank picked up a carving knife and began swiping it against the sharpener. "Sure," he said to Piper, "go talk to Lyella. See if she has an alibi. Someone that upset? No telling what she might do."

Piper nodded but wondered about Uncle Frank's sudden lip twitch. When he ducked his head and began poking at the roast with the carving fork, she decided he must be starving and got out the butter and milk for the potatoes to get things moving along.

By midafternoon on Sunday, Piper's wares had been released by the crime scene crew and safely hauled back from the fair to her store with the help of many. Since she wouldn't have opened for business that day anyway, and Aunt Judy had assured her the library would be open, Piper decided to run over to see if she could catch Lyella Pfiefle. She headed off on foot to cover the few blocks there, enjoying the exercise but also appreciating the shade offered by the trees that lined both sides of Beech Street on that warm day.

Piper had visited the library often during her summers with Aunt Judy and Uncle Frank but hadn't been back since her move and all the hustle and bustle of setting up her new shop. But she remembered many happy hours spent browsing through the children's books, then graduating to more grown-up sections. She may have seen Lyella among other library workers in those days, but the adults might as well have had fuzzy blobs for faces, focused as Piper had been on finding the perfect book.

She turned off Beech Street, remembering that the library would be one more turn off of Third Street two blocks ahead. With her thoughts busy with what she wanted to learn about Lyella, Piper forgot for the moment about the library's drastic color change. As she turned onto Maple, however, it hit her full force.

"Whoa!"

Her informant from the fair's livestock barns had compared the look to a bottle of Pepto-Bismol, and he hadn't exaggerated. The library, which Piper remembered as a stately, decades-old converted house with white siding and black shutters, had been turned into an amusement park fun house. The shutters were still black, but that only served to emphasize the garish pinkness of the rest of the building.

Piper was at once horrified and on the verge of giddy laughter. It was just too awful. She could only imagine how Lyella Pfiefle must have felt to see it and to hear her beloved library become the butt of jokes. Did it make her mad enough to want to kill the person responsible? Piper hoped to find out.

Fighting down the feeling of walking into a giant clown's mouth, she entered the library and was relieved to find the interior pretty much as she remembered it. A scattering of patrons browsed among tall shelves of books, and one or two sat at computer tables. The overall quiet gave an air of both study and coziness and brought back all of Piper's good feelings of years ago. To her, going to the library had always been like a treasure hunt, with riches only waiting to be discovered. Today, however, she was on a totally different kind of hunt and wasn't all too sure what she might find. Piper went up to the checkout desk and asked the plump, friendly-looking woman there if Lyella Pfiefle was around.

"She's in the meeting room right now," the woman said. "It's story time for the preschoolers. You can go in if you like and wait. She'll be done in a few minutes."

"Thanks." Piper headed toward the meeting room at the back, catching the sounds of a woman's reading voice and children's titters as she drew closer. The open doorway allowed her to slip in quietly, and she joined a line of mothers—and a few fathers—at the back, who shuffled together to make room for her. Once Piper settled in and got a good look at the librarian standing at the head of the room, she sputtered out a laugh—luckily during a loud shriek from the children.

Lyella Pfiefle looked about as unlikely a murderer as anyone could. She was tiny, for one thing, barely reaching five feet tall by Piper's estimation. Most storytellers who Piper remembered from her childhood days had perched cozily on chairs to read to their groups. But it was clear if Lyella sat, she'd disappear from view.

The librarian was slim to the point of too thin, causing Piper to think a rogue puff of wind from the window might easily blow her over. Piper would, at first guess, have put her at late middle age. But a look beyond the simple blouse and cotton skirt showed an unlined face framed by dark, shiny hair that, despite being pulled back severely into a ponytail, signaled a woman at least ten years younger.

Taken altogether, though, Piper could not imagine Lyella Pfiefle—currently describing the antics of bunnies and turtles—having the strength to kill a man plus lift his body into Piper's pickle barrel, no matter how furious she might be.

Piper flashed back to the kitchen and Uncle Frank's twitching mouth as they discussed Lyella as a possible suspect. She shook her head and laughed silently at herself. After all these years, she still fell for her uncle's jokes. Still, since she was here, she might as well talk to the woman.

The story ended, and the children scrambled to their feet, a few dillydallying but most rushing over to their parents. Lyella gathered up a small pile of books and waited for the group to move on. Piper made her way to the front of the room.

"Miss Pfiefle?"

"Mrs.," she swiftly corrected, then offered an efficient smile. "What can I do for you?"

Piper introduced herself and asked, "Would you mind talking a bit about Alan Rosemont?"

The librarian's smile disappeared, but she nodded. "Quite a shocking turn of events."

"Yes, it was. I was the one who found him, along with Ben Schaeffer. It was my pickling booth."

"Oh! So you're the owner of the new pickling shop."

A little girl with blond curly pigtails dashed over and gave the librarian's knees a hug. "Thank you, Mrs. Pfiefle."

"You're welcome, Kayla. See you next week."

The girl ran back to her mother, and Lyella murmured to Piper, "A pleasant age. Ten years from now she'll be shooting me dirty looks for breaking up a giggling session in the stacks. But you had a question about Alan Rosemont?"

"Yes. I never met the man, but I witnessed a nasty argument he instigated the afternoon before he was murdered. I've since heard that was fairly typical of him—that he was difficult to get along with."

"Horrible man," Lyella said flatly. "I was hoping for years that his business would go belly-up and that he'd leave town for parts unknown. Preferably Siberia. Who would have guessed it would be he who'd go belly-up? But life," she said, looking down at the books in her arms and shifting them, "is unpredictable."

"I heard he was responsible for the paint job on your building."

Lyella gave a choking laugh. "Lovely, isn't it?" The group of mothers and children had cleared, and Lyella made a move to leave. "Let's continue this out there, shall we? I need to reshelve these books." With Piper hustling to keep pace, the librarian spoke as she briskly led the way toward the children's books section. "Alan claimed he chose the paint to save the town money, which would be bad enough. But I know he took a special satisfaction in doing something he knew would aggravate me."

"Oh?"

"I once had the audacity to organize a petition against one of his council proposals. He wanted to stop funding for maintenance of our town's historical marker. No way was I going to let that happen. He didn't like that."

"There's a historical marker?" As soon as Piper said it she could have bitten her tongue, for Lyella threw her a severe look.

"In front of the courthouse. It details Cloverdale's founding in 1821, among other things."

"I'll check it out," Piper promised. "Alan Rosemont apparently didn't like opposition."

"Alan Rosemont liked being a big fish in a small pond." Lyella slipped two of her slim books into place on a shelf.

"A fish that liked to play the bagpipes, apparently. His pipes were found next to him at my booth."

Lyella rolled her eyes. "He took that up after digging into his genealogy here. We have quite good resources for doing so," she said and slipped another book onto the shelf. "He traced his roots to a particular clan and suddenly became more Scottish than Rob Roy. Unfortunately for Cloverdale music lovers, having Scottish genes doesn't guarantee you can play the bagpipes. Alan seemed to think the more he played them, the better he'd be. He was wrong."

"Do you think he was practicing when he was killed?"

"That'd be my guess."

"But you didn't happen to see him that night?"

"Oh no! Gordon and I were home all evening. We retire early. From what I understand, what happened to Alan occurred late, after the fair had closed down."

"Yes, it must have. Gordon's your husband, of course?"

"Of course." For the first time, Piper saw a softening in Lyella's face and warmth creeping into her smile. She became close to lovely for the moment or two it lasted. Then the efficient-librarian face returned. "I have things to do in my office. Was there anything else?"

"No, but thank you very much." Piper glanced around. "Perhaps I'll go look over your cookbooks."

"Section 641," Lyella pronounced crisply, indicating the area with a quick wave. She bid Piper a good day and strode off.

Piper started to head for section 641—there was always the possibility of new pickle recipes to be found—when she heard, "Psst." A stooped, gray-haired woman dressed in wrinkled beige linen was beckoning her over. Piper glanced toward the office to check that Lyella had disappeared into it before going over to the woman.

"I overheard you talking with Lyella," the woman whispered. Her deep-set eyes fairly glittered. "She and Gordon don't always retire early."

"No?"

"That Gordon Pfiefle worships the ground she walks on. Anyone who upsets Lyella, upsets Gordon, if you take my meaning." The woman nodded vigorously before pulling a balled-up handkerchief out of a pocket and dabbing at a corner of her mouth. "I'm Martha Smidley. I live right across the street from the Pfiefles. Not that that meant Lyella ever condescended to save a person a bit of trouble by bringing a book or two back for them." She sniffed.

"Did you see the Pfiefles go out Friday night?" Piper asked.

"No," Martha Smidley said, shaking her head with regret, "I didn't. I'm just saying it could happen. Their lights aren't always out by nine. Oh, there you are, Betty," she exclaimed as a younger woman—a daughter?—approached. "I'm ready to check out now, dear." Martha turned away from Piper without a further word and walked off with Betty, gabbling energetically to her about the particular book she'd chosen. But she managed to shoot a meaningful look over her shoulder at Piper before she'd gone too far.

Well, Piper thought, looking after Lyella's watchful neighbor. *What do I do with that?*

6

~~~

Piper left the library—with one checked-out cookbook in hand—and paused for a moment outside to think. A tan pickup pulled over near her.

"Lost your way, little girl?"

"Uncle Frank!" Piper poked her head into the open passenger window, leaning one arm on the edge. "If I had, I'm not sure you'd be the one to ask for directions."

Uncle Frank chuckled. "You met Lyella."

"Yes, I certainly did. I think I can safely cross her off my list, don't you?"

"Detective work not as easy as it looks on TV? Maybe you should stick to pickling and just let the sheriff do his job. What do you think, peanut?"

"I won't get in Sheriff Carlyle's way. I hope he finds

whoever killed Alan Rosemont. Who really killed Rosemont, not just who's conveniently handy."

"Well, now, that's not fair. George Carlyle's an honest man."

"You're right. I take that back. But I'd hate to think that some things might be overlooked if the sheriff—and those around him—rushed to judgment. I just want to check out what might be the forgotten fringes of the situation." She paused. "Do you know Lyella Pfiefle's husband?"

"Gordon Pfiefle, the fellow who manages the supermarket? What, is he the next suspect on your list?"

From the crinkles around Uncle Frank's eyes, Piper assumed Gordon Pfiefle was just as unlikely a suspect as Lyella had turned out to be. She shrugged. "I just wondered what he did, since Lyella happened to mention they always turn in early."

"Well, I suppose he might have early hours at the market. I wouldn't know. Want a lift to your place? I'm just heading back from the fairgrounds and have a few things to drop off at Bill Vanderveen's down the way, there," he said, gesturing toward Third Street.

"No, go ahead." Piper knew her uncle would want to stay and visit with his friend for a while instead of hustling her on home. "I feel like a walk. But give Bill my best." She pulled her head out of his truck and waved him off.

As she strolled toward Beech Street, Piper thought about what Martha Smidley had hinted to her. She seemed to have a grudge against Lyella and might also have something against Gordon that could color her opinion. Perhaps he hadn't shoveled her snow-covered walk when she needed it, or an oversight similarly unforgivable in her eyes?

Was Gordon worth checking out? Piper at least knew where to find him, thanks to Uncle Frank—assuming he wasn't putting her on again. The supermarket, Piper knew, wasn't that much out of her way. She could always use a few fresh items for her kitchen, and once she reopened her shop the next day her time would be limited. Having thoroughly talked herself into it, she turned right at Beech instead of left and headed for TopValuFood, Cloverdale's largest food market.

P iper strolled about the supermarket, a bright yellow basket slung over one arm, wondering just how she should approach this. It was one thing to walk in at the library and question Lyella Pfiefle. However, if Lyella's husband, Gordon, informed her that Piper had shown up at his market and done the same with him, she'd get a tad suspicious. If they had nothing to hide, of course, the worst that would come from it was an icy glare the next time Piper visited the library. If they did have something to hide, though, such as murder—well, that's what kept Piper wandering through the produce section uncertainly.

After about ten minutes of sniffing melons and pinching grapes, she heard a voice on the public address system say, "Manager to register number three, please." Piper's head snapped up. She plopped a bag of seedless reds into her basket and scurried toward checkout number three.

Checker three stood motionless at her register, gazing

expectantly over the heads of those in her line. Soon, a man in a white dress shirt with sleeves rolled up to his elbows came barreling toward her, an expression of "eager to help" on his broad face. Whether or not it was genuine or pasted on for the public, Piper could only guess.

"Mr. Pfiefle," the checker said, "Mrs. Diehl has a question about the price coming up on this bag of cat litter."

Piper picked up a copy of one of the tabloids from a nearby rack and pretended fascination with its latest alien-baby headline but flicked her gaze between the newspaper and the burly manager.

Close to six feet tall, Gordon Pfiefle had the broad shoulders, biceps, and chest of a weight lifter. He clearly would have no problem lifting Alan Rosemont into Piper's pickle barrel once he had knocked him dead. Interestingly, Piper noticed red scratches on Pfiefle's neck, visible at the open collar of his shirt, and at least one near his ear. A struggle with Rosemont before killing him? Was that white shirt possibly hiding bruises?

Don't jump to conclusions, Piper warned herself, which was exactly what she didn't want Sheriff Carlyle to do. First she needed to establish if Pfiefle had the opportunity. She had at least the hint of a motive for him, if Martha Smidley was to be believed.

Gordon Pfiefle settled the price problem with Mrs. Diehl—to the woman's satisfaction, judging by her pleased smile—and left the checkout area. He stopped to chat briefly with another customer, then walked on. Piper followed at what she hoped was a discreet distance.

A clerk stood partway up one aisle, stacking cans in rows, and as she added a final one the entire lineup toppled.

The clerk—a young girl—cried out in dismay, and nearby customers jumped out of the way. Pfiefle hurried over and caught a few cans rolling his way, then helped the clerk scramble after the rest. Piper listened to him advise the girl to stack the cans in the sturdier pyramid formation, demonstrating. He then moved on, waving off the clerk's grateful thanks. Piper waited until he'd disappeared around the corner before sidling up to the young woman.

"Guess you lucked out, there, huh?"

The girl grinned. "I could have really been chewed out, right? But I've never seen Mr. Pfiefle get really mad at anyone. I've only been here a few weeks, though." She tapped lightly at her stacked cans. "Guess I'd better not press my luck."

Piper picked up an overlooked can of green beans and handed it to the girl. "He seems very conscientious. Probably gets here at the crack of dawn, I'll bet."

The girl wrinkled her nose, melding together the freckles that were dotted across it. "I don't think so. I've seen him mostly come in around eight thirty. Patty Wright opens up for us at seven."

"Eight thirty's not bad," Piper said, nodding, "unless of course he stays till closing time. I've known managers who get pretty obsessive about their stores."

"No, that's not Mr. Pfiefle." The girl smiled. "He says the sign of a good manager is training good employees, and if he can't trust them to do their job, he hasn't done his job." She quoted Gordon Pfiefle with obvious admiration. Keeping in mind that the girl had only been employed there a few weeks, Pfiefle sounded like an ideal boss and possibly a very nice man.

Should Piper cross him off her list of suspects? She shook her head. There were still those scratches to be explained. Plus, if he wasn't working late that night, his only alibi so far came from his wife, Lyella, who could safely be assumed to be biased. Piper also hadn't yet spoken with the man. But she preferred to do that away from his workplace where his public face would always be on. Piper wanted to make sure she saw the real Gordon Pfiefle.

O n her walk back to her shop, Piper spotted Charlotte's Chocolates and Confections up ahead. An encounter with Charlotte once every few days, she felt, was more than enough, so she crossed the street. As she did so, Piper noticed the interior of Tina Carson's coffee shop was lit and open for business. The delicious aromas of coffee and cooked bacon wafted her way, reminding her that she hadn't had a decent lunch and drawing her toward the cozy, plaid-curtained shop. She went in.

"Hi, Piper," Tina called from the other side of the counter where she set down a plate for a customer. "How's it goin'?"

"Not too bad." Piper slid onto a stool. "Feeling better?"

"Lots," Tina said. "All I needed was to get out of that sun. Even my headache's gone."

Piper smiled, though the dark shadows still under Tina's eyes hinted at possible lingering symptoms.

"Get you something?" Tina asked.

Piper ordered iced tea and a BLT on toasted wheat, and Tina turned to the work counter behind her to assemble it.

"Some doings at the fair, yesterday," the lanky, pony-tailed man sitting two stools down from Piper said.

"That's all everyone's been talking about today," Tina said as she dropped two slices of bread into the toaster. She glanced back at Piper. "A shame it happened at your booth."

"Oh, it was your pickle barrel?" the man said, studying Piper with interest. His work boots and stained denims seemed a tad out of place at Tina's shop, whose clientele tended to be more tidily dressed. But Piper was less put off by his attire than by the uncomfortable vibes she was getting from him with his roving gaze.

"Yes," she answered, not inclined to elaborate.

"Bummer," the man said, though his weak attempt at sympathy vanished as a grin slowly spread over his face. "What a way to go, eh? In a barrel of pickles. Alan Rosemont—Pinky—was pickled pink!" He laughed heartily at his own joke, then started coughing as the laugh turned into a choke.

Piper looked uneasily at Tina, but apparently she'd gotten used to the fact of Rosemont's murder since her episode of the day before. When the man's coughs gradually died down, Tina said, "Take it easy, Dennis. Do one thing at a time. Eat or talk."

"Yeah," he agreed. "One thing at a time." He coughed again, then cleared his throat. "Hey, I think I'll take the rest of this with me," he said, looking down at his plate. "Got something I can wrap it in?"

Tina handed him a sheet of waxed paper, and he rolled the remaining half of his sandwich in it before standing up. "I'll see you around."

"Okay, Dennis," Tina said. "Thanks again for coming over."

After he left, Tina explained to Piper, "That's Dennis Isley. He does odd jobs around town, and I had to call him in to fix a pipe in the back that sprang a leak." She rolled her eyes. "Just what I needed to bring on another headache, huh? Anyway, I promised I'd fix him something to eat afterward if he came right away." She slid a plate with a thickly layered BLT and a generous side of potato chips on it across the counter, then poured out Piper's iced tea.

"Thanks," Piper said.

"Dennis did a fair amount of work for Alan Rosemont," Tina said, "but he didn't like him much."

Join the crowd, Piper thought as she bit into her sandwich.

Tina picked up a mug of coffee and took a sip, leaning back against her work counter. "Alan hired Dennis to paint the library that awful color. Have you seen it?" When Piper nodded, her mouth full, Tina added, "From what I heard, Dennis was the only one he could get to do the job in a hurry when he heard Lyella Pfiefle was out of town. But even though he wanted a rush job, Alan still hassled Dennis afterward about sloppiness and tried to whittle the payment down. That's one reason Dennis obviously wasn't too broken up over Alan's death. I mean, with that 'pickled pink' comment." A grin started spreading across Tina's face until she bit her lip. "I shouldn't laugh."

Piper couldn't help a snuffle herself, though she worked to control it. Besides being wildly inappropriate, considering the man had been murdered, she definitely didn't want to have a choking fit like Dennis Isley's.

"I was just talking to Lyella at the library," Piper said, after a sip of her iced tea. "She's still pretty angry over what Alan did."

"Yeah, well, who wouldn't be?"

"You don't happen to know her husband, Gordon, do you? He manages the TopValuFood market?"

Tina shook her head.

Piper paused. Tina had always struck her as a sensible, genuine people person, which had helped make her coffee shop a popular place in a short time. She'd listened to the older woman's tales of the endless, obscure food service regulations that Alan Rosemont had come up with and the countless hoops he'd forced her to jump through to get her license. Tina had persevered, though, with minimal complaints and was on her way to becoming a Cloverdale casual dining tradition. It was this daily access to town gossip and Tina's ability to put people at ease that interested Piper.

"I'd like to explain why I'm interested in the Pfiefles, if you'll keep it to yourself."

Tina set her coffee mug down. "Absolutely."

"I know Sheriff Carlyle will work hard at finding Alan Rosemont's murderer."

Tina's head bobbed. "It must have been a mugging, right? I figure maybe somebody from out of town who thought they'd have easy pickings at our fair."

"The sheriff doesn't seem to think so. Dumping Rosemont into the pickle barrel looks more like someone making a personal statement. He's been questioning Nate Purdy."

"What!" Tina's jaw dropped in horror. "I can't believe it!"

"There've been no charges, yet. But Nate is worried enough to talk to a lawyer."

"But that's preposterous. I've heard Nate perform at A La Carte. Lovely, gentle songs. You can't tell me anyone who can sing like that is capable of murder."

If only it were that simple, Piper thought, but aloud she said, "Nate's a great guy who finds himself in a tough situation and with only a few supporters. I want to help him out by digging up anything that will legitimately shift Sheriff Carlyle's focus to someone else."

"Oh my, Nate! Such a sweet guy. I couldn't stand to see him falsely accused. You can add me to that list of supporters, Piper. Just let me know what I can do to help."

"Would you keep your eyes and ears open here? There's a chance you could overhear something useful."

"You got it."

"One of the things I'd love to know more about is how Gordon Pfiefle got the scratches I saw today on his neck and face. They looked pretty fresh."

"I'll see what I can learn. If any of Gordon's friends stop in, I'll try to get them talking."

"Just be careful," Piper warned. "Discreet. We don't want anything getting back to him. And Gordon's only the beginning. I'm sure there are others in this town who wanted Alan Rosemont dead." As she said that, Piper wondered about Dennis Isley. Tina had shared at least one reason he didn't like Alan. Perhaps there were more?

Before she could throw out the thought to Tina, a young couple with two small children walked in. Tina straightened up and greeted them as they headed toward one of the tables, and Piper turned to polishing off the last of her meal. As she settled her bill, Tina thanked her, adding, after a careful glance at the nearby customers, "I'll be in touch, Piper." She pulled at one ear, wiggling it, and gave a quick wink. Then she picked up menus and headed over to the young family.

"Hey, guys," she said. "Nice to see you. Been to the fair?"

7

"I should start writing a list of all the people who had something against Alan Rosemont," Piper said.

"You'll need a big sheet of paper," Amy advised. She was shelving a shipment of spices that had arrived early Monday morning.

"Wasn't there anybody who liked the man?"

Amy paused, thinking. "Mrs. Franklin, I suppose. She showed up at A La Carte a few times with him for dinner."

Piper remembered Aunt Judy mentioning a Brenda Franklin. "Mrs.?" she questioned.

"She's a widow. I don't remember a Mr. Franklin, but I think he was killed a long time ago in some kind of accident. He must have left her pretty well-off, because she lives in that big house on Willow Street and fills her time with things like the garden club and stuff. Maybe she likes antiques and that was why she and Alan got along."

"Maybe," Piper said. "I—" Amy suddenly dropped a jar of curry powder, which bounced but luckily didn't break.

"Oh! I'm such a klutz! I was doing stuff like that at the restaurant all last night."

"Your mind is understandably on other things. How is Nate doing?"

"Not good." Amy picked up the spice jar and sat down, shaking her head. "He's a wreck, I know, though he won't admit it. It showed, though, in his performance last night at the restaurant. I'm worried he might lose his job there if the management decides he's losing them business." Amy hesitated, her pretty face wrinkling worriedly. "And something more has come out."

"To do with the murder?"

Amy nodded. "More motivation, if you want to look at it that way." She sighed. "It seems Alan Rosemont blocked another job that Nate wanted besides the talent show. Something Nate applied for when he first arrived in Cloverdale—teaching at the summer music camp for kids. Again, he would have been perfect for it. He plays lots of other instruments besides the guitar, and he's great with kids. The elementary school music teacher practically begged for Nate to be hired as her assistant. But Alan made sure Nate didn't get it."

She paused. "Now this is where it gets tricky. Someone who was there at the time apparently told Ben Schaeffer that Alan laughed in Nate's face when he let him know he'd been turned down, and that Nate was furious. Nate doesn't remember it that way. He says Alan, who he barely knew at the time, simply told him he didn't get the job, and Nate shrugged it off thinking something like, 'win some, lose some.' "

"Hmm. Ben's version makes Nate look much worse."

"I know! Who could have told Ben something that wasn't true and put Nate in such a bad light?"

Who indeed? "Maybe we could ask Ben?"

"We could. But I know Ben. Even though he's an auxiliary police officer, he'll get as official sounding as my Dad and say things like 'he's not at liberty to say,' or 'he can't discuss an ongoing case.' He can be really pigheaded when he wants to be."

Plus he's really in love with you, Piper thought, *and probably highly biased against his rival.* "Well," she said, "although I believe Nate's telling the truth, unfortunately Ben's version of how Alan handled it sounds credible. In fact, the more I hear about Alan Rosemont, the more surprised I am he lasted this long. How did he grab so much influence?"

Amy shook her head. "Beats me. Maybe he just started volunteering for jobs nobody else wanted and worked his way up. I knew a kid in school who did that, taking on things like study hall monitor. Before we knew it he was student council president, even though nobody much liked him. They just got used to seeing him be in charge."

"That could have been the case with Rosemont, I suppose," Piper said. "Or he might have simply lucked out by settling in a town full of nice people who never encountered someone as nastily manipulating before."

Piper grabbed a large spiral notebook from behind her counter and flipped it open. "Okay, here's the people I know of so far who might have liked to kill Alan Rosemont. There's Lyella Pfiefle, and her husband Gordon Pfiefle. I'm also putting down Dennis Isley, although all I know about him is that he's done work for Alan and wasn't treated well. Do you know anything else?"

"I think he's kind of creepy," Amy said. "But people hire him, so they must trust his work. Or maybe it's just that he works cheap. I don't know."

"If he's worked for a lot of people in town maybe someone can tell us where he was Friday night. We can ask around. Who's next?"

Piper's shop door opened and a woman about Aunt Judy's age walked in. "Good morning," she said with a dimpling smile. "I'm hoping you have more of those delicious sweet-and-sour zucchini pickles. My family loves them."

"Hi, Mrs. Peterson," Amy said. She pulled a jar of zucchini pickles off the shelf and handed it to Piper.

"Wonderful!" Mrs. Peterson cried. "You know, I did canning and pickling a few years ago but got away from it, what with one thing or another. But these reminded me how good 'homemade' can taste—so much better than store-bought. Though I never did anything this exotic."

"This recipe's as easy as anything you've done," Piper assured her. She opened the cookbook that had her sweet-and-sour zucchini pickle recipe in it and let Mrs. Peterson look through it awhile.

"You know, I'm going to take this book, too, and study it at home. I just may talk myself into doing this again. I'm sure I still have my canning things. Wouldn't some of these relishes be wonderful to serve when I have the whole family over for Thanksgiving?"

"Definitely," Piper said, bagging up the pickle jar and cookbook. "And if you need anything new in canning equipment, we have that, too."

Mrs. Peterson beamed, her interest in pickling again obviously revived, and handed over her credit card. "I went to your booth yesterday," she said, as Piper totaled up the sale, "for these pickles. That's when I found out about Alan Rosemont. Terrible thing."

Piper nodded but could see that the woman wasn't too broken up about it. As she slid over the receipt for Mrs. Peterson to sign, she asked, "Did you know him?"

"Oh, I went into his antique shop once or twice." Mrs. Peterson scribbled her name on the dotted line. "He carried a nice collection of carnival glass for a while." She lowered her voice to a whisper. "But then I heard what he did to poor Mrs. Taylor."

The way she said it, Piper was almost afraid to ask, but this wasn't the time to get squeamish. "What was that?"

"Ah!" Mrs. Peterson lifted her chin and straightened her shoulders, looking about as indignant as a cat in a bath. "The Taylors have been in this county for generations, you know, and scads of their things have been passed down through the family. Most of it ended up in Dorothy Taylor's big attic. It was a real jumble, and she's getting old and grew awfully tired of dealing with the mess. Alan Rosemont got wind of that and offered to look through her attic and see if there was anything of value."

Uh-oh. Piper could guess what was coming.

"Well!" Mrs. Peterson exclaimed, then went on to

describe how Alan had convinced Dorothy Taylor that the contents of her attic was more trash than treasure but out of the goodness of his heart he was willing to pay her a modest sum and take it all off her hands. She agreed, believing she'd at least saved the cost of hiring someone to haul it away. "I remember her telling me how glad she was her son wouldn't have a mess of a house to deal with after she passed on, poor soul. Her son, Robby, lives in Poughkeepsie, you know."

Mrs. Peterson dropped her receipt into her purse before continuing. "When Robby came to visit and learned what she did, he was terribly upset. Poor Dorothy didn't realize there were things he cared about in her attic. But children do that, don't they? They think of their parents' house as their personal museum and their parents as caretakers."

Did they? Piper thought guiltily of the piles of school yearbooks and other memorabilia she'd left behind after college, blithely assuming they would be preserved without question. But with archeologists as parents, perhaps that wasn't such a bad assumption?

"Was Robby able to retrieve those things?" she asked.

Mrs. Peterson shook her head with much drama. "Alan Rosemont sold off the smaller items—toys in good condition, trunks of wonderful vintage clothing—as fast as he could. Some of the larger pieces like antique furniture in good condition were still in his shop but with astronomical price tags attached. Alan told Robert he had interested buyers but that Robert could make a bid if he liked. Imagine that! Asking him to buy back his own family's things."

"Robby must have been unhappy," Piper said.

"Furious is more the word for it. Not only did he lose family mementos, but Robby felt his mother had been fleeced. He complained to Sheriff Carlyle, but that didn't get him very far. Apparently, since Dorothy is of sound mind, the contract of sale she signed was valid."

"Too bad Mrs. Taylor didn't consult with her son before signing it. I guess living in Poughkeepsie, she doesn't see him all that much?"

"Oh, Robby visits fairly often," Mrs. Peterson said. "And since this episode, he's stepped it up. Worried, maybe, that Dorothy might sign away her house next. Dorothy entered her quilts in the fair, you know, and he was here to cheer her on."

"Was he, now?"

"Oh yes. He's a good son."

Mrs. Peterson picked up her purchase and took her leave. Once the door closed behind her, Piper turned to Amy.

"Well, I think I have a name for line three on my list."

Later that afternoon, Amy had taken off for her job at A La Carte, and Piper was in her back room, checking that she had a good supply of white vinegar, jars, and other items for her next pickling project. Her radio, still tuned to the classical station, played Gilbert and Sullivan, and Piper started humming along as Yum-Yum sang about the sun and moon in a song from *The Mikado*.

Since she was alone, her hums progressed to singing, and she soon became a Japanese maiden in full costume.

"—I mean to rule the earth as he the sky," she warbled. "We really know our worth, the sun and I."

"Must be a nice feeling!" a male voice said from the front of the store, startling Piper to immediate silence. She clicked off her radio and peeked out. Will Burchett stood there, grinning. He'd chucked the white apron and had exchanged the tee and shorts for a plaid shirt and khakis. But his eyes were just as blue as she remembered and currently were crinkled in high amusement.

"I didn't hear you come in," Piper said, wincing and aware of heat rising in her cheeks.

"Your singing may have drowned it out. But don't stop on my account. It was good."

"You're too kind. Way too kind. I sing with enthusiasm, and that's the best that can be said of it." She cleared her throat and came out to her front counter, setting down her clipboard. "So, how did the youth group concession go? Did they raise a good amount?"

"Enough to buy some new basketball equipment and maybe sponsor a hiking trip."

"Great! That was good of you to pitch in like you did."

He shrugged, then laughed. "I got roped into it at the last minute. Their regular grill man came down with some sort of bug. Who knows how many others Bill Vanderveen ran through before he called me, but he sounded pretty desperate. I wasn't too sure about handling it, but it turned out fine. They're a good group."

"Now you'll be at the top of their list, you know."

He laughed. "I know." He glanced around and said, "Nice shop."

"Thanks. I'm pretty proud of it, but I couldn't have set it up without help from a lot of generous people. I hear you bought the Andersons' tree farm?"

"Christmas trees. Right. Ever been out there?"

"Once or twice a long time ago."

"I've made a lot of changes. You might not recognize it." He leaned over to read the label on one of Piper's pickle jars. "Zucchini?"

"The Peterson family loves them."

"Ah. Well, there you go."

His lingering look of skepticism prompted Piper to grab a jar and hand it to him. "On the house, just to prove you'll like them."

He took the jar from her, studied it, then looked up at her. "I'll try them, but only if you'll let me show you around my tree farm."

"Oh! Well, ah, that's fair." She smiled. "Deal."

"Great. How's tomorrow evening?"

Piper thought that sounded pretty good, and they agreed that Will would pick her up around seven. He took off with a firm hold on his jar of sweet-and-sour zucchini pickles, and Piper watched as he headed toward a Christmas tree–colored van and climbed in. Then her cell phone dinged, signaling a text message. Piper turned from the window to check the phone.

"Saw this beautiful statue. Reminded me of U," a text from Scott read. The photo he attached, possibly of an ancient Indian goddess, was graceful and lovely in itself but looked nothing whatsoever like Piper. Still, it made her smile. Just like Scott, she thought, to come up with such a ridiculous comparison.

And with such an uncanny sense of timing.

8

~~~~

Piper was closing up shop for the evening when she noticed Tina Carson hurrying toward her. Since Tina's coffee shop closed around three, she'd changed from her work clothes to loose shorts and a blouse that deemphasized her extra pounds.

"Good, I caught you!" Tina called out. "I thought I'd pick up that pear chutney and save you a second trip."

"Oh, right," Piper said, realizing the chutney had totally slipped her mind. She held the door open for Tina, then flipped her sign to "Closed," wondering where in the world she might have stashed Tina's chutney. Things had been distracting, to say the least, in the last two days. After poking around a bit, Piper found the jars right where they should have been, between sweet pickle relish and pepper relish, where she suspected Amy must have efficiently set them.

Piper slipped the two jars into a bag and handed it to Tina, who said, "I've been really concerned about Nate. He hasn't been arrested or anything, has he?"

"Not last I heard. But more reasons to charge him seem to be cropping up. We're only hoping they won't seem so to Sheriff Carlyle."

"Oh, I hope so, too." Tina's look of distress touched Piper. "I'm afraid I haven't picked up anything very useful yet from my breakfast or lunch customers," Tina said. "Whenever I manage to bring Gordon Pfiefle into the conversation—which isn't all that easy," she added with a laugh, "they get to complaining about how the price of food keeps going up. Nobody blames Gordon for the high costs, though. They generally find a way to pin it on Congress, and then the political grousing takes off."

"Anything come up about Pfiefle's scratches?"

"One woman said she'd noticed them, but at other times, too, not just this weekend. Maybe they just have an ornery cat? Or he grows plants like roses with thorns in his yard?"

"Maybe." Piper thought the Pfiefles' neighbor, Martha Smidley, might know a little more about that. A visit to the lady with a complimentary jar of piccalilli could be in order.

"I was wondering about Dennis Isley," Piper said. "You said he didn't like Alan Rosemont. Was there anything that might have tipped him over the edge toward murder?"

"Oh, gosh, I don't think so. Dennis complains a lot. But

I get the feeling he's used to life being a string of just one lousy thing after another. I doubt he'd ever get mad enough for murder."

"When he came to fix your leaky pipe yesterday, did he mention where he had been late Friday night when Alan was murdered?"

"Hmm. Let me think. He was talking about baseball." Tina brightened. "Yes, that was it. The Yankees played two nights in a row, Friday and Saturday. Both games ran late on TV, which is why he didn't appreciate me dragging him out early Sunday morning. And there was a fight in the stands during Friday night's game, which Dennis seemed to enjoy even more than the game. It sounded like he watched again Saturday night just hoping there'd be another fight." Tina rolled her eyes.

"Well, I'll still keep him on my list of suspects for now. But Dennis Isley probably won't make my call list of handymen."

"Yeah, I know what you mean. Sometimes, though, he's the only one available. If you need another suspect, Lynn Jackson did say she remembered a guy hanging around the fair on Friday, someone she never saw before. She said he looked up to no good."

"Did she get anything that would help the sheriff, like a name or a license plate number?"

Tina shook her head. "'Fraid not. Only that he looked kind of scruffy and shifty. A youngish guy. Maybe someone else noticed him, too. I'll let you know if I hear more."

As Piper let Tina out, a distant voice called, "Just a minute, there, young woman." Charlotte Hosch was striding their way purposefully, and the sight made Piper want to step back into her shop and pull down the shade. Instead, she pasted on a polite smile and waited.

"You're going to have to do something about the horrendous odors coming from your shop," Charlotte demanded, as she drew near.

"Odors?" Piper asked.

"Your pickling odors! Vinegar and that other stuff you cook with. They're flooding the entire neighborhood."

Piper's smile stiffened. "I really don't think so, Charlotte."

"They certainly are! It's horrible. Everyone on the street can smell it, and who's going to think of buying my candies when they're smelling pickles, I ask you. I won't have it. You've got to do something about it or I'll have to take matters in my own hands. You have fair warning!"

With that, Charlotte spun on her heel and marched away toward her own shop. Tina turned a sympathetic eye toward Piper. "She complained to me, too, about my fried onions. I wouldn't worry about it. There's nothing in the town regulations that say you can't have normal cooking odors coming from your establishment."

"Even if there were," Piper said, "I've taken pains to manage mine with a HEPA air cleaner. I don't want my own shop overwhelmed with the aroma of vinegar and spices. So I couldn't be choking the neighborhood with them, either."

"Unfortunately, you probably haven't heard the last of it from Charlotte." With that, Tina took off, and Piper locked up, thinking ahead to the next day when she and Amy planned to cook up a batch of summer savory wax beans. She pictured Charlotte Hosch sniffing outside her door, cell phone in hand and finger hovering over her call button for 911. Piper sighed.

The next morning, however, no SWAT team burst through the door as Amy and Piper worked in the shop's back room, following Aunt Judy's recipe, which Piper had tasted—and loved—Saturday night. The pint jars had just been taken from their boiling water bath to cool, and the two set about cleaning up the scraps and trimmings of wax beans and red peppers. Piper's air cleaner, she noted with satisfaction, had worked so well they hadn't even needed to open the windows and thus lose her cool, air-conditioned air—or flood the neighborhood with any odors.

"I can't wait to try these," Amy said. "Adding that slice of gingerroot and a bay leaf to each jar along with all the other spices we simmered into the mix should make them totally delish."

Piper was about to comment on the delicate flavor she'd tasted in Aunt Judy's batch, when she heard her front door open. She'd rigged a simple bell system the night before to cut off any chance of being caught unawares—singing or anything else—ever again, feeling proud of herself and pleased that those hours of following Uncle Frank around as a youngster while he did his farm repairs had paid off. The bell, attached to a wire that she'd strung through metal eyes along the ceiling of her shop, rang clearly in the back room, and two female voices chimed along with it, calling out, "Hellooo."

"It's Erin and Megan," Amy said, brightening, which Piper was glad to see. Though Amy had made a strong effort to be upbeat as she'd worked beside her, Piper could tell that she was feeling down from worry over Nate. Piper grabbed a towel to wipe her hands and followed Amy, who'd hurried out.

"We just came from my brother's office," Megan said, referring to Ben Schaeffer. "I asked him point-blank who told him that Alan Rosemont had laughed in Nate's face when he didn't get the music camp job."

"And?" Piper asked.

"And nothing!" Megan swiped her long blond hair off her neck in disgust. "You'd think he was CIA and I was asking him to divulge state secrets. He's an idiot."

"No, he's not," Erin argued softly. "He's just trying not to step on Sheriff Carlyle's toes by giving out information."

"I'd like to stomp on *his* toes," Megan said, and Piper realized how little resemblance she saw between Megan and her brother, either physically or personality wise. She could never imagine Ben Schaeffer threatening to stomp on anyone. Piper could, however, see him carefully writing up a warning that, if not followed, could lead to a significant fine—and take much satisfaction in having done his part toward making Cloverdale a safer place.

"Don't worry about pressing Ben for now," Piper said. "If the story turns out to be a problem for Nate, he'll find out soon enough where it's coming from."

"I just hate that anyone could think so badly of Nate," Amy said. "If they took the time to really know him, they'd see how totally incapable he is of hurting anyone." Amy looked so distraught that Megan and Erin closed in for a double hug.

"That's what we're trying to do," Erin said, stepping back first. "We're talking to everyone who'll listen about all the great things Nate does. Like how he spent hours learning all those 1960s songs so he could sing them when the O'Neills celebrated their fiftieth wedding anniversary at A La Carte. Nobody paid him extra for that. He just thought it'd be a nice thing to do."

"You guys are the greatest," Amy said, her eyes shining.

"Say," Piper said, "if you're going to keep Amy company for a while, I'm going to run out for a bit, okay?"

"Sure, no problem," they answered practically in unison.

"Just call my cell if anything urgent comes up," Piper told Amy as she shed her apron and grabbed a jar of piccalilli from the shelf. "I shouldn't be too long." As she left, Piper saw Amy leading her friends to the back room to finish the cleanup rather than just stand and chat. The girl was worth her weight in gold.

Piper had looked up Gordon and Lyella Pfiefle's address the night before, then Martha Smidley's, which appeared to be on the opposite side of Locust Street. The direct way to Locust meant walking past Charlotte Hosch's candy shop, so she struck out on the longer route, having decided it was a fine day for a walk.

Locust Street, Piper soon found, was lined with a variety of brick and clapboard homes tucked cozily together and fronted with meticulously kept lawns. The Pfiefles' house was on a corner lot and therefore had a side yard as well. There were no thorny rosebushes that Piper could see, nor raspberry brambles, nor anything else particularly scratch producing. Just nice, soft grass edged with a few marigolds and other colorful and tidy annuals.

Piper turned to Martha Smidley's house, which sat directly opposite. It was similarly well kept with its healthy grass, sprinkling of flowers, and clean, white siding. The only thing remarkable about the place, Piper realized, was the aged face peering at her from the window. Piper gave a little wave and headed toward the door, which opened before she reached it.

"You're the woman at the library," Martha said. She'd exchanged her wrinkled beige linen of the other day for an apple green housedress. Her feet were clad in sandals and white cotton socks.

"I am. I'm also Piper Lamb, and I've brought you a complimentary jar of piccalilli from my shop, Piper's Picklings."

"Thank you." Martha smiled as she took the jar, but her sharp eyes examined Piper closely. "I had a feeling you might stop by. Come in."

Martha's living room contained a collection of mix-and-match furniture—a sofa, upholstered chairs, an ancient, console television set—that looked to have been acquired over decades. Interestingly, one comfy-looking chair was turned toward the large bay window that was free of view-blocking draperies or sheers.

"Piccalilli," Martha said, turning the jar about. "I haven't had that for ages. This will be a nice treat. Would you care for some iced tea?"

"That would be great, thank you."

Martha trundled off to her kitchen, and Piper took a seat on the plump, brown and gold–printed sofa. She glanced around, seeing a sprinkling of knickknacks and family photos. On the padded cushion of the bay window perched a pair of binoculars.

"Here we are," Martha said, carrying a tray with two large glasses of tea and a plate of cookies. Piper jumped up to take it from the elderly woman and set it on the coffee table for her. "Thank you. It's always nice to get company during the day. So many of the younger people are off at jobs nowadays. How did you manage to leave your shop?"

"I have a great assistant," Piper said. She handed a glass of tea to Martha and took the second. "Amy Carlyle."

"Oh yes. The sheriff's daughter. She used to babysit for the Crandalls down the street. I don't think they were aware that her two friends, Megan Schaeffer and Erin Healy, sometimes joined her. But I don't suppose there was any harm in it, do you?"

Knowing Amy, she had most likely cleared her friends' visits with the Crandalls, but Piper said, "Probably not. You obviously keep an eye on things, Mrs. Smidley." Piper nodded toward the binoculars.

"I like to know what's going on in my neighborhood. You hear about burglars pulling moving vans up to houses where nobody's home and pretending they have the right to walk off with everything. That won't happen around here. I know who's moving and who's not, as well as who's a legitimate house painter or gutter cleaner and who isn't. Nobody will be putting up ladders where they shouldn't on my street!"

Was Martha Smidley possibly related to Ben Schaeffer? Piper wondered. She took a sip of her tea and said, "That's very conscientious of you. At the library you mentioned being aware of the Pfiefles' routines. I see you have a clear view of their place."

"I do." Martha smiled. "Of course, I wouldn't dream of invading anyone's privacy."

"Of course not."

"But I can't help seeing what's right before my eyes, can I?"

"Certainly not."

"And I did notice that their lights were on the night of Alan Rosemont's murder—I assume that's what you're interested in—though I didn't see them leave." Martha took a sip of her tea. "That's not to say they—or he— couldn't have left the house. It's just that it's impossible for me to see everything." She sighed. "Like that time Gordon got into a shouting match with Hal Brockway. Unfortunately, I was at the doctor's that morning." She gestured vaguely toward her abdomen, indicating a not-to-be-mentioned ailment in that area.

"What was it about? The shouting match, I mean."

"Well," Martha said, leaning forward, "it seems the Brockway boy—a horrible child, if you ask me—trampled over Lyella's newly planted flowers in pursuit of a soccer ball, or, more likely, on purpose. When she called him out on it, he responded in an extremely rude way. The father either denied the incident or claimed it was no big thing." Martha's eyes snapped in indignation as she straightened her back. "My belief is it was the latter. After all, where did the child learn his ways? This infuriated Gordon and very nearly, from what I heard, led to a physical fight. As I said before, Gordon worships the very ground Lyella walks on and is very protective of her."

"So Gordon Pfiefle has a temper?"

Martha nodded firmly. "He keeps it in check most of the time. But when it comes to standing up for Lyella, well, I'd have to say Hal Brockway had a lucky day, that morning."

9

On her way back to the shop, Piper mulled over her conversation with Martha Smidley, who had, much to her regret, been unable to come up with a good explanation for the scratches on Gordon Pfiefle's neck and face. No ill-tempered cat or other pets, no habit of hiking through brushy terrain. Nothing.

She suddenly spotted Sheriff Carlyle standing near his patrol car, chatting on the sidewalk with Jim Reilly, one of Cloverdale's barbers. Piper slowed, planning to catch the sheriff when he'd finished. She pretended interest in a pair of lavender, multi-strapped, stiletto-heeled sandals (not quite her style) displayed in a shoe store's window. When she heard, "Okay, Jim, see you later," and saw Jim Reilly disappear into his barbershop, she hurried forward and called out, "Sheriff?"

Sheriff Carlyle turned. "Well, good day, Miss Piper," he said, touching his hat. "How are you today? My little girl watching your shop?"

"She is, Sheriff. Amy also has Megan and Erin with her."

The sheriff chuckled. "Those three never get too far apart, do they?"

"Sheriff, I've been talking with a few people since Alan Rosemont's murder."

"Now, don't let anyone upset you, Miss Piper. We know it was just your bad luck that Alan's body was left in your pickle barrel. No one should be blaming you the least bit for what happened. We're hot on the trail of knowing exactly what happened."

"I know you'll come up with the truth, Sheriff. I just thought I should tell you that Gordon Pfiefle's name has come up in this regard."

"Gordon?"

"You know, of course, he's married to Lyella Pfiefle, the librarian whose building Alan Rosemont painted that terrible pink color. Gordon, I understand, is quite defensive of Lyella, and he's known to be willing to fight on her behalf. I wondered if he might have confronted Alan about the library situation late Friday night on the fairgrounds? I've seen Alan's temper, and I can imagine any confrontation with him turning ugly."

The sheriff looked thoughtful. "I hope these people you've been talking to haven't been tossing around accusations."

"No, nothing to that level. Because, of course, unless there's concrete evidence pointing to a particular person, nobody would want to upset anyone's life that way."

"Understood. Ah, Piper," the sheriff said—and Piper noticed her demotion from "Miss"—"I'm sure my daughter has given you an earful about the part of our investigation that's involved her friend, Nate Purdy. I'm very sorry that she's upset, but as I've assured her, and I'm now assuring you, we will not pass over anyone simply to avoid upsetting those near and dear to us."

"I know you won't, Sheriff. Which is exactly why I'm passing on what I've learned about Gordon Pfiefle. He seems to be a well-liked man, and I'm sure Lyella, in particular, won't be happy if you question him about Alan Rosemont. But as you said, you'll need to be thorough in your investigation."

Sheriff Carlyle's face suddenly looked like he had simultaneously bitten into a sweet spiced apple and a tart mustard pickle. "I thank you for your confidence," he said politely, "and for the information. It will be dealt with appropriately."

With that, the sheriff touched his hat once more and climbed into his patrol car. Piper watched him drive off, hoping that his definition of appropriate matched hers but having the feeling she'd just been dismissed. Don't call us, we'll call you.

A glance at her watch made her gulp. It was almost time for Amy to leave for her second job. Piper took off, taking the direct route and picking up her already swift pace significantly as she passed Charlotte's Chocolates and Confections. When she hurried into Piper's Picklings, Amy appeared at the doorway to the back room, looking upset.

"I know. I'm late. I'm so sorry—" Piper began, but Amy waved her hands, stopping her.

"No, no! That's not the problem. Come look." She spun around and Piper followed, wondering what was wrong.

"Erin and Megan helped me clean up back here, and I dumped all the garbage into the can out back, like we always do. After they left—just a few minutes ago—I found a bit of trash we'd overlooked, so I carried it out. See what I found?" Amy opened the outside door and stepped aside for Piper to see. The garbage can had been turned upside down and all its contents—piles of vegetable scraps and soggy papers— were spread across the alley pavement. Piper gasped at the mess.

"What happened?"

"I have no idea. I didn't hear a thing."

"Kids?" Piper asked.

"That was my first thought, but look." Amy pointed to the garbage cans up and down the alley behind other establishments. All were upright and covered. Piper's was the only mess. "Kids in the mood for this kind of mischief would have tipped over as many as they could."

Amy looked at Piper worriedly. "I think someone's got it in for you."

Piper scurried about her upstairs apartment, running late getting ready for her date with Will Burchett. Was it a date? She wasn't really sure. Her hair was still wet and wrapped in a towel from her shower. Should she pull it back or leave it down? And what did one wear for a tour of a Christmas tree farm? Tinsel?

She grabbed a bite of the chicken sandwich from the plate on her bed as she switched on her hair dryer. She'd been late closing up the shop because of two lingering, chatty customers, then still had to clean up the garbage disaster in the alley. Amy had offered to do it, but Piper shooed her off to her restaurant job. When Piper finally made it up to her apartment, a sandwich was all she'd had time to throw together before jumping into the shower, and Will would be there in minutes!

Settle down, Piper ordered herself. Will could wait in her small living room if he had to. However, someone had to open the door to let him in, and guess who that someone would be? Did she really want his first sight of her to be in her ratty bathrobe with a towel wrapped around her head? Piper switched the hair dryer to high and waved it furiously at her hair.

When the doorbell rang, Piper had somehow managed to get herself dried and dressed, as well as powdered and glossed. She took a deep breath, then walked slowly down the steps to her apartment's street door.

"Hi," Will said. "Sorry, I'm a little late. A delivery truck drove up just as I was ready to leave."

"Oh, no problem," Piper said smoothly and wished multiple blessings on that timely deliveryman. "Shall we go?"

As she buckled herself into the passenger seat of Will's green van, Piper felt herself relax. Something about Will made that very easy. She was glad she'd decided to go with shorts, sneakers, and her favorite yellow tee, which Scott had once said made her brown eyes look like deep, dark chocolate (but she wasn't going to think of Scott right then). Will had dressed just as casually, a signal that the evening would be a simple tour of his farm and a prompt return home, which was fine. It was a nice evening to be out.

"So," she said as he slid into the driver's seat, "Aunt

Judy said you bought the Christmas tree farm a couple of years ago?"

"Right. It was pure luck that I happened to be in the market at the same time the Andersons were ready to sell." He put his van in gear. "The farm was in great shape, so taking it over went very smoothly, and I was able to get started right away on the changes I wanted to make."

Will drove down Beech Street for a few blocks, then turned toward the highway. Piper's stomach gurgled, a complaint, probably, on the recent scarfing down of her sandwich, and she was glad the van's motor was on the loud side.

"I tried those zucchini pickles, by the way," Will said.

She turned to him with a smile. "And?"

He grinned. "Not bad."

Piper laughed. "Not bad? Well, I'll take that as high praise from someone who was extremely skeptical of them."

"My apologies. My mother would probably tell you I was a picky eater as a kid, though I always thought of it as being sensibly cautious. I think I've grown out of most of that, but those pickles caught me by surprise."

"Then I'm honored that you decided to risk it." Piper thought of Scott's fondness for sushi, one more difference between the two men since she couldn't picture Will clamping chopsticks around a salmon and seaweed sushi roll. But then, sushi had never been a favorite of hers, now that she thought of it. She had only tolerated it for Scott's sake.

They talked about Will's family—one older brother and a younger sister—and where he'd grown up—

Vermont—then how he became interested in Christmas tree farming—a college major in plant sciences, which ultimately convinced him he preferred hands-on to theoretical work, specifically with Christmas trees.

By the time they got through all that, they'd arrived at the turnoff for Will's farm, marked by a colorful sign pointing to Burchett Tree Farm and Christmas Shop. As they drove up the long, private road, memories of Piper's childhood visit to the place with Uncle Frank and Aunt Judy came floating back—except that all the trees had looked a lot bigger to her eight-year-old self.

"How long does it take to grow a Christmas tree?" she asked.

"About ten years until it's ready to cut."

"Wow. So I guess that's why you'd want a farm that's already established?"

Will nodded with a smile. "It helps."

The top of the road widened into a small, graveled parking lot. "We'll switch here," Will said, "to something that'll handle the bumps in the field better. It's sturdy but doesn't look that great, so I generally drive the van into town." Piper walked with Will over to a mud-splattered, scraped, and dented four-wheeler, then held on for dear life as they bounced their way in it to the various fields, Will pointing out plantings of firs, spruce, and white pines. The scents coming from the dark green trees were wonderful, and Piper commented on it.

"My farm is all organic," Will told her. "That's important to me, when you think of people bringing one of these trees into their homes. I wouldn't want those branches loaded with pesticides."

"Some people say they have artificial trees because they hate the thought of cutting down a live tree for a few weeks' decoration."

Will laughed. "I've heard that before. Christmas trees are planted specifically for cutting. Nobody's clearing wild forests. And when a live tree is taken down after Christmas, it gets ground up into biodegradable mulch. How long do they think those artificial trees sit in a landfill once they toss them out?"

"Good point," Piper said, and thought a tad guiltily about the plastic tree she'd owned but had at least passed on to the girl taking over her apartment in Albany instead of dumping it. Would that new tenant also pass it on when her time came to move? She hoped so.

Will drove her through fields he said were designated for "cut your own" customers, and much larger fields of trees that would be cut in late fall by crews and shipped off to other vendors. He talked about the new netting and tie-down equipment he'd invested in, and Piper found, to her surprise, that a subject she'd never dreamed could be interesting actually was. Will's enthusiasm probably had a lot to do with it, and she liked the idea of someone investing their time and savings into doing something they really loved—much like herself. Will Burchett also had obviously discovered "who he was," as opposed to Scott, who was currently on the other side of the world trying to figure that out.

The tour ended at a small building Will said he'd put up just that year. "The Burchett Christmas Gift Shop," he announced with a wave. "We'll offer hot and cold refreshments during our busy season, when I'll also have someone here to handle it. Right now, all I can offer is Coke, 7 Up, and a variety of chips."

"Sounds great," Piper said, pleased at the prospect of extending her time with Will. The more she learned about him, the better she liked him.

Will pointed her to a small round table with two wire-backed chairs as he went to gather their snacks. The gift shop had a counter where Piper imagined Will's future employee would dispense food and drink orders to families hungry after tramping through the fields in search of the perfect tree. The shelves throughout the shop currently held only a few sealed cardboard boxes, but she could picture them loaded with Christmas knickknacks and toys, the entire shop decorated with fresh greens and lights, as well as smelling of pine, and maybe cinnamon and cloves. The image made her smile.

Will brought the sodas and chips and sat down.

"You have a wonderful place, Will," Piper said truthfully.

Will beamed. "It's a lot of hard work, but I love it. But now it's your turn. Tell me all about how you ended up in Cloverdale with your pickling shop."

Piper smiled, certain he didn't really want to know about all the ins and outs of her developing love of the pickling process, learned in Aunt Judy's kitchen and fueled by Uncle Frank's farm-grown vegetables. She gave him the condensed version, though, tossing in mention of her long engagement to Scott, which she made clear no longer existed. Will nodded without comment, but she thought she saw a smile in his eyes.

Eventually, the conversation worked its way, between

crunches on BBQ-flavored corn chips and salt and vinegar crinkle cuts, to Alan Rosemont's unsolved murder.

"I've been looking around for possible suspects, for Amy's sake," Piper said. "And for mine, too," she admitted. "I just can't see Nate Purdy as the guilty one, despite Sheriff Carlyle's apparent interest in him."

"Isn't Sheriff Carlyle Amy's father?"

Piper nodded. "He's doing his best to keep that fact from influencing him. I just hope he isn't leaning too far in the other direction in his efforts to be impartial." She took a swallow of her soda.

"So you're looking for other suspects. I hope that's not why you came here tonight?" Will said it with a smile, but Piper realized with shock that he'd asked a reasonable question.

"Not at all!" But what could she say that didn't get her into more trouble? That she'd come because she liked his blue eyes and honest face? "You shouldn't be a suspect, should you?"

"No, but maybe you should have verified that before riding alone with me to this remote spot? As it happens, besides never having met Alan Rosemont in my life, I have a pretty good alibi for Friday night." He paused, grinning, and Piper realized she was holding her breath. "I was playing cards with Sheriff Carlyle and three other men. Low stakes."

Piper laughed. "I guess you can't do much better than that."

"Probably not. But I hope when you're looking around for suspects, you'll always keep your own safety in mind."

Will looked so serious, but Piper knew he was right.

She was getting involved in something that could have dangerous repercussions. Her tipped-over garbage can came to mind. Certainly nothing that could be called dangerous—more annoying than anything. But could it also have been a warning?

10

"So, how did you enjoy your tour of Will's tree farm?" Aunt Judy asked casually as she browsed through Piper's spices. Uncle Frank had dropped her off along with a fresh bushel of his black-spined cucumbers.

Piper looked up in surprise. She'd intended to mention the evening tour to her aunt, but in an "oh, by the way" manner. "How did you know about that?"

Aunt Judy smiled. "You're still not used to small-town living, are you? Not much gets missed."

"Other than the occasional murder, I presume?"

"Well, that," Aunt Judy agreed. "But when a young lady gets picked up on a bright summer evening and heads off in the direction of the driver's tree farm, somebody's bound to notice. Will's very proud of his setup."

"He should be. I was impressed." Piper was sorting

through the bushel, but it was clear Uncle Frank had already done so. She hadn't found a swollen or pinch-ended cuke in the bunch. Plus they'd been thoroughly washed, though she'd give each cucumber a second scrub before packing them into her crocks. "To answer your question, I enjoyed the tour very much. But it was simply a tour," she added. "Will's a nice guy, and I'm glad to get to know him. Nothing more."

"Of course not." Aunt Judy replaced a jar of Sichuan peppercorns that she'd been examining. "It's always good to make new friends. And I agree. Will's a very nice young man."

Piper thought it was time to change the subject. "I've been checking out a few possible suspects that might deflect Sheriff Carlyle's investigation away from Nate. Lyella Pfiefle and her husband Gordon, as you know. But I also learned about Dorothy Taylor's son, Robby, who was pretty ticked off about Alan Rosemont's fleecing of his mom, and rightfully so, I'd say. According to Mrs. Peterson, Robby was in town during the fair. Do you think he's the kind of guy whose anger could turn violent?"

Aunt Judy frowned. "I haven't run into Robby very much since he was a teenager, and we all know how volatile teenage boys can be. They usually grow out of it, though whether or not Robby did I just can't say. I could drop in on Dorothy if you like. If she's aware of anything bad Robby might have done I think I'd be able to tell. And if she's in the dark—and I have to say Dorothy doesn't always pick up on things that others do—I might at least be able to pin down his whereabouts late Friday night."

"Would you? That'd be great."

"I do want to help. I feel the same as you, that it's just too unbelievable that Nate could do something so terrible as murder. There's a few too many in this town, though, who are ready to jump to conclusions when a stranger is involved."

"I guess I'd better watch my step, then, too," Piper said, only half joking. She was thinking of her overturned garbage, which she hadn't mentioned to her aunt and didn't plan to.

"You're not a stranger, dear," Aunt Judy said, patting her hand. "At most you're a newcomer, but plenty of people know you, or at least about you, through us. Nate doesn't have any connections here, though, and that's the problem. It makes some people uneasy when they can't fit a person into a slot."

"It is odd that he's so alone," Piper said, "although I can think of plenty of reasonable explanations for that."

"I'm sure we'll learn more when he's comfortable sharing. For now, I'm happy with accepting the boy for himself."

The shop's door opened, and two ladies entered.

"Good morning, Mrs. Lamb," the older of the two said to Aunt Judy. The other nodded politely.

Aunt Judy responded in a polite but reserved manner, which told Piper these women might belong to the group of "some people" her aunt had just referred to. Aunt Judy introduced the two to Piper and slipped in a recommendation or two for Piper's newer pickling spices to the women. Then she took her leave.

"I'll let you know what comes up," she said to Piper, who nodded, hoping her aunt would be able to dig up something useful for Nate. She then turned to her customers, who were picking and poking about like gulls on a search for bread crumbs.

"Ladies," she said, bracing herself for a challenge, "can I help you?"

An hour or so later, when Amy arrived for her shift, the first words out of her mouth were, "So, how was your date with Will Burchett?"

"How did you know about that?"

Amy looked puzzled for a moment, as though Piper had asked how she was aware the sun was shining or that it was Wednesday. "Megan saw you riding off together. That was you, wasn't it?"

Piper sighed. "Yes, it was. But I wouldn't exactly call it a date. Will was just showing me his tree farm."

"Ah." Amy stowed her purse under Piper's counter. "Did he feed you?"

"Y-yes. Just chips and a soda, though."

"Was he cleaned up and changed out of his work clothes?"

Piper nodded, aware of where this was going.

Amy whooped. "It was a date!"

Piper sighed. "Okay, maybe it was. But just a 'friends' date."

"No such thing," Amy declared, "if the guy goes to some pains—and I'll bet you did, too, right?"

Piper half shrugged, but then nodded honestly.

"Then it was an honest-to-goodness date. Yay! Piper has a boyfriend."

"No! Don't call him that, especially not to anyone else—not even Megan or Erin."

"Okay," Amy promised, "I won't." She grinned slyly. "But I think it's great."

The phone rang, and Piper grabbed for it thankfully. "Piper's Picklings."

"Piper, it's me," Aunt Judy said. "I've been to see Dorothy Taylor."

"That was fast." Piper pulled up a stool and sat down as Amy headed toward the back room. "How did it go?" Piper asked.

"It was . . ." her aunt said, hesitating. "Odd."

"Odd? In what way?"

"Well, as I mentioned, Dorothy was never exactly the brightest bulb in the chandelier. But either her mental capacities have gone downhill significantly, or she's hiding something."

Piper began penciling inward-turning spirals on a nearby notepad as she listened.

"You asked her about Robby?"

"Oh yes. And normally she's quite chatty about him, going into more details than you ever want to know. But today she simply said he was fine and stopped there. So I said I was sorry to have missed him since I understood he'd been in town for the fair. That's when she got this funny look on her face and changed the subject altogether."

"That is odd."

"Yes! I didn't know what to do about turning the conversation back to Robby—I didn't like to make poor Dorothy uncomfortable when she'd clearly signaled she didn't want to talk about her son. I'm so sorry, Piper. I make a terrible detective!"

"Not at all. You found out that Robby Taylor is a person

we should be checking into more closely—just not through his mother, obviously."

"Oh, I do hope it's not Robby who did in Alan Rosemont. Dorothy would be so upset. But there! Another reason I'd make a bad policewoman. I'd feel so sorry for anyone I arrested that I'd probably end up letting them go."

"No you wouldn't, Aunt Judy, because you'd feel even worse for their victims."

"Maybe so." Piper heard a sigh. "But it's just as well I went into farming with your Uncle Frank, isn't it? I can be quite hard-hearted over a less-than-perfect parsnip when I have to be. Which reminds me, Frank will be picking me up any minute. I'd better go."

Piper thanked her aunt for her efforts and hung up the phone. As she did, Amy came out from the back room, tying on an apron.

"I'm going to have to find out where Robby Taylor was on the night Alan Rosemont was murdered," Piper said. She told Amy about Dorothy Taylor's evasiveness.

Amy's face lit up with excitement. "I'll ask around, too. Wouldn't it be cool if we find it was him?" she said, inadvertently expressing the exact opposite opinion from Aunt Judy's.

"It'll be great to find out who the real murderer is and be able to tell your father. Which reminds me, do you happen to know if your father was playing cards Friday night with Will?"

"The night of the murder? I know he played cards, and that Will often joins that group. I'd have to check whether he was there that night. You asked Will for an alibi?"

"He offered it. It hadn't even occurred to me until he brought it up. Which was foolish, I know."

Amy grinned. "It's hard to see straight when there are stars in your eyes."

"Enough!" Piper cried, but with a smile. "Just find out from your father, if you would. Discreetly." Piper reached for her own purse. "Since you're here, I'm going to run over to Tina's coffee shop for lunch. She's been keeping her eyes open for us, too. Maybe she's picked up something."

"Hope so. While you're gone, I'll get started on that bushel of cukes back there, okay?"

"That'd be great. Bring you anything?" Amy shook her head, and Piper pulled open her door. "I won't be long."

The coffee shop was busy, so Piper ordered her sandwich and coffee, then nibbled on it as Tina tended to her other customers. Tina's part-time waitress, Darla, who was there only on the busier weekdays, bustled about as well, and it wasn't long before all were served and the crowd began to thin. The coffee shop seemed to have become the top choice of many who enjoyed the food but had jobs or other things to get back to, so few dawdled over extra cups of coffee.

When the place had about emptied out, Darla announced it was time for her to pick up her youngest and took off. Piper was down to her final potato chip crumbs when Tina pulled out the chair opposite.

"Whew! Glad that's over."

"Business is doing well," Piper said.

Tina nodded. "Not too badly, though yesterday wasn't nearly this busy. You never know what to expect. Want some more coffee?"

"I'm fine, thanks. Got anything to report?"

Tina smirked. "I did hear that a certain pickling shop owner has started seeing a certain Christmas tree farmer, but maybe that's not what you meant?"

"Oh good Lord!"

"But don't worry, Janice Hockley approves, though Betsy Testerman has a few worries about the level of debt Will might be carrying and whether he's in a position to think of settling down yet."

"Let me know when they've booked the church," Piper said. "I'd hate to miss my own wedding."

Tina laughed. "They're just having fun with it. A few of these older people have time on their hands."

"Next time, send them to me. I'll show them better ways to keep their minds occupied—and their pantries filled at the same time."

"Will do. Nothing more has come up on Gordon Pfiefle, by the way. Sorry."

"That's okay. Keep listening, and while you're at it would you keep an ear open for anything on Robby Taylor?"

"Sure. Who's he?"

Piper explained about Robby, and his mother's uncharacteristic evasiveness when asked about him."

"Sounds like she knows something that she doesn't like, doesn't it? Of course, that could be anything from 'he lost his job' to 'he murdered Alan Rosemont last weekend.'" Just then, a man of about sixty walked into the coffee shop, and Tina slid back her chair. "Hi, there, Mr. Laseter."

"Afternoon," Mr. Laseter said cheerily, including both women in his greeting. "Mind packing up one of those tasty egg salad sandwiches for me to take along, Ms. Carson?"

"Coming right up."

As Piper made her way to the counter to settle her bill, Mr. Laseter said, "You're that lady owns the pickle shop."

Piper smiled. "Yes, I am."

"Shame about what happened at your booth. I hope it didn't hurt your business none."

"Thank you. I can't really tell, yet, since my shop's barely gotten off the ground."

"Well, I hope not, anyway. I hate to see anyone get hurt, even that miserable Alan Rosemont. My friend Ralph Farber, though, has been dancing a jig since it happened."

"Oh?"

Tina turned from her sandwich making and threw a look at Piper, but Piper didn't need any prodding.

"Why is Mr. Farber so happy?"

"Throw in a bag of chips with that, would you?" Mr. Laseter said to Tina before answering Piper. "Ralph's delighted because he doesn't have to listen to that infernal bagpipe wailing anymore. He lives next door to Alan Rosemont. Or he did, since Alan's not there anymore, is he?"

No, he isn't, Piper thought.

11

~~~~~

Mr. Laseter took off, but before Piper had a chance to discuss with Tina the interesting tidbit he'd dropped, Dennis Isley pushed his way into the coffee shop, wearing the same stained denims as before, which, from the whiff Piper caught, may not have been off his lanky frame since then.

"Hey, Tina!" he called, while giving Piper a blatant once-over. "I've been working hard patching old Mr. Perkins's roof. I need a cold drink." He winked at Piper, who decided it was time to take off.

As she turned to say so to Tina, she noticed a pained look on the shop owner's face as she loaded ice into a tall, take-out cup, and hoped that didn't signal another of Tina's headaches coming on. At least Dennis wouldn't be hanging around. What a shame, Piper thought only half seriously, that Tina was able to give Dennis an alibi for Friday night.

When she stepped out the coffee shop door, Piper spotted Charlotte Hosch standing halfway up the block, apparently venting her complaints of the day to a younger—and obviously very patient—woman. Not caring to provoke a headache of her own, Piper turned in the opposite direction to circle the block.

Once she'd rounded the corner and was out of range of any "Just a minute there, young lady!" calls, Piper relaxed, and she continued on, soon coming upon a small park she'd forgotten existed. It looked invitingly cool, with its bubbling fountain framed with shaded benches. But as Piper drew closer, she spotted a dejected-looking figure sitting on one of the benches. Nate Purdy stared at the ground as his guitar lay silently on his lap.

"I hope you haven't had more misery piled on lately," Piper said, approaching.

Nate looked up and managed a wan smile. "Nothing I can't handle. I just thought I'd come out here and give my neighbors a rest from listening to me practice."

"With what you play, I can't imagine they'd really mind." Piper thought of Alan Rosemont's neighbor, Ralph Farber, having to put up with his bagpipe wheezes and wails, and knowing what she did of Alan, probably not at the best time of day—or night.

"Thanks." Nate lifted his guitar and dispiritedly plucked out the beginnings of a tune.

"I've been digging up information on other possible murder suspects to pass on to Sheriff Carlyle," Piper said, hoping to cheer him. "It's early days, but I think he'll pay attention as more things come up. A lot of people are pitching in."

"That's great of you, trying to help. But that friend of the sheriff's—Ben Schaeffer—really seems to have it in for me, and he has Carlyle's ear. As soon as I've explained away one problem, he comes up with another. He's like one of those terriers convinced a rat is in a hole and just keeps yapping and digging. I don't understand why Schaeffer seems so bent on my being the guilty one."

"We'll just have to prove Ben wrong," Piper said. And somehow shake him out of love with Amy, if that was possible. "How would you like a job in that respect?"

"Sure! Anything."

"You could check out Alan Rosemont's next-door neighbor, who might have been driven to murder by Alan's incessant piping."

"Who wouldn't?" Nate said with a grin. "What's his name?"

"Ralph Farber." Piper pulled out the smartphone that Scott had talked her into getting, and that she hadn't yet totally mastered. She started a search on Ralph Farber, muttering a bit over one or two missteps before crying, "Aha! Got it!" She whipped a sheet of notebook paper out of her purse. "Here's his address," she said, scribbling. "And, let me see . . ." She tapped a few more times. "Oh! Ralph Farber runs a plumbing business. It's over on Fourth Street." Piper wrote that down, too.

"I'll try to catch him there," Nate said. "Better than knocking on his door at home."

"It'd be great if you learned that he was at the fair late Friday night."

Nate laughed. "Wouldn't it? And if he'd mention that he happened to bash Rosemont in the head with a lead pipe while he was there, it would be very helpful."

Piper grinned, happy to see life returning to the musician. "You never know. But just getting a feel for the man and maybe his thoughts about Alan could tell us a lot."

"I'll see what I can do," Nate said, packing his guitar into its case.

They took off in separate directions, Piper hoping she'd both turned Nate's worries toward a productive use and that the mission she'd sent him on would in fact produce something positive.

Later that afternoon, Piper was alone in the back room of her shop when her newly installed bell signaled a visitor. She wiped her hands on her apron and hurried out to find Will on the other side of her counter.

"Hi!" Piper said, pleased to see him but also uncomfortably aware of all the recent interest and speculation about the two of them. Had he heard it, too, and come to put an end to it?

To her surprise, though, Will asked, "Are you free tonight?"

Piper hedged. "What did you have in mind?"

"Right," Will said. "Sorry, I should have explained. I just came from the barbershop." Piper had thought something was different about him but hadn't put a finger on it. Will, in fact, did that for her, running several fingers through his hair and returning the too-perfect combing to its normal rumpled state.

"Anyway," he continued, "that's where I picked up on the fact that Nate is on the verge of losing his job at A La Carte."

"No!"

"'Fraid so. Seems the owner has seen a significant drop-off in business since the murder and thinks Nate might be the cause because of his 'person of interest' status."

"That must be why he was so down when I ran into him today. Though he never said a word about it."

"It's not a done deal, from what I could tell. So I thought maybe if we went there for dinner tonight and also pulled in a few more customers, we could make Nate's boss happy enough to keep him on awhile longer." Will suddenly looked uncertain. "Or is that a completely lame idea?"

"I think it's a great idea! I'm sure I can get Aunt Judy and Uncle Frank interested. And they could get a few of their friends."

Will brightened. "I was hoping you'd think so. I'll see if I can spread the word to people I know, and maybe not all for tonight. It'd be good to keep it going for a few more nights."

"From what Amy told me, A La Carte gets people coming in just for drinks and nibbles later in the evening when Nate is still performing. So everyone doesn't have to spring for an expensive dinner. And that'd be fine with me, too," Piper said, giving Will an option he might not have thought of.

He smiled. "Dinner works for me, if it does for you. How about I pick you up at seven?"

Piper nodded. "Sounds great," she said, happy because it really did sound great. Will had come up with a very thoughtful way of helping someone they both believed was being treated unfairly, and in the process she had a pretty nice evening to look forward to.

A t six forty-five, Piper was dressed and ready, glad to have avoided the frantic rush of the night before. She'd picked out a summery dress to wear with strappy sandals, and as an afterthought grabbed a light shawl to throw over her bare shoulders if the night—or the restaurant—were cool.

Was this an official date? she wondered as she plopped down onto her sofa. Or was she simply Will's accomplice in his "saving Nate" plan? She sighed, thinking it didn't matter—either way, the Cloverdale townspeople would likely be placing bets on the date of their wedding, as well as the number and names of their future children. Much as she loved Cloverdale, there were times she missed life in the big, anonymous city.

Her doorbell rang, and Piper picked up her purse to meet her date-accomplice-escort, who, it turned out, had slipped a light sports jacket over a polo shirt and slacks. Piper could just hear Amy hooting, *It's a date! It's a date!* which she ignored as she let Will take her hand and walk her to his van.

T his was Piper's first visit to A La Carte, at least in its present form. She vaguely remembered that the place had once been an Italian restaurant, but it had changed nationalities and currently offered, according to Amy, country French cuisine.

The front entrance hinted at that with its old-brick façade, blue canopy, and hanging baskets of flowers. Inside, the large space had been made cozy with wood ceiling beams and a brick fireplace presently filled with flowers instead of logs.

As the hostess led the way to a white cloth–covered table, Piper glanced around and saw no sign of Nate, though a small stage was set up against one wall with a microphone and tall stool—a good sign that he was expected. At the moment, soft music floated through a speaker system, and patrons, of which Piper saw a gratifyingly decent number, conversed quietly in keeping with the congenial atmosphere.

"Oh, there's Bill Vanderveen," Piper said as she took her seat, spotting the man who was Uncle Frank's friend and the one who had pulled Will in to help at the youth group's concession stand. Vanderveen sat with his wife, Gloria. "Did you call him, or did my uncle?" Piper asked.

"Must have been your uncle," Will said, glancing over the wine list the maître d' had left behind. He looked up. "Is he here with your aunt?"

"I don't see them, but I know they're coming."

Piper studied her menu for a while, then said with a hint of a smile, "The frog legs look good. What do you think?"

Will lifted an eyebrow, then caught on to the teasing. "Maybe next time," he said. "If they come with zucchini pickles."

"I'll have to see what I can do about that."

They placed their orders, and Will added a bottle of white wine to share, Piper thinking as he did what an upgrade this was from the soda and chips they'd had the night before in the undecorated Christmas farm gift shop. Would there be a third evening out? Piper wondered, then reminded herself she was here for Nate's benefit, not her own. But that didn't mean she couldn't enjoy herself, which so far she definitely was doing.

As their entrées arrived, poached salmon for Piper and filet mignon for Will, Piper spotted Aunt Judy and Uncle Frank walking in with another couple—the Tollivers. Aunt Judy waved brightly before taking her seat at their table for four, and Piper knew they'd join them eventually. She liked seeing Uncle Frank spruced up beyond his usual dungarees, though he appeared a tad uncomfortable and was probably wishing he could have put his feet up in front of the television. Piper felt sure, though, that whatever Amy sent him from the kitchen would change his mind.

Midway through their dinner, the piped-in music cut off, and a male voice introduced the live entertainment "for your dining pleasure." Nate hopped up to the stage accompanied by a smattering of applause and took his seat behind the microphone. It was a very different Nate from the dejected person Piper had spoken with that afternoon, and she was impressed with his stage presence, which, while low-key, was commanding. Every eye, she saw, was on the musician as forks were set down and elbows leaned on.

Nate began with a genial patter, speaking about French folk music as he strummed soft chords on his guitar and illustrated his words with a couple of simple but charming songs. He then moved on to more modern music.

"He's pretty good," Will whispered at one point. Piper nodded enthusiastically as she lifted her wineglass for a sip.

More patrons arrived, and Piper saw Megan and Erin join friends at the "drinks and nibbles" tables near the bar. Will and Piper had just been served their coffee when Piper spotted Tina Carson standing at the doorway and looking around uncertainly.

Piper leaned toward Will. "Do you mind if I ask Tina to join us? I called her about coming tonight, and she's alone."

"Fine with me," Will said, and Piper caught Tina's eye and waved her over.

"Hi, guys," Tina said as she slipped gratefully into the chair Will snagged from a nearby table. "Looks like a good crowd showed up." A waiter appeared at her side, and she ordered coffee and a dessert. Tina had clearly gone to some pains for the evening, with sparkly barrettes in her hair and a pretty lavender tunic and slacks replacing her usual coffee shop garb. Piper thought Tina's face looked a bit drawn, though, and feared she may have dragged the hard-working woman out after a tiring day.

Nate opened his performance to requests, and the first one came from the lively bar area—a shout-out for the Cloverdale High fight song—which drew laughter.

"'Fraid I don't know that one," Nate said, genially. "Want to sing a few bars for me?"

Two young men who looked like former football players belted out the song together with beer mugs swinging. Nate quickly picked up on the tune and strummed accompaniment, eventually adding his voice to theirs at the final "Fight, Cloverdale, fight," to much laughter and applause.

That loosened up the crowd considerably, and more

requests were called out. Nate honored them, one by one, and Piper was glad to see waiters bustling about, delivering orders for more food and drink. Gradually, the requested songs turned more sentimental, and a few couples grasped hands and leaned a bit closer together. Piper was surprised when Tina suddenly raised her hand and asked for "Deep in My Heart, Dear." "It's from *The Student Prince*," she explained, and Nate nodded.

"I always loved that song," Tina whispered to Piper, "since somebody took me to a performance when I was young."

Tina didn't seem very old to Piper, but she knew that revivals of *The Student Prince* popped up regularly. The song was sweet and sentimental, and obviously meant something to Tina, since Piper noticed her dab at the corner of an eye during the performance.

Finally, Nate thanked the crowd for being such a great audience, and the spotlights illuminating the stage dimmed. Nate hopped down and headed toward Piper and Will's table, his progress slowed by people complimenting his performance along his way. By the time he reached them, Will had grabbed a fourth chair for him.

"Nate, that was just wonderful," Tina said, and Piper and Will agreed.

"Thanks," Nate said. "And thanks for coming tonight. I just might have a job for a while longer because of this turnout."

"That'd be great," Piper said. "Did you get a chance to talk with the plumber?" she asked, adding, "Tina's been helping with our information gathering, too."

Nate threw Tina a grateful look, then said, "I did have a talk with Mr. Farber this afternoon." He paused, taking a thirsty gulp from the beer he'd snagged along the way. He wiped his mouth, then said with a lopsided grin, "It was quite interesting."

12

～～～

"I went to the shop right after we met up this afternoon," Nate said, describing his visit to Ralph Farber's plumbing showroom. "When I walked in, Farber was on the phone with one of his employees, and he wasn't happy with the guy."

Nate laughed. "Farber would be an intimidating man when he was in a good mood. He's got shoulders at least three feet across and biceps that make you wonder if he does daily curls with the sinks and sump pumps he sells. When he's in a bad mood, as he sure sounded when I walked in, well, let's just say I felt like backing out of there, pronto."

"What was he mad about?" Tina asked.

"Something to do with a job he'd sent one of his workers out on. It sounded like the guy messed up and Farber was trying to figure out how he could make things right. Eventually, with plenty of cuss words, Farber worked out a solution, though when he hung up, he looked ready to spit nails. That's when he noticed me and said, 'Yeah?' like I'd better have a darn good reason for taking up his time."

"Ouch!" Piper said. "What did you say?"

"Luckily," Nate said, smiling, "I had time on my way over there to come up with a story. I still didn't know if I'd end up being thrown out of his store, but I gave it a shot. I told him I'd seen an old-style sink at Alan Rosemont's shop—which was true, actually—but that since the antique shop was now shuttered, I wondered if Farber carried anything like that."

"Oh, a vintage sink?" Tina asked. "I love those."

"Farber doesn't," Nate said. "But he did pull out a catalog that he was willing to order from if I found something I wanted. As I flipped through the book, I talked about Rosemont's inventory, which led pretty smoothly, I thought, to Rosemont himself."

"Good for you," Piper said. "Did you get Farber talking about him?"

"Yeah, and without too much trouble. Farber's not one to keep his thoughts to himself. I'd love to play poker with him sometime."

Will grinned and said, "Me, too!" then added, "Assuming he's not our murderer, of course."

"What do you think?" Piper asked. "Could he have done it?"

"Well," Nate said, and took another swallow of beer, "he sure didn't have much use for Rosemont. He might have barely tolerated his existence if Rosemont didn't happen to live right next door. Farber shared at one point that he would have liked to wrap Alan's bagpipe around his neck more than once."

"Wow!" Tina said. "That's incriminating. Except," she added, "would a murderer come out and actually say that?"

"Good question," Nate agreed. "However, I did learn that Farber was at the fairgrounds Friday night."

"Really?" Piper said, excited. "What for?"

"He told me one of the toilet facilities had backed up, and he had to run over and take care of it. He mentioned it because we got talking about my having to work late hours, and he said it beat getting called out in the middle of watching a good game on TV."

"Right," Piper said. "There was a Yankees' game on that night, wasn't there, Tina?"

Tina looked blank until Piper reminded her that Dennis Isley had been watching it. She then nodded vigorously. "Of course! The game with the fight in the stands."

"Was Farber at the fairgrounds alone?" Will asked, and Nate shrugged.

"It sounded like it, but he didn't actually say. He just groused about having to miss his game."

Just then Aunt Judy walked up, giving Piper a squeeze on her shoulders and gesturing for the two men to keep their seats. "I loved your performance, Nate," she said. "I can't think why we haven't come before, but we'll certainly be here again."

Nate thanked her, and Piper jumped in to tell her what he'd learned that day.

"Ralph Farber?" Aunt Judy said uncertainly. "He came to our place last May to install the new water heater. He's not exactly what you'd call a charmer, but he does good work. I can't imagine him murdering anybody."

"Maybe that's because you never had to listen to somebody's incessant bagpiping ten feet from your bedroom window." Uncle Frank had come up behind and caught most of what had been said.

"No, I haven't," Aunt Judy agreed, "but still. Ralph Farber?" She shook her head. "It's just hard for me to imagine anyone I know doing such a terrible thing. But I need to focus on keeping Nate from being wrongly accused."

"Amen to that," Tina said. "We're all working toward that."

Amy suddenly appeared at the swinging doors to the kitchen, dressed in her white chef's jacket and hat. She waved to Nate, and he pushed back his chair.

"If you'll excuse me, I think I have some dinner waiting for me." He took off, and Aunt Judy slipped into his chair.

"Such a nice young man," she said, watching him head toward the kitchen. She shook her head slowly, adding, "But I wish for his sake that he'd never come to Cloverdale."

The next morning, Piper woke to bright sunlight streaming into her bedroom and the sound of birds chirping outside her window. She stretched leisurely, thinking pleasant thoughts of her preceding evening with Will until she read the digits on her bedside clock: seven forty-five. She'd overslept! Her stretch ended with a rapid whipping off of the covers. As her feet hit the floor, her thoughts raced over her morning schedule. Mrs. Peterson had arranged to come at eight to take a refresher course from Piper on canning.

Piper needed to be dressed and ready for her arrival within fifteen minutes.

Water splashed and clothes flew as Piper dashed about, brushing her teeth with one hand while closing buttons with the other. At four minutes past eight, she hopped down the stairs to her shop, one shoe on, the other still in hand. As she slipped her foot into the second shoe, Piper paused to take a deep breath, then raised the shade on her shop door. There stood Mrs. Peterson, hands crossed in front over a large purse and a strained look on her face.

Piper unlocked her door and pulled it open. "I'm so sorry to be late, Mrs. Peterson," she began, then stopped as she realized her customer wasn't looking at her but rather to the right.

"Miss Lamb, did you see that?" Mrs. Peterson asked, pointing.

Confused, Piper couldn't think for a moment. Then an ominous feeling fell over her. Piper stepped out to see what Mrs. Peterson was pointing to and groaned. On the brick section of wall between her shop window and the outer door to her apartment, someone had splashed paint—lots of it, and white, all the better to show up against the dark red brick.

"Oh no!"

"I think you'd better report this," Mrs. Peterson advised solemnly. "It couldn't have been an accident."

"So, you didn't see this when you arrived home last night?" Sheriff Carlyle asked. He'd responded to Piper's call within the hour with Ben Schaeffer, for some reason, at his side.

"No, I didn't." Piper didn't add that she hadn't exactly been focusing on her shop's front wall at the time, having been escorted to her door by Will and thinking of other things, such as the possibility of a good-night kiss (which, happily and quite pleasantly, had occurred). But surely she would have noticed something as glaringly obvious as that paint splash, especially since the streetlight illuminated the area quite well (much to the delight, she was sure, of any Piper-and-Will watchers).

"And you didn't hear anything during the night?"

Piper shook her head. "But I'm a fairly sound sleeper."

"The paint is dry," Ben said, stating the obvious, as all three of them had already pressed a finger against it. "Taking last night's temperature and humidity into consideration, I'd say this was perpetrated no later than four A.M."

"It was already dry at eight, when I discovered the mess," Piper said. "Including the dribbles along the sidewalk. I checked to make sure paint wouldn't get tracked into my shop."

"Three A.M., then," Ben amended.

"Let's just say sometime between twelve, when you stated you turned out your lights, Miss Lamb," the sheriff said, "and daylight, when we'll assume our vandal wouldn't want to be seen out and about."

"Shouldn't be too hard to track down, wouldn't you say?" asked Ben. "Just look for kids with white paint on their sneakers."

"Possibly," Sheriff Carlyle said, nodding. "Do you have any thoughts as to who may have done this?" he asked Piper. "Any problems or threats recently?"

Piper frowned. "The only thing I could mention is what happened two days ago. My garbage can was tipped over in the middle of the day, causing a huge mess for me out back. I would have thought it was kids except that my garbage can was the only one pushed over in a long string of cans in the alley."

"Hmm," Sheriff Carlyle said as Ben's chin shot up in indignation.

"Such behavior can't be tolerated in Cloverdale," Ben said. "As we all know, juvenile delinquents left undisciplined grow up to be hardened criminals, and we don't need that element in our town."

"The garbage thing I can see as kids fooling around," Sheriff Carlyle said. "But defacing a shop front with paint in the middle of the night seems much more than a prank. If it was graffiti, maybe. But this strikes me as something done in anger, as if someone was sending a message to you, Piper."

"A message? To me? But what would that be?"

"I guess we're going to have to figure that out."

Sheriff Carlyle looked so serious that Piper shivered, though the temperature had already climbed close to eighty. But almost immediately she shrugged off the thought. Surely no grown person could be so upset with her, except . . . Charlotte Hosch suddenly popped into her mind. The candy maker had been angry and threatening over what she claimed were noxious pickling odors oozing from Piper's shop. But Charlotte's threats involved legal complaints, not petty vandalism. Piper couldn't really imagine the woman sneaking about in the middle of the night and . . .

"Daddy! What's going on?" Amy called out as she climbed out of her orange Toyota. Erin Healy was with her, and the two rushed over, soon spotting the cause of everyone's concern. "Oh gosh!" Amy said. "What happened?"

"Nothing to worry about, sugarplum. Piper can fill you in," the sheriff said as he jotted something in his notebook. Ben gazed at Amy with an odd combination of pseudo-official sternness and dewy-eyed pining, while Erin, Piper noticed with surprise, watched Ben with similar enthrallment, though in her own, much shier way.

Piper explained what she knew to the two girls, and the sheriff flipped his notebook closed. "Well, I've got to be going." He gave Amy a peck on her cheek, then said to Piper, "You think about what I said. Get back to me if you come up with anything."

"What?" Amy asked as her father and Ben took off. "What are you supposed to think about?"

Piper hustled them into her shop. "Your father thinks this might have been done by someone with a vendetta against me." She pulled the Cloverdale phone book from under her counter and started flipping through the yellow pages.

"A vendetta? Who could have anything against you?"

Charlotte Hosch, for one, Piper thought but didn't say out loud. The idea still seemed too far-fetched to be true. "I don't know. All I know is I have to find someone to clean that mess off in a hurry or I'll be losing more customers. Mrs. Peterson already took off instead of staying for her pickling and canning lesson."

"She'll be back," Amy said.

Piper smiled, hoping she was right about that. But the thought of anyone doing such damage to her property deliberately and out of anger or spite lingered, making her highly uneasy.

13

As Piper waited to hear back from her insurance agent as well as the handyman she'd left messages with about her paint problem (did anyone answer their phones anymore?), she pulled out from under her shop counter the spiral notebook that contained her list of suspects.

"Did Nate tell you about his visit to the plumber yesterday?" she asked.

"Oh yes," Amy said, looking pleased.

"And Amy told me," Erin said. "It sure sounded like Mr. Farber was angry enough to kill Alan Rosemont."

"Plus he was at the fairgrounds late Friday night," Amy said.

"Where he must have heard Rosemont playing his bagpipes," Piper said, nodding. "Which just might have tipped him over the edge if he truly wanted to wrap Alan's bag-pipes around his neck. I think he deserves to be added to our suspect list." She wrote Ralph Farber's name into the notebook under Robby Taylor's.

"So we have Gordon Pfiefle, Robby Taylor, and Ralph Farber. I'll have to cross off Dennis Isley since he has an alibi." Piper's pen moved toward Isley's name.

"What's his alibi?" Amy asked.

"He was home watching a Yankees' game—alone, but he knew about the fight in the stands. I checked, and there was a fight that night."

"He could have heard about that from someone else," Amy argued. "I'd say keep him on."

"Hmm," Piper said. "It seemed credible to me because he'd mentioned the fight to Tina in passing, not as a defensive answer to 'Where were you Friday night?' But maybe you're right and that's not enough. I'll keep him." She set down her pen.

Tina walked in at that moment, her eyes wide with shock. "Good heavens, Piper! What happened to your storefront?" A faint aroma of coffee and cooked bacon wafted in with Tina and reminded Piper she hadn't had time for any breakfast. She told Tina all she knew about the vandalism, while Erin quietly excused herself and took off, promising to give Amy a call.

"Who could have done such a thing?" Tina asked.

"That's what the sheriff and I have been wondering. I can't imagine who."

Tina's eyes took on a funny look as her lips pursed. "I can," she said. "That fudge-making harpy, Charlotte Hosch."

"Oh my gosh, you're right!" Amy cried.

"No, it couldn't be," Piper said. "Though I admit her name crossed my mind."

"There! See?" Tina said. "I'll bet she took her complaints to the town council and got no action. So she took her frustration out in another way." Tina paused. "She's also been heard ranting against Nate, wondering why he hasn't been arrested yet for Alan Rosemont's murder."

Amy gasped.

"Don't worry," Piper assured Amy. "I'm sure Charlotte's opinion won't weigh heavily with your father."

"Probably not," Tina agreed. "But now that I think of it, maybe she's throwing out the accusation as a smoke screen. Maybe she killed Rosemont."

"Why do you say that?" Piper asked.

"Oh," Tina said, shrugging, "just because she's so nasty, I suppose. But I'll bet if we looked hard enough, we'd find a pretty good motive for her to have done it."

Piper had to admit the idea of locking Charlotte up for the crime was appealing, but she said, "We'll keep her in mind. I've been thinking we should probably be looking into Alan Rosemont's background. Maybe there's something in his past that brought about his murder."

Piper's phone rang. It was one of her spice wholesalers calling with an urgent question concerning Piper's latest order. Did she want regular yellow mustard seed or whole brown or both? Piper scrambled to find her order list and found that she needed both. She'd barely settled that and hung up when her phone rang again.

"You got some bricks need cleaning? How soon d'ya need it done?"

Instantly came to mind, but Piper got into a discussion of method and cost, knowing she'd need to run it by her insurance agent. As she finished with that call, a customer in a bright pink tee walked in.

"Why don't I do that background search for you," Tina offered. She'd been browsing the shelves while Piper was occupied and laid several jars of chutney on the counter. "I'm pretty good on the computer, and I'll have time."

"Would you?" Piper said, happy to have one chore taken off her plate.

Amy packed up Tina's purchases as Piper turned to the pink-clad woman, asking, "How can I help you?"

Clutching her bag of chutneys, the coffee shop owner waggled her fingers and headed for the door, promising, "I'll get back to you." Piper waved back, then continued her discussion with her new customer on the various merits of white, cider, and malt vinegars for use in the pickling process. Her phone rang again, but Amy picked up, and as she did, Piper's empty stomach grumbled its own bid for attention. Piper sighed, mentally telling it to get in line.

For the next couple of hours it seemed half the town popped in—one or two at a time—to ask about the paint on the front of Piper's shop. With all the repeated explanations—and no return in the form of helpful information on the vandalism—Piper felt her energy draining to near zero despite the two cups of coffee she managed to down from the pot Amy set to brew. As soon as there was a lull, Piper scurried up to her apartment for a bite of lunch, leaving Amy to hold down the fort.

With the need for speed in mind, Piper popped a cheese sandwich into her toaster oven, then added two homemade bread-and-butter pickles to her plate. She'd just taken her first, absolutely delicious bite when she heard a clear-pitched woman's voice carry up the stairs.

"I wish to speak to Miss Lamb. Immediately."

The voice was familiar, and Piper found herself inexplicably picturing bunny rabbits and dancing turtles. Then it hit her: her visitor was Lyella Pfiefle, children's librarian and wife of Gordon Pfiefle, chief suspect on Piper's murder list!

Piper coughed, choked, then managed to swallow her food with the help of a gulp of water. About that time, Amy's head poked up from the stairwell. "There's a . . ." she began, but Piper nodded.

"I heard."

"She looks mad," Amy whispered, her eyes wide.

Amy's head disappeared from view, and Piper got up to rinse the crumbs from her hands. She could well imagine what Lyella Pfiefle might be mad about. The question was how did she know about it?

"Miss Lamb," Lyella said as Piper appeared, then paused and shot Amy a stern look. "Leave us, please." Amy glanced at Piper—who nodded—then disappeared into the back room.

With false bravado, Piper said, "How nice to see you again, Mrs. Pfiefle." The librarian looked dressed for work in a tidy, though bland, blouse and skirt. Her hair was pulled into the same severe ponytail she'd worn before, and though she stood with a ramrod-straight back and chin jutting high, she still didn't reach five feet above the floor. Her manner, however, did, and more.

"I'm not here for your pickling spices, and I have to be at the library very soon, so I'll get right to the point. Miss Lamb, I realize my husband is a very attractive man. You are a single woman, whose heart, I'm sure, must be more than ready to be engaged. I fully understand that, as well as the weaknesses of human nature. Understanding, however, does not mean overlooking. Gordon Pfiefle is my husband and fully intends to remain so. I strongly advise you to keep that in mind and to look elsewhere for your romantic interests."

"My—?" Piper's lips continued to move but produced no intelligible words.

Lyella misinterpreted Piper's shock. "There's not much I miss, I assure you. And believe me, Miss Lamb, you're not the first woman I've had to speak to in this way. I've never held it against any of them, and I won't hold it against you. In fact," she said, "I feel I'm doing you a favor—saving you from a waste of time and certain disappointment."

"I, ah," Piper stammered, floundering for a response. If she protested that she had no romantic interest whatsoever in Gordon Pfiefle, how would she explain what her true interest was? That she saw him as a possible murderer?

"That's all right," Lyella said, again interpreting Piper's silence in her own way. "No apologies necessary. We'll simply leave it at that. There'll be no need to speak of this again. Good day, Miss Lamb."

Piper nodded, knowing she should say something. But

since "thank you for coming" seemed totally inappropriate, she simply raised one hand in a weak farewell as Lyella turned and left the shop.

As the door closed behind the librarian, Amy peeked out from the back room. "Did I hear what I think I heard?"

Piper turned a stunned face toward her assistant and nodded.

"She really thinks you're after her husband?"

"Apparently so."

"But she forgives you!"

"Generous of her, isn't it?"

"Oh!" Amy cried, pulling out a stool to support herself as she collapsed in laughter. "That's so amazing! Gordon Pfiefle! I mean, he's nice and all, but . . . And doesn't she know you and Will Burchett are an item?"

"We're not an item," Piper said. "But since Lyella seems to be the only person in town who hasn't heard about us, the question is how did she link me up with her husband?"

"GPS?" Amy suggested, then suddenly grew serious. "What if it's all a smoke screen? Like what Tina said about Charlotte Hosch? What if she knows you have good reason to be suspicious of her husband and is doing this to throw you off the track?"

Piper looked at Amy. Good question. "I don't know if that's the case. But I'm starting to realize that we probably all need to be much more circumspect in our investigations."

14

Amy had left for A La Carte, and Piper had just been informed by her insurance agent that she needed a second cost estimate on the paint clean-up job, when a woman she recognized from the fair entered the shop.

"You look like you just bit into a sour pickle," the woman said.

"Biting into a sour pickle generally makes me smile," Piper said. "Having to drum up another handyman in a hurry doesn't."

Piper explained the situation as the woman's name percolated to the top of her brain—Emma Leahy, with whom Piper remembered discussing the many ways of pickling okra. "I can't stand okra itself," she remembered Emma stating. "Slimy things, aren't they? But I remembered trying a pickled okra once, and it was delicious."

A no-nonsense type of woman in her late sixties, Emma looked like she might have come straight from digging in her garden (and had looked pretty much the same a few days ago at the fair). She brushed back a loose strand of salt-and-pepper hair, cut sensibly short, and dug into the canvas tote that seemed to be filled with enough items to get her through the night. She pulled out a cell phone and began scrolling through her contact list.

"Dennis Isley would probably give you the lowest price," she said as she searched, "but I wouldn't recommend him. Besides, he's working on Ira Perkins's roof right now. I saw him on my way here."

Piper nodded, aware that she wouldn't have chosen to hire Dennis, anyway.

"Here you go. Max Noland." Emma recited Noland's number for Piper to write down.

"Great! Thanks. Now how can I help *you*?"

Emma, as Piper expected, wanted to know more about pickling okra, specifically which recipe Piper could suggest that might come closest to the one Emma had once sampled. Piper walked her through six different recipes, including a no-salt version and a couple with celery and either mustard seeds or hot red peppers, and even found one for candied okra, made with brown sugar, cinnamon, and cloves. Emma liked the recipe with green, rather than hot, peppers, plus garlic and mustard seeds, and Piper gathered up the spices and equipment she'd need.

After Emma left, Piper tried Max Noland's number and got a "please leave your name and number and I'll get back to you" message. She sighed and did so for perhaps the fifth time that day. Her aggravation was short-lived, however, since she soon spotted Will Burchett's green van pull up in front of her shop. She watched as Will climbed out and slid open his side door. He reached in and dragged out a four-foot-tall—at least!—potted Christmas tree.

"What in the world?" Piper ran to her door as Will staggered over with his tree.

"Hi," he said, seeing her. He lowered the heavy pot gently to the sidewalk. "I heard about your problem," he said and jerked his chin toward the now-famous paint splash. "I have plenty of these sitting around and thought you might like one."

"A Christmas tree?"

"Yeah, a spruce." He looked fondly at it, then suddenly blinked. "Not for Christmas! It's to keep outside here, as a, you know, decoration, and to maybe make you feel a little better after what some creep did to your wall." He looked down at his tree, again, doubt crossing his face. "It'll grow, you know. I probably should have picked a bigger one, except lugging it here might have been a problem."

Piper laughed, shaking her head. "That's so nice! But I really can't accept such an expensive gift."

"No! It's nothing! I just dug it up and plopped it in the pot. I have plenty of them, you know. I would have thinned out the row, anyway. This way the little guy gets to hang around awhile longer."

Piper was skeptical but said, "Well, then, great! That really is very nice of you, Will. Thank you!"

"I'll just leave it here for now, okay? So it won't get in the way of the work. Water it once in a while."

"I will." Piper found herself grinning broadly at her unexpected and unusual gift. It might have been the first tree she'd ever gotten.

Will checked his watch. "I'll be off, then. I'll give you a call, okay?"

"Please do. And thanks again, so much."

Will left, and Piper stood gazing at her new tree. How tall would it grow? Could she put lights on it in December? She'd have to ask Will if that would hurt the tree. Piper went back into her shop but found herself wandering to the window often, just to look at her potted spruce.

She wasn't the only one who admired it. Customers who walked in the rest of the afternoon said, "Nice tree!" which was such a welcome change from the comments and questions she'd been fielding about the ugly paint splash. About fifteen minutes before closing time, Aunt Judy surprised Piper by popping in.

"I had to come see it for myself," she said, referring to the tree, which told Piper news of her gift had made the rounds. "What a lovely thing for Will to do!"

Piper agreed. "He tried to downplay it, but I'm sure he went to a lot of trouble. It certainly cheered me up."

"Yes, I felt so bad when I heard about the paint being thrown on your wall and was planning to come just on that account. But this is so much better. Your paint mess will go away, but that beautiful tree will last for years."

"Will it?"

"Oh yes. Of course, eventually you'll have to put it back in the ground. We can bring it to our farm if you like. Or . . ." Aunt Judy paused, her eyes twinkling, then simply said, "Yes, your tree will last a good, long time."

Just then, another van pulled up to Piper's shop. This one was white and had "Flowers by Fredericka" written on it in green paint. *Uh-oh*, Piper thought, not sure what to make of that.

"Oh my goodness," Aunt Judy said as she turned to follow Piper's gaze. They both watched as a young man of about eighteen bounced out, then reached into the back to lift out a huge bouquet of roses. "Look at that!" Aunt Judy cried, and she hurried to get the door for the teen.

"Piper Lamb?" the delivery boy asked as he walked in. Close-up, the bouquet he held was even more enormous. When Piper nodded weakly, the young man grinned and set the bouquet on her countertop, saying, "Enjoy!"

"Thank you," Piper croaked.

"There must be two dozen roses in there," Aunt Judy said, her eyes popping. "How can Wi—, I mean, who sent it?"

Piper found a white envelope tucked into the blooms and plucked it out. She pulled the flap open and slipped out the card, closing her eyes a moment before she read what was on it. "Oh Lord," she moaned.

"What? What is it?"

Aunt Judy looked so fearful, Piper couldn't keep her in suspense. "They're from Scott."

"Scott! But I thought you, I mean, he, that is . . . Didn't you two break up?"

"We did. At least I did. Scott doesn't seem to have realized it. He just sent me two dozen roses on the anniversary of our first date."

"Oh," Aunt Judy said. "Oh my." She looked searchingly at Piper. "Well, that's . . . very nice. I suppose."

At that moment, Nate Purdy walked into the shop,

halting as he spotted the roses. "Wow! I was going to say, 'Good-looking tree out there,' but that's one gorgeous bouquet in here. Who's the lucky guy?"

Piper groaned, then hustled her bouquet, which seemed to be growing larger by the minute, up to her apartment before anyone else could see and comment on it. Aunt Judy had looked on the verge of asking how Piper felt about it, but all she felt at the moment was confusion.

Why would Scott make such a romantic gesture? He'd rarely done so when they'd been together, and now that he was half a world away he feels the urge? The phrase "absence makes the heart grow fonder" popped into her head, but did Piper want Scott's heart to grow fonder? She thought she'd ended that episode in her life, partly because she'd felt taken for granted. Now, just when someone new had entered her life, a man who was clearly very thoughtful, Scott suddenly becomes the gallant knight? Had he also become clairvoyant? It seemed as though every time Piper's feelings toward Will stepped up a notch, Scott did something to shake the ladder.

"Piper, do you want me to ring up the purchase for Nate?" Aunt Judy called up the stairwell. "He's picking up tarragon for Amy on his way to A La Carte, and he has to go now."

"I'm coming down," Piper answered, giving one of Scott's wonderfully fragrant roses an impatient tweak. She trotted down to the shop and wrote up a bill that Nate could give to the restaurant owner instead of paying out of pocket.

"More people have said they intend to go to the

restaurant to hear you play," Aunt Judy told him. "Your fame is spreading."

Nate grinned. "I think it's Amy's cooking that's doing it, but either way it'll be good for both of us. Thanks again." He made a snappy salute and took off.

"Want to come by for dinner?" Aunt Judy asked Piper. "It won't be up to the A La Carte offerings, but I've made your favorite chicken and biscuit stew."

"Your cooking will always be tops with me," Piper said. "Just give me a minute to close up shop." *And to get my head together.*

Since Aunt Judy had been dropped off by Uncle Frank to run her errands in town, she rode with Piper to the farmhouse, first calling to let her husband know she had a ride back.

"Take a peek at the Crock-Pot, would you, Frank?" she told him over the phone. "If my stew is bubbling too much, turn the switch to low."

As Piper pulled onto the highway on the outskirts of town, they heard sirens in the distance.

"Oh dear," Aunt Judy said. "I hope nothing serious has happened."

"If it has, we'll be sure to hear about it soon," Piper said, checking her mirrors but not spotting any flashing lights.

"Caitlin Walker's little boy is prone to asthma attacks. Sometimes it's a bad one. Or old Mr. O'Hara's heart might have—"

"It could just be Ben Schaeffer in his auxiliary officer

role catching a driver going five miles over the speed limit. You know how super-seriously he takes things like that."

"Maybe . . ." Aunt Judy said.

Piper glanced over and saw her aunt's face still looking worried, so she bit the bullet and brought up the subject sure to distract her. "Will's gift of that live Christmas tree was such a surprise."

Aunt Judy's expression instantly brightened. "He's such a nice young man. I liked him from the first. I remember saying to your Uncle Frank, 'That Will Burchett has an honest face.' Of course, Frank laughed and reminded me that I'd said the same about the man who drove up to the house and offered to reseal our driveway at a big discount with his 'leftover material from another job.' That was a long time ago, though. I think I've learned a thing or two about scam artists since then."

"You're probably safe in your opinion of Will."

"So, you like him, too?"

"I think he's a very nice guy. And I know half the town is already planning what to wear to our wedding. But we're still getting to know each other. Being a great guy and being the right guy aren't always the same thing."

"Of course, dear." Aunt Judy paused. "Scott's gesture—sending those beautiful flowers—does that cloud the waters?"

Piper shook her head, laughing ruefully. "You could say that. It's so unlike him, at least the Scott he was toward the end. But I haven't seen him for weeks while he's been traveling the world and 'finding himself.' Maybe this separation has been doing him some good? Or maybe he's experiencing a touch of temporary insanity. I just don't know what to think."

Aunt Judy reached over and patted her arm. "Don't overthink it, would be my advice. You have two men vying for your attention. Enjoy that for now, and as they say, 'Just go with the flow.' "

Piper grinned at her aunt, and they lapsed into a comfortable, thoughtful silence the rest of the ride.

As Piper pulled into the farmhouse driveway, she saw Uncle Frank step out onto the front porch. Jack, their lovable mixed breed, barked and ran excitedly to meet them. Piper climbed out and ruffled Jack's fur before he darted to Aunt Judy's side of the car.

Uncle Frank trotted down the porch steps to give each of them a peck on the cheek. Piper thought his greeting fairly restrained and expected to hear that a large piece of farm equipment had gone on the fritz or some such complaint. But what her uncle said turned out to be much worse.

"Bill Vanderveen just called," he said, his bushy brows knit tight. "There's been a bad accident in town. Dennis Isley took a fall from Ira Perkins's roof. They're not sure he's going to make it."

15

After that glum news, Aunt Judy's excellent dinner was consumed but hardly enjoyed. Several calls concerning Dennis Isley interrupted them as well as ensured that any conversation in between would be somber.

"Bill thinks he might have tripped over his own tools," Uncle Frank said at one point.

"Ira Perkins's roof is so steep," Aunt Judy responded, her lower lip trembling. Gracie, the plump gray cat, took this as a cue to jump onto her lap, something Aunt Judy normally disallowed during meals. But that night she held on to the cat and gently stroked its fur.

When they finished the meal, Piper helped clean up, then felt there was nothing more she could do and bid her aunt and uncle good night. She left, with hugs and a basket of fresh-picked tomatoes, knowing little more about

Dennis's condition. However, not long after she arrived home, her uncle called.

"We just got word, peanut. Dennis died at the hospital."

Piper gasped softly. Though the handyman hadn't been anywhere near a friend of hers, his death was still a shock. He was, after all, a person Piper had very recently seen and spoken to. Feelings of guilt flooded in as well, both because she'd disliked the man when he was alive and had been more than happy to suspect him of murder. She tried reminding herself that death tended to transform villains into angels but still found the news hard to deal with.

The next morning, Piper dragged herself from bed, knowing she faced a day of nonstop talk about the accident. She pulled out her box of quick-cooking oatmeal to fortify herself and brewed a generous pot of strong coffee. When she raised the shade on her shop door, the sun was shining brightly, and Cloverdale looked quiet and peaceful. Piper was sure that would change, though, and was soon proved right. Within minutes Mrs. Peterson popped in, professing to have come to reschedule her canning and pickling class but getting around rapidly to Dennis Isley.

"I understand that Ira Perkins heard the fall," she said, "but thought Dennis had dropped a load of shingles. Dennis had a rope system for pulling the shingles up to the roof, you know, so he wouldn't have to carry them all up the ladder. Mr. Perkins's hearing isn't the best, of course, which is why I suppose he didn't mind staying home while Dennis was banging away overhead. When I had my roof redone a few years ago the noise was so awful, it sent me running to my sister's. I can only imagine if you listened to that all day, one more thud would barely be noticed."

"Then why did Mr. Perkins think he heard Dennis fall?" Piper asked.

Mrs. Peterson winced. "Because he also heard Dennis cry out. But Ira put it to his having dropped the shingles, as I said. Poor man—Dennis, I mean. Who knows if he might have survived if he'd gotten help sooner."

"I don't think so," Emma Leahy said as she pushed through Piper's door. "Dennis landed on alley concrete, and his head injuries, I heard, were terrible. There's no way he could have survived except maybe as a vegetable for the rest of his life, and who'd want that?" Emma turned to Piper. "I came by to get another canning jar for my pickled okra, by the way."

As Piper went to get the jar, a third person entered her shop, Mr. Laseter, the man who had first clued her in about the plumber, Ralph Farber.

"Did you ladies hear about the accident?" he asked.

Needless question, Piper thought, and he paid for it by getting an earful and then some from both women. Mr. Laseter, it seemed, had come by to buy a jar of Piper's pickles—any kind—having felt concern for how her business might have suffered after Alan Rosemont's murder. Her business, however, wasn't currently suffering at all, and as the morning wore on, the sight of two or more people in conversation inside her shop seemed to suck in several others to pick over the grisly details and, by the way, pick up spices or pickles while they were there.

Piper was relieved when Amy finally arrived, which would give her a chance to rest her ears as well as her feet. She'd been bustling about, gathering merchandise while listening to the same information—and plenty of off-the-wall misinformation—shared and repeated, contradicted and dissected. Amy, however, seemed uncharacteristically quiet as she tucked her purse under the counter, and Piper asked, "Are you okay?"

Amy's brow puckered. "Nate's not answering my calls and texts."

Piper handed a customer her bagged purchase of spices before turning back to Amy. "When did you last hear from him?"

"Late last night. I'd stayed behind at the restaurant to finish a few things in the kitchen and texted him when I got home. He answered to say good night and that he'd call me in the morning. But he didn't."

Piper didn't know what to say. Normally, not hearing from one's boyfriend for a few hours wouldn't be much to worry about. But things had been far from normal lately. So much so that Piper was beginning to forget what that state was like.

"Maybe it's just a cell phone problem," she offered. Then, thinking the ongoing busyness might be a good distraction, she asked, "Mind taking over? I'm in huge need of a break." Amy nodded, managing to put some enthusiasm into it, and Piper left care of the shop to her.

She trotted upstairs and headed for a soft chair in her living room, kicking off her shoes and pulling the hassock closer. As she stretched her legs out, Piper heaved a sigh of pleasure. Unfortunately, besides comfort, her position also provided a direct view of Scott's roses. Of course, a bouquet that large was hard to miss from nearly any spot in her small apartment.

Piper shook her head as she stared at it. Was she the

only woman in the world who was less than thrilled to receive such an amazing gift of flowers from a boyfriend? An ex-boyfriend, she reminded herself. But maybe Aunt Judy was right. She should just go with the flow.

Piper inhaled the flowers' pervasive perfume, which was lovely. It reminded her of one of their early dates, when Scott had taken her to a very nice dinner. As they'd strolled away from the restaurant toward his car, Scott had stopped at a street vendor's cart and bought her a small bouquet of violets. It was a spontaneous, romantic gesture that made Piper smile even now, just thinking about it.

There had been fewer of those gestures, however, as their relationship progressed. Scott's career kept him busier, and he began to take her more and more for granted. He'd won her over, his attitude seemed to say, and now he didn't need to work at it anymore.

Had Scott's travels caused him to rethink that attitude? Had it finally begun to sink in that Piper had broken up with him and that he was going to have to get busy at winning her back and changing his ways if he had any hopes of a future with her? Did Piper want him to win her back?

A screech from below jerked Piper forward in her chair. Amy's voice! Piper scrambled up and rushed to the top of her stairs.

"No!" she heard Amy cry. "No! That's not right!"

Piper grabbed her shoes and rushed down to the shop. Erin and Megan stood beside a distraught Amy. Erin spotted Piper first and explained.

"Nate's been taken back in for questioning."

"Questioning about what?" Piper asked. "I thought he answered everything he could about Alan Rosemont."

"Not Alan. For Dennis Isley."

"Dennis! But that was an accident. Wasn't it?"

"Once in a while my idiot brother, Ben," Megan said, "turns into someone who's actually useful." She tossed her blond hair away from her face. "He told me Amy's dad is suspicious that Dennis's fall was murder. First of all, it seemed too coincidental for someone with a connection to Alan Rosemont to die within days of Alan's murder. Dennis, you know, did plenty of odd jobs for Alan, even though he didn't like him much."

"Right," Piper said. "And Dennis got the library painting job through Alan."

Megan nodded. "Then, there was the fact that Dennis knew how to handle himself on a roof. He was experienced and had all the right safety precautions in place. He had a rope system for pulling up shingles, and the rope ran through a clip of some type on his tool belt." She turned to Erin. "What did Ben call it?"

"A carabiner."

"Yeah. Anyway, it's a gadget that roofers use to keep from losing the rope. Ben said there was no reason Dennis should have been pulled off the roof by that rope under normal circumstances. There was nothing for it to accidentally catch on and so forth. The only thing that could have happened is that someone down below pulled on it and surprised Dennis, making him fall." She added, "And Mr. Perkins claims he saw a figure—that's all he could say, 'a figure'—outside his window around that time."

Piper gasped at the picture Megan had drawn. It was horrible. But she couldn't fill in the rest of it with Nate's face. It just wouldn't fit. "Why Nate?"

"Nate was seen going into the alley around that time," Erin said, her face glum.

"Oh Lord," Piper said. "He might have. He was here at the shop picking up the tarragon for you, Amy, before heading to work. It wasn't long after when we heard the sirens. Would that alley have been a shortcut to A La Carte?"

"Yes," Amy said, shaking her head. "But that doesn't mean anything. Nate might have walked behind the Perkins' house, but he never would have done such a terrible thing. Never!"

"How did he seem when he arrived at the restaurant?" Piper asked.

"Perfectly fine! Normal. Happy! There's no way he could have just killed someone and been so cool. He'd have to be some kind of monster, and he's not!"

"No, definitely not," Piper agreed.

"Tell your father that," Erin urged. "Tell him how natural Nate was when he showed up."

"Oh, I will," Amy said. "I definitely will. I just don't know that it will make a difference. Daddy's always pointing out that he needs facts, not opinions."

"Well, we'll have to dig up the facts, then," Piper said. "If that rope was yanked, it was by someone else. We'll just have to find out who that was."

Brave words, Piper thought. Now to accomplish it. She took a deep breath. "So, first we have to see who benefits from Dennis Isley's death. Any thoughts?"

She looked from one to the other, but all she got were blank stares. Not a great start.

"Okay," she said, pulling out her notebook of suspects

from under the counter and dragging over a tall stool. "Let's assume Dennis's death had something to do with Alan Rosemont."

"Can we?" Megan asked.

"Two violent deaths within days of each other in a small town? There has to be a connection. Unless you know of any other reason for Dennis to be murdered?"

Megan shook her head. "He didn't have anything anyone would want that I know of."

"Then we could go with the theory that Dennis was a difficulty that needed to be removed. Maybe he knew or saw something, possibly without even realizing its significance. Otherwise, wouldn't he have reported it?" Or maybe not, knowing Dennis. But that was another problem.

Piper looked at her list of names. "We have the Pfiefles, Ralph Farber, and Robby Taylor as suspects in Rosemont's murder." She quietly drew a line through the fourth name on the list—Dennis's. Piper looked up at the three friends. "We need to know where these people were when Dennis was pulled off the roof."

"Erin and I can check on Gordon Pfiefle, find out if he was at his supermarket or not."

"I can stop at the library on the way to the restaurant and check on Lyella," Amy said.

"Good," Piper said. "I'd just as soon not have to go there myself for a while." That coaxed a wan smile from her helper. All four looked up at the sound of voices as two chattering women approached the door to the pickling shop. "Go ahead," Piper told Erin and Megan. "Let us know what you find out."

As they left and the two new customers came in, Piper braced herself to be bombarded with round two of the Dennis Isley accident story, hoping that amid all the whirlwind of gossip, something helpful might actually fly out—and that Amy could hold it together if Nate's name came up.

16

Amy kept her composure at the shop, but only because Nate's name didn't come up during the customers' continual rehashing of Dennis Isley's death. Apparently word of Nate once again being a "person of interest" hadn't gotten around yet. It was only a matter of time, though, so Piper sent Amy off early to stop at the library and check on Lyella Pfiefle's activities at the time of Dennis's fall, before heading on to A La Carte. There was still Robby Taylor's and Ralph Farber's whereabouts to pinpoint, and Piper was thinking about how to do that when Charlotte Hosch walked in.

"Oh!" Charlotte said as she glanced around, her mouth pursed into a sour look. "She's gone."

"Do you mean Amy?" Piper asked.

"Yes, of course! I wanted to offer her a word of advice."

Oh Lord, Piper thought, and felt that at least one piece of luck had graced Amy's day—disappearing before Charlotte arrived.

"Advice?" Piper asked to be polite, though Charlotte had been sinking rapidly on her list of "Those Who Deserve a Modicum of Courtesy."

"Concerning that young man she's been spending time with. The musician." Charlotte pronounced that last word as Piper might have said tomato blight or fruit rot.

Piper stood a bit straighter. "What about Nate?"

"He's trouble, obviously. Pure trouble. As the sheriff's daughter, Amy Carlyle needs to steer clear of him, and for her own good, as well. I felt it was my duty to make that clear to her."

At that moment, Tina walked into the shop. "Piper, did you know Nate—oh! Charlotte!" Tina rocked back on her heels at the sight of the not-so-sweet confectioner.

"You came to tell Miss Lamb about Nate Purdy being taken in for questioning, I presume?"

"Y-yes," Tina said. "I guess I didn't need to." She turned to Piper. "It's just so upsetting! Why should they harass the boy like that? First because of Alan, now about Dennis. It doesn't make any sense!"

"It makes all the sense in the world," Charlotte countered. "Nobody knows a thing about that young man. There's no reason whatsoever to trust him. I'm convinced he saw Alan as an obstacle and therefore removed him. The same with Dennis, though I don't know exactly why in that case. But he acted as soon as he saw the opportunity."

"What are you talking about?" Tina said, her voice rising. "What opportunity?"

"Nate was seen entering the alley," Piper said. "Apparently close to the time Dennis fell."

"That's crazy!" Tina cried. "Who keeps track of foot traffic in an alley? Nate couldn't have been the only person walking through there, anyway. What bonehead picked him out specifically as the one to report?"

Charlotte drew herself up to her full, five-feet-eight height, looking, with her prickly mop of steel-colored hair and pointed nose, not unlike an angry ostrich ready to strike. "I did."

"You!"

"Somebody has to act with more than an ounce of intelligence around here! I saw Nate Purdy slip furtively into that alley and thought to myself that he was up to no good. Little did I know how right I was."

"You don't know anything!" Tina's face had turned florid. "You're just a busybody who thinks the worst of everyone. Do you know how much trouble you've caused that boy?"

"I never shirk my duty simply to avoid unpleasantness."

"No, you go looking for unpleasantness, you miserable—"

"Ladies!" Piper cried. "Enough, please. Tina, it's no good getting yourself worked up. That won't help Nate at all. The only thing that will help him is finding out the truth."

Charlotte turned on Piper. "You're protecting that villain? I might have known! Well, obviously I'll have to speak directly to Sheriff Carlyle about his daughter. Perhaps he'll be able to talk sense into her—if it's not too late! I expect he'll also rue the day he allowed her to take employment at this—" She paused, obviously searching for the most scathingly descriptive words she could think of, then spat out, "—this pickle den!" With that, Charlotte stalked out, slamming the door behind her.

Tina stared after her with hands clenched into fists, her face beet red. "Oh! That horrible woman!"

Piper stared, too, but mainly in astonishment over Charlotte's exit line. Pickle den? What the heck was that supposed to mean? She turned to Tina, realizing the coffee shop owner looked upset enough to have a stroke. Or a migraine, at the very least.

"Don't let Charlotte get to you," Piper soothed. "She thrives on stirring up trouble."

"Don't I know that." Tina took a deep breath. "But you're right. My ranting won't help Nate." She pulled her gaze from the sight of Charlotte marching away, which seemed to help her regain her composure. In a moment Tina asked, "What can I do that will help him?"

Piper thought a moment. "Would you find out where the plumber, Ralph Farber, was when Dennis fell to his death? I already have scouts checking up on other suspects."

"You got it. That shouldn't be too hard." Tina's normal color was returning, and she even managed a wan smile. "Though I'd hate Ralph to be the one. Nobody likes to lose a good plumber." She glanced at her watch. "I'd better get back to the coffee shop. Darla will need to take off soon."

Tina moved toward the door, and Piper asked, "Any luck with your search into Alan Rosemont's background?"

Tina turned back and shook her head. "Not much, so far. He seems to have kept a low profile. But I'll keep working at it. I'll let you know as soon as I dig up anything good."

"Great. Thanks." Tina took off, and Piper heaved a huge sigh. She'd known at the start that it was going to be a rough day. And the day was only half over.

Within an hour, Erin returned alone with a report on what she and Megan had learned about Gordon Pfiefle. Piper was glad it was only Erin. Though she genuinely liked both girls, on this near-siege of a day she was particularly grateful for Erin's quieter ways.

Erin's large brown eyes looked troubled, and she began by saying, "I really like Mr. Pfiefle. His supermarket sponsored our softball team back in high school, and he always showed up to cheer us on."

"By himself?" Piper asked.

"With his wife."

Of course. "It sounds like you learned something that doesn't rule him out."

Erin nodded. "He was out of the store from three until a little after five."

"Doing what? Do you know?"

"Mrs. Pfiefle had car trouble—a flat tire—and he rushed out to take care of it."

"That's interesting. Amy might be able to tell us if Lyella Pfiefle told the same story, although I expect she would. Those two seem joined at the hip. If one of them was up to no good, they both were."

"Maybe it really was a flat tire." Erin said it so earnestly that Piper realized she'd been jumping the gun and back-tracked.

"You're right. And we'll have to check up on that, some-how. But for now he's still on our list." Piper looked at Erin's worried face and said, "It'll have to be someone, you know. Even someone who seemed likable. Try to remember that whoever it is, that person wasn't as nice as everyone once thought to do such terrible things. And we don't want Nate to be blamed for crimes he didn't commit."

"Oh, I know! Absolutely. I just wish . . ." Erin winced. "I wish none of this had ever happened."

"As do we all," Piper said—particularly, she thought, Alan Rosemont and Dennis Isley. "If this is too hard on you, Erin, we'll all understand if you want to step away."

"No," Erin said, shaking her head firmly. "I want to pitch in." She paused. "I hope Ben understands that what we're doing isn't anything against him. It's just that we know Nate so much better than he does."

So Piper hadn't been mistaken about the feelings she'd picked up from Erin toward Ben Schaeffer. "I don't think he'll take it personally if we can prove the murderer is someone other than Nate," Piper said. "Maybe you could talk to Ben, explain your view of the situation." *And in the process let him see that there are other nice girls around besides Amy.*

"Oh!" Erin flushed. "I couldn't! That is, he'd be . . . I'd be so . . ."

"That's okay," Piper said, helping her out. "It was just a thought." Piper's cell phone rang, and she glanced at it. "It's Amy. Let's see what she's found out."

"Lyella Pfiefle wasn't at the library yesterday afternoon," Amy said as soon as Piper picked up. "She was supposed to drive to Appleton for a meeting, but that got canceled at the last minute. Since she'd already arranged for someone to fill in for her at the library, she decided to stay home."

"Well, that's interesting."

"Why?" Amy asked.

"Because," Piper said, "it doesn't exactly match her husband's story."

17

Piper closed up shop at six with a sigh of relief, although her day still wasn't done. She'd called the Pfiefles' inquisitive neighbor, Martha Smidley, and arranged for a visit that evening. Martha was more than agreeable but chose six thirty as the time.

"*Wheel of Fortune* comes on at seven," she said in a tone that indicated she was stating the obvious.

That didn't give Piper much time for a badly needed refueling, so she hurried upstairs and pulled open her refrigerator. Her eyes lit on the tomatoes Aunt Judy had sent home with her the night before. Was there anything better than fresh-picked, vine-ripened summer tomatoes? she wondered. Well, maybe pickled green tomatoes, but there wasn't time for that.

Piper pulled out a fat red one and sliced it, piled the

slices on wheat bread, then slathered it all with mayonnaise. Her first bite oozed juice and mayo down her chin but was the most delicious, satisfying thing she'd had all day. Piper took a few gulps of iced tea, then grabbed a raisin-loaded oatmeal cookie (also from Aunt Judy) to nibble on the way to Martha's, taking along a complimentary jar of pickled beets.

To save time, Piper drove to Locust Street. She'd barely climbed out of her car in front of Martha's house when the front door was opened by the elderly woman, who had obviously been watching for her as she watched most everything on her street. Piper hoped she'd been as vigilant yesterday afternoon.

"Hello, Martha!" Piper called and trotted up the front steps. Martha's smile broadened as Piper handed her the pickled beets.

"How nice! Thank you. Coffee?" Martha asked as Piper stepped into the foyer.

Piper saw a tray was already in place on the coffee table. Her hostess obviously didn't want to waste much time. "That'd be great," she said and slipped onto the chair opposite as Martha poured the brew into two daintily flowered china cups, then passed over Piper's. After a quick sip, Piper drew a breath, ready to jump in with her questions, but Martha beat her to it.

"You want to know what was going on around here when that handyman fell off the roof, don't you?"

Piper nodded. "I do. Were you home then?"

"Luckily, I was." Martha raised her cup to her lips, keeping Piper in suspense. She was wearing a crinkle-cloth matching top and pants, along with the sturdy sandals

Piper had seen before. This time her socks were pale blue, which matched her pants outfit. Piper waited for her to speak.

"Well," Martha said as she set down her cup. "Things were quiet the first part of the afternoon. Mrs. Donohue took her grandson out for a stroll after lunch. She watches him on Mondays and Thursdays, and occasionally on Friday afternoons."

Piper nodded, though she didn't care a fig when Mrs. Donohue babysat. Martha apparently needed to run through her list of the goings-on of her street from the beginning, since they were all fascinating to her. Skipping ahead was not her method of choice.

"Then, the Patterson boy came by and mowed the Riveros' lawn, which was way overdue for a cutting. He's fifteen, now, and gotten quite tall."

"Has he?" Piper glanced at the clock behind Martha and saw the minute hand creeping closer to *Wheel of Fortune* hour. "Did you happen to see the Pfiefles?"

"Why, yes. Yes, I did. Which really surprised me. They both are normally at work at that time. I saw Lyella first. She came home around two thirty. Looked a little more dressed up than she generally is for the library, wearing a light-colored suit and high heels."

"I understand she had some sort of out-of-town meeting to go to."

Martha nodded. "That explains it."

"When did you see Gordon?"

"He showed up about three fifteen. Very odd. Not exactly lunchtime, though he rarely came home for lunch, either. Why would he, when he's surrounded by food at work?"

"Could you see Lyella's car? How did her tires look? Any flat ones?"

"Her car was parked out front. I can't say I noticed her tires, but I think if she had a flat I would have heard it thumping as she drove up, don't you? And she would have fussed over it when she got out. All she did was walk into her house like she does every day."

"So Gordon didn't change any tires while he was there?"

"Certainly not. He came home, parked behind her car, and disappeared into the house."

"And when did he leave?" Piper asked.

"Ah, now that's a sticky part. Since they have a corner lot, all I can see is this side of their house where their front door faces Locust. But they have a back door that's out of my line of sight, and what with all the shrubs and trees on that side, anyone can slip out onto Third Street without me knowing it." Martha's mouth puckered with frustration. "I noticed Gordon getting back into his car at five. But I can't guarantee that he—or she—was inside the house that entire time. There've been times they surprised me by going for walks together but leaving from the back door, and I didn't know they'd gone out until they came sauntering down the street from the other direction."

How very inconsiderate of them, Piper thought, though in this case she shared Martha's frustration. Martha glanced at her clock. It was five minutes till showtime. Thinking that was all there was to be said, Piper set down her cup, ready to leave.

As she was in mid-rise, Martha said, "There's one other thing."

"Yes?"

"The look on Gordon's face as he came back out to his car around five o'clock."

Piper sank back down and waited as Martha seemed to search for the best way to describe Gordon Pfiefle's expression.

"It was . . . almost . . . well, smug. Yes, that's what I would call it. Smug." She looked up at Piper. "Now, what do you suppose he had to feel smug about?"

Piper drove home, thinking over Martha Smidley's account of the Pfiefles' activities. It made them look bad. Gordon Pfiefle had left work with the explanation that he needed to fix Lyella's flat tire. Yet, according to Martha, there was no flat tire. Then, either of them could have slipped out of the house without Martha's knowledge—Piper suspected they were aware of their neighbor's surveillance activities—and could have gone to the alley behind Ira Perkins's house and killed Dennis Isley.

But why? That was the missing puzzle piece. But nobody else had a motive for killing Dennis, either, so far as she knew. All the suspects on her list had strong motives for murdering Alan Rosemont as well as opportunities to do so, but all she had to work with on Dennis's death was opportunity.

Tina was looking into the plumber, Ralph Farber, for her. Piper was going to have to find out where Robby Taylor had been yesterday afternoon—and the sooner the better on both counts. There'd been two murders already in the small town of Cloverdale, and the sheriff was surely under pressure to arrest the murderer. Unfortunately, Nate was the person who kept drawing his attention.

Piper parked in the alley behind her shop and let herself in, happy to avoid the sight of the paint splash on the front of her building. She'd have to check with Max Noland as to when he was coming to power wash that ugly blot away for her. It occurred to Piper that if the splash had happened as a simple accident, it wouldn't be quite so disturbing. It was the negative vibes connected to someone defacing her bricks on purpose that made the splotch so unsightly—and made her that much more eager to get rid of it.

She shook her head, willing herself to think pleasanter thoughts, and smiled when the image of Will's Christmas tree popped in her head. Who else, she wondered, would come up with such a super-thoughtful gift at just the time she needed it? Piper climbed the stairs to her apartment and flicked on the lights, bringing her second unexpected gift into view—Scott's rose bouquet, which was much less smile producing. She sighed, knowing she hadn't e-mailed him yet, what with all that had gone on since the flowers arrived. She'd handle that task right away, she decided, since—grim thought—who knew what might happen next?

Martha's dainty cups had barely provided two decent swallows of coffee, so Piper set about making herself a mugful before tackling a job that she knew would require brainpower—wording her note of thanks to Scott politely but clearly enough that he would stop thinking of her as waiting breathlessly for his return.

As the water heated in the microwave, she changed into comfy sweats, then switched on her laptop. She left it to power up while she went to add instant coffee crystals to her steaming mug and, as an afterthought, snatch another of Aunt Judy's oatmeal cookies, carrying both to the table that held her laptop. She sat in front of it, then logged into her e-mail and set up a message for Scott. Once that was done, she stared at the screen and watched the cursor blink.

What to say? How to say it? After five minutes, all she'd typed was, "Dear Scott," her mind going blank after that. Piper's phone rang, and she lit up at the sound, not caring enough who might be calling to check caller ID. At that point she would have been happy to talk with a fund-raising solicitor for the mental health of gerbils. However, she was spared descriptions of rat phobias and psychoses as she heard Will's voice.

"Hi," he said. "How's it going?"

"Hi," Piper responded happily. She made a series of clicks to put her laptop to sleep, promising herself to wake it back up and finish her task soon. "Things are fine," she said. "That is, all things considered."

"You mean what happened to Dennis Isley? That was a shocker. But at least he didn't fall from *your* roof. Alan Rosemont ending up in your pickle barrel was bad enough."

"That's the truth. Having a second death too close to home might have tipped a few people over the edge about me."

"What? Have you been accused of something?"

"Not exactly. I've been wondering, though, if that paint thrown on my wall was a message, a 'We don't want your kind in Cloverdale' message."

"If it was, whoever did it is a bigger idiot than I thought—and that was pretty big to begin with." Will sounded genuinely angry, which touched Piper but at the same time made her instinctively pull back. She didn't want Will feeling responsible for her, well-intentioned as he was. She was fine with handling that herself.

"What I'm most worried about," she said, changing course, "is Nate. He was taken in for questioning this morning after someone—well, Charlotte Hosch, actually—reported she'd seen him go into the alley behind Mr. Perkins's place just before Dennis was killed."

Will grunted. "Not good."

"No, and not fair, either. That alley is a shortcut for any number of people. To pick out Nate and not worry about who else may have been passing by there around the same time is a mistake."

"Do you know for sure the sheriff isn't looking at anyone else?"

"No, but I haven't heard of anyone else being questioned as closely as Nate. Have you?"

"Can't say I have, but then I didn't know about Nate until you just told me. The sheriff's office isn't likely to broadcast every step of their investigation, so maybe certain happenings just haven't gotten around, yet."

"I certainly hope they're casting a broader net." Piper didn't like to mention her worries that the sheriff might be predisposed to suspect the worst of Nate, who, besides being of unverifiable character and in suspicious circumstances, had captured the affections of his daughter. Uncle Frank had a high opinion of Sheriff Carlyle's professional abilities and ethics, but could he say for sure that Carlyle was able to separate fatherly protectiveness from his job? Mama bears had a reputation for fierceness on behalf of their young, and the sheriff had needed to be both mother and father to Amy for years. Would heightened concern for his daughter affect his judgment?

"Tell you what," Will said. "I'll check around, see if I can find out if other townspeople are being looked at in connection with Dennis's death."

"Would you? That'd be great."

Their conversation moved on to less serious topics, and Piper remembered to ask if hanging lights on her live Christmas tree would hurt it. (It wouldn't.) They chatted about the latest movies, Will asking if Piper would like to go see the newest one. (Yes, but not until after the current situation was resolved.) Finally, it ended with Will promising to stop by if he had anything to tell her—and even if he didn't.

After they hung up, Piper glanced at the dark screen of her laptop. She should get back to her message to Scott, she knew, then saw that the time had flown by astonishingly fast. She set the laptop aside and picked up her empty coffee mug, telling herself that it wouldn't hurt to put off writing her note to Scott tomorrow. Such an important e-mail should, after all, be composed when her mind was well rested and clear.

That settled, she turned off her living room lights, brushed her teeth, and went to bed.

18

~~~~~~

The next morning, Piper dragged herself out of bed earlier than usual in order to accomplish what she'd promised herself to do: send off the e-mail to Scott that would set him straight on their relationship. She showered, dressed for work, then headed for the kitchen, planning to eat her breakfast from behind the laptop. She set coffee to brewing, then set a couple of scrambled eggs to frying. As they cooked, she popped toast in her toaster and pulled a jar of homemade apple butter from her refrigerator.

Her laptop sat waiting on her small kitchen table, and Piper bustled about doing enough things at once that she barely glanced out the window over her sink, though the sun streaming through it told her it would be another bright and warm day. It wasn't until she'd scraped the cooked eggs onto her plate and carried the empty pan to the sink that she actually looked outside. Her car was parked in the alley below, where she'd left it the night before. A fine coating of dew sparkled on the hatchback's hood, which Piper knew would burn off as soon as the sun rose a little higher.

She squirted soap into her pan and added hot water, but as Piper picked up the yellow-checked dish towel to wipe her hands, she took a second look out the window. Something struck her as odd about her car. She stared at it a moment then gasped. Her tires were flat! Not just one, but both tires on the driver's side.

Piper tossed the dish towel aside and trotted down the stairs, hoping against hope it had been a trick of the light or her not-quite-awake eyes. She reached the bottom of the stairs and hurried through her back room to the alley door, fumbling with the bolt before finally throwing it open.

She paused on the threshold, not really wanting to see what she feared she would, then stepped out and approached her car from the passenger side. She groaned. Both tires on that side were flat, too, rubber spreading outward on the concrete like overripe, gray tomatoes.

This was no fluke. There was no way she'd picked up nails in all four tires while driving through the paved streets between Martha Smidley's and her shop. This was deliberate, malicious vandalism. Not to mention costly. Piper allowed herself a single screech, then spun around and marched back into her shop.

"Sheriff's office?" she said, able by then to dial the number from memory. "I need to report a problem."

~~~~~~

Sheriff Carlyle arrived within minutes, this time without Ben Schaeffer. Carlyle stood looking down solemnly at Piper's flat tires after having examined all four closely.

"You seem to be having a rash of real bad luck lately."

He'd already agreed with Piper that four flat tires at once was way too incredible to have happened accidentally. Paint on her brick storefront. Tipped garbage cans. Now this! Someone was trying to tell her something, but what, and more importantly, who?

"I don't suppose there's any way of identifying the culprit?" she asked.

The sheriff shook his head. "We don't have the money for video cameras on every Cloverdale street corner, not to mention the back alleys. I can have my deputies swing by a little more often during the night, but my manpower will only stretch so far. Things like removing tire stems—which is what looks like happened here—or throwing paint at walls don't leave clues like fingerprints. Now if you happened to look out and see anything . . . ?"

Piper shook her head. "I have a quirky habit of sleeping in the wee hours of the morning—or whenever these things occur. As do most of my neighbors, I suspect."

"I'll ask around. Maybe one of them saw or heard something." Sheriff Carlyle didn't look hopeful. "In the meantime, think hard about who might have a grudge against you."

Piper had been doing that but was reluctant to bring up the one name that kept popping into her head because of Tina's wishful reasoning—that Charlotte Hosch's disagreeableness made her guilty of other crimes. She shook her head. "I just don't know," she said, then shrugged. "Maybe it's simply troubled teens acting out, and I happen to be a convenient target."

"Maybe," the sheriff said, but he didn't look convinced.

He finished his examination and took off, and Piper went back into her shop to call a garage about fixing her tires. She wasn't at all surprised to get voice mail and glumly left her message. Good thing she had no urgent need to drive anywhere, she consoled herself, and wondered how much this latest "prank" was going to cost her. Then she had a sudden frightening thought. With all her attention focused behind her store, she'd never thought to check out front!

Piper hurried through her shop and out the front door. She heaved a sigh. No sign of more damage to the front of her shop, and—perhaps more importantly—her new Christmas tree appeared untouched and in good shape. Thank heaven for small favors! She patted the healthy-looking dark green branches and leaned down to check the pot. The dirt felt dry, so she went back inside and filled a quart-sized measuring cup with water. As she emptied it slowly into the pot, she listened to the soft *glug-glug* as the roots gradually absorbed it, surprised at how good that made her feel—possibly how feeding hungry strays made Aunt Judy feel. But Piper, at least, hadn't started talking to her spruce, though she feared a few more "incidents" just might turn her in that direction.

Piper trotted back up to her apartment where she gazed, hands on hips, at her cold scrambled eggs and toast. She could reheat both in the microwave but found she had lost her appetite. Instead she tossed them into the garbage and poured out coffee from the still-hot carafe, then closed up the laptop that sat waiting for her to compose the e-mail to Scott. That message would have to wait a bit longer, as life had once again pushed itself in the way of her best-laid plans. It was time to open up Piper's Picklings as well as think hard about other things.

P iper pulled out the basket of zucchini Uncle Frank had given her, feeling the need for action after the not-so-great start of her day. What better way to ease anger and frustration than to grab a sharp knife and chop? The primitive side of her brain, she was sure, would appreciate that sort of activity. Perhaps she could even use it in her advertising brochure?

Put that aggravation to use—chop and pickle those veggies. Your family will thank you—both now and later.

As her distress-fueled chopping took on a certain rhythm, an appropriate tune, "I've Got a Little List," eased its way into her head, keeping time with the action of her knife, and soon Piper was humming along with Ko-Ko's list of all the annoying people who "never would be missed." As she worked, Piper easily thought of a few of her own to add. But she felt her mood steadily improve and instead of grabbing a pen and paper simply reached for another onion.

The bell attached to her shop door jingled, and Piper

grabbed a towel to wipe her hands and head out. Her visitor was Megan, and they met midway.

"You're here bright and early," Piper said.

"Amy's not answering her cell, but she probably just hopped in the shower or whatever after working late at A La Carte. But I wrangled some pretty interesting news from my brother, Ben, that I thought both of you would want to know." Megan was dressed in denim shorts and a tee and Piper figured she was on her way to the SPCA for her weekly volunteer work.

"What is it?"

"Dennis Isley's checking account had two deposits of three thousand dollars each this week."

"Payment from Ira Perkins for the roofing job?"

Megan shook her head. "Mr. Perkins gave Dennis his down payment for the new roof a month ago. He was going to pay the rest when the job was done. Plus he paid Dennis by check. These deposits, Ben said, were cash."

"Wow! That much in cash? That's pretty suspicious."

"It sure looks like someone was paying Dennis off, and it started right after Alan Rosemont was murdered."

Piper nodded excitedly. "That must let Nate off the hook. He surely didn't have that much money."

Megan's face darkened. "My thoughts exactly. But Ben," she said with an impatient flick of her long hair, "not surprisingly, doesn't agree. Which means the sheriff probably doesn't think so, either. Ben claims Nate could have had a secret cache of funds or had someone to call on for the money."

"That's ridiculous! Nate's been living hand to mouth ever since he arrived in Cloverdale."

"I know! But typical Ben thinks that could have been all for show."

Piper sank down on a stool. "Poor Nate. He can't win for losing, can he? Either he's a penniless, no-good drifter, or he's secretly rich but hiding his money—for what? In case he needs to pay off a blackmailer?"

"Apparently."

Piper shook her head in frustration. "Well, at least we now can guess why Dennis was pulled off that roof."

Megan nodded. "Blackmailers really need to be careful about climbing up on roofs. Or doing anything, for that matter, like walking down dark alleys or driving on deserted roads. They just set themselves up."

"The scary thing about Dennis's murder," Piper said, "is that it happened in broad daylight when anyone could have come along. It was a pretty gutsy thing to do."

"Plus," Megan said, "whoever did it wasn't a stranger who might have been noticed and remembered. It was someone who blended right in." She grimaced at the thought. "That gutsy person—who's killed two people already—could be anyone we know."

19

After Piper promised to bring Amy up to date on this latest information, Megan left for the animal shelter. As she returned to her pickling prep in the back, Piper puzzled over the obvious question: who was Dennis blackmailing—a risky venture that ended up getting him killed instead of making him richer?

As manager of a supermarket, Gordon Pfiefle would have been able to easily lay his hands on six thousand dollars in cash to pay Dennis off. Ralph Farber, owning his own plumbing business, might also have had accessible money. What about Robby Taylor, Dorothy Taylor's son? Piper still hadn't pinpointed his whereabouts on Thursday when Dennis was killed. Would he be able to scare up six thousand in a hurry?

Piper finished slicing the zucchinis and onions and

mixed pickling salt in with them in a large bowl. She covered all with cold water, then left it to sit as she returned to her front counter. Her phone rang, and—miracle of miracles—it was the garage returning her call about her tires.

"I'll send my guy out to look at them," garage owner Rodney Knotts promised her. "Might be he can fix them in place. If not, we'll have to tow."

That call reminded Piper to check with Max Noland about his plans for cleaning off the paint splash. *Can't let these damage repairs start piling up*, she thought grimly. Her call to Noland reached only his answering system, so she left a second inquiring message that was a tad testier than her first.

Two customers stopped in within a few minutes of each other. Piper helped them out, learning from the second woman that she was a longtime pickler who was delighted to find a shop nearby that catered to her particular culinary joy. As this customer was gathering up her purchases, Amy arrived, looking more down than she had the day before.

Piper was eager to share Megan's news, certain that would perk Amy up. But her latest customer continued to linger, coming up with one pickling anecdote after another, each remembered after making what Piper hoped was her final good-bye. Finally the woman went out the door, and Piper turned to her assistant.

"Megan stopped in earlier," she said and shared the story of Dennis Isley's mysterious bank deposits. "We both think that should let Nate off the hook, since where would he come up with that kind of money? Ben has a differing theory on that, but I think your father would surely agree that he should look elsewhere for a blackmailer and murderer."

Amy didn't look as excited as Piper expected. "I don't know what my father's thinking," she said, "but I do know what A La Carte's management is thinking."

Uh-oh.

"They fired Nate last night. Or, as they put it," Amy said, making air quotes, "temporarily suspended his performances until this unfortunate matter is cleared up."

"Oh, shoot!"

"I used stronger words than that. Out of management's earshot, of course. I have to keep my own job there, for now." Amy looked at Piper with a mixture of anger and anguish in her eyes. "It's so unfair! None of this is Nate's fault! I don't know what he'll do without a job. How will he pay his rent?"

"We can figure something out. Nate's not exactly friendless. There are people who believe in him and who will help."

"He won't take charity, I'm sure of that."

"It shouldn't have to come to that. Something will surely come up." Piper said it with confidence for Amy's sake, and she truly did hope so herself. But at the moment things looked bleak for Nate. How many openings were there in a small town for a singer-musician? Especially one whose reputation was rapidly spiraling downward?

"Until another job materializes," Piper said, "the best thing we can do for Nate is uncover the actual murderer of Alan Rosemont and Dennis Isley."

"Are we getting any closer to that?" Amy asked.

"We're learning more every day," Piper said, hoping

that sounded more encouraging than it felt. "What you learned about Lyella Pfiefle's activity on Thursday, plus Megan and Erin's information about her husband Gordon's false excuse to leave TopValuFood around the same time, sent me for a chat with Martha Smidley. All stories combined put the Pfiefles in a very suspicious light. But probably not enough to convince the sheriff yet.

"I still want to find out more about Robby Taylor," Piper continued, "and haven't been able to figure out how to do that. When Aunt Judy last tried talking to his mother about Robby, Mrs. Taylor clammed up."

Amy grew thoughtful. "I remember seeing Robby going in to the Yeager Real Estate Agency not too long ago. I was pulling up to get a hair trim at Alexander's next door. Maybe Robby's planning to move back to Cloverdale, in which case Mr. Yeager might be keeping in touch with him."

"Hmm. Worth a try," Piper said. "It's certainly more than what I have otherwise, which is close to zilch. Maybe I'll run out there right now." Piper started untying her apron. "While I'm gone, there's a big bowl of zucchini in salt water in the back that'll need its first drain and rinse in a few minutes."

"I'm on it," Amy said.

"Oh, and someone from the garage might show up." She explained, to Amy's dismay, about the flattened tires. "And if Max Noland happens to call here instead of my cell to schedule the paint cleanup, grab the earliest available time."

At that, Piper stuffed her apron under the counter and snatched her purse. She caught her reflection in the wall mirror behind the register and realized she could greatly benefit from a visit to a hair salon herself. Unfortunately, the mounting need for repairs was gobbling up any spare funds for such luxuries. Piper ran her fingers through her chin-length hair and wondered how she'd look with a thick braid hanging down to her hips, which might be the hairstyle of choice if the vandalism wasn't stopped.

S tan Yeager had helped Piper in her search for a suitable shop with living quarters not too long ago, and she remembered him as a friendly, chatty man who seemed to have forgotten that Piper had spent many summers in Cloverdale and therefore had at least a basic knowledge of the town. Today she didn't care if he remembered anything about her. What she wanted was information on Robby Taylor.

Piper walked into the real estate agency and spotted the fifty-something Yeager at his desk, talking on the phone. He nodded cheerily to her and held up an index finger to signal he'd be with her shortly. The agency was a small one—Yeager being the agent-owner with one other part-time associate. But Cloverdale was a small town that wasn't exactly booming with development, which seemed to suit most of its inhabitants just fine.

"Well, young lady," Yeager said as he finished with his call. "What can I do for you today?" He unfolded his lanky frame from the desk chair to stand several inches over Piper, smiling affably.

To be on the safe side, Piper reintroduced herself, reminding Yeager of the pickling shop he'd helped her establish.

"Right! Right! How's that going? A big success, I hope? And now you're ready to branch out in a second location?"

He seemed to be only half joking, and Piper hurriedly assured him that though doing well enough, she had a long way to go before thinking in those terms. "I'm here, actually, with a question about Robby Taylor."

"Robby Taylor?" Yeager's eyes lit up. "Are you interested in Dorothy's place?"

"Um—"

"It's not officially on the market, yet, but I can let Robby know you'd like first dibs on the house. It's a grand old place, just perfect for a discriminating young person like yourself looking for something out of the ordinary. Loaded with charm, plenty of room to spread out, and for"—he actually winked at this—"the kiddies someday. And the price—as is—should be real attractive. The bit of fixing up it needs should be no problem whatsoever for that young man of yours, who—"

Oh good Lord. "So Robby's mother is selling her house?" Piper interrupted.

Yeager pulled up at that, saying cautiously, "It looks highly possible. The place is certainly much too big for Dorothy and more than Robby can maintain for her long-distance. She hasn't signed on the dotted line yet, but I'm convinced she's on the verge. Robby was here just the other day—"

"Thursday? Someone mentioned they thought they'd seen him in town then."

"Why, yes, it was Thursday, as a matter of fact. Thursday afternoon. Anyway, he'd just spoken with his mother, and he stopped in to let me know he'll probably have the signed papers for me very soon. I can let you know when they're ready to show it. Nice big yard. A little paint and plaster and the place could be ready to move in by—"

"That's okay, there's no hurry at all. I think Dorothy told me her son lives in Poughkeepsie. Is that right?"

"Yes, that's exactly right. He moved there, let me see . . . good heavens, it must be at least twenty years ago! He took a job at a fitness gym, you know, one of those places with all the weights and treadmills and other instruments of torture." Another wink. "He was a personal trainer, if I remember rightly. Must have been pretty good at it, because a couple of years ago he invested in a gym of his own. Of course, Dorothy may have pitched in some, financially. He was always the light in her eye, and she'd do anything for him."

Including giving up her house if he asked? Piper wondered if Dorothy was really ready to do that, or if Robby had suddenly become desperate for cash and was tightening the screws on a doting mother. Piper had never met Robby, but Stan Yeager's information about Robby's line of work told her he would certainly be strong enough to do away with Alan Rosemont if he were so inclined, plus lift his body into Piper's pickle barrel.

That last part still rankled Piper. If Robby—or anyone else—murdered Alan Rosemont, why did they have to involve her pickle barrel? The instant she had the thought, Piper chided herself. A piece of equipment—proud as she'd been of it—was the least of the problems. Two men were dead, and a third was under deep suspicion for their murders, his life in danger of being ruined forever.

Robby Taylor had been in town on Thursday. That, on

top of his having been furious at Alan for fleecing Dorothy out of her antiques, certainly kept him in the running with her other suspects.

"Thank you very much, Mr. Yeager."

"Not at all. As I said, I'll let you know as soon as the Taylors are ready to show the house, and you can bring your young man—"

"Hey, look at the time! Gotta run." Piper left Stan Yeager in mid-thought, delighted to hear his phone ring, which would hopefully distract him from images of her house hunting along with Will.

Poor Will. If he only knew what he'd gotten himself into by giving her that Christmas tree.

Or did he?

20

~~~

"Piper," Aunt Judy asked over the phone, "what's this about you being in the market for a house?"

Piper glanced at the clock above the shelf of assorted pickling spices. It had been over two hours since she spoke with Stan Yeager. What took so long?

"I'm not looking for a house, Aunt Judy."

"But Mrs. Peterson said that Stan Yeager told her that—"

"I only visited with Mr. Yeager to find out where Robby Taylor was on Thursday afternoon, when Dennis Isley was pulled off the roof."

"Oh, of course! I told Mrs. Peterson . . . well, never mind. So what did you find out?"

Piper explained about Robby having been in Cloverdale

on Thursday to discuss selling his mother's house with Stan Yeager.

"Maybe that's why Dorothy was so closemouthed when I tried to talk to her about Robby," Aunt Judy said. "Do you suppose she really wants to sell her house?"

"You know her better than I do. What do you think?"

Piper's aunt went silent for a moment before saying, "First and foremost Dorothy wants to make her son happy. She probably felt she was doing that when she let Alan Rosemont clear her attic, thinking she was saving Robby from the job later on. Instead, Robby went ballistic when he learned what she'd done and realized she'd been essentially swindled by Alan.

"Dorothy might have convinced herself that since she'd lost a chunk of what would have been Robby's inheritance," she continued, "she now needed to make it up to him. I doubt Dorothy wants to give up her house, but she might if Robby asks her to."

"Is the house Mrs. Taylor's only asset? I mean, if Robby needed a significant amount of money from her, would she have any on hand to give him? Or is selling her house the only way she could come up with it?" Piper was thinking of the six thousand Dennis had received after Alan Rosemont's murder.

"That I don't know, dear." Piper heard a soft chuckle come from her aunt. "Small towners know a lot about one another, but that doesn't generally include bank balances."

"No, I don't suppose it would," Piper agreed. And thank heavens for that, though in this case she wished there'd been an exception.

"There's bad news about Nate, Aunt Judy." Piper told her about Nate's loss of job at A La Carte.

"That's terrible! That poor boy. But tell Amy not to worry. I'll ask around. I'm sure we can find something for him."

"Would you? Thanks, Aunt Judy."

Piper ended the call as a woman walked into her shop, announcing she'd come for a fresh supply of pint jars and lids. As Piper gathered them up, her customer chatted, as most seemed to do, about her intended use for the equipment.

"My husband loves to grow tomatoes," the woman said, "and we get so much more than we can eat or give away. So I turn some of them into catsup—my own recipe—and give them away here and there. Everyone seems to love it!"

"A great idea," Piper agreed. After all, who didn't like catsup?

When the woman left, Piper went into her back room to work on her zucchini pickles. Amy had drained and rinsed the soaking vegetables while Piper was at the Realtor's office. She'd also combined the vinegar, sugar, and spices and boiled it all briefly as required. Piper had continued the project when she'd returned, and it was time for the next step.

She brought the squash and vinegar mixture back to a boil, and after five minutes of cooking, ladled her pickled squash into clean, hot jars, sealed them, and set them into her water bath canner to process. She heard her front door open and Tina's voice call out, so Piper carefully set her timer, then went out front.

Tina got right to the point. "A couple of people in my

lunch crowd told me they saw Rodney's garage truck pull into your alley this morning. Is everything okay?"

Tina appeared a bit frazzled, with her normally tidy hair hanging limply and her face flushed and shining from the heat. *Must have been a busy lunchtime at the coffee shop*, Piper thought, and she was touched that Tina had put checking up on a friend's well-being ahead of her own need for rest.

"I had a little problem with my car's tire stems," Piper said. "Someone did a number on them, pulling them out during the night, which left me with four flats."

"Oh, that woman!" Tina glared in the direction of Charlotte Hosch's confectionary shop.

"Hold on, Tina. There's no proof it was Charlotte. And really, can you imagine Charlotte skulking about in the middle of the night fiddling with tires or throwing paint?"

"Maybe she got someone to do it for her," Tina persisted.

"And trusted they wouldn't rat on her someday? I don't know, Tina. Charlotte's pretty disagreeable, but I just can't see her going to such lengths."

"Piper," Tina said as she swept a drooping lock of hair from her face, "you don't know her like I do. Her shop is right across the street from mine, and I see and hear that woman every day. I really think she's capable of much more than you realize. Even if you don't think you can report her, you should really watch out for her."

"I'll do my best," Piper said, shaking her head, "but if Charlotte—or anyone—is inclined to cause damage when no one's around, I'm afraid they're going to get away with it. I can't expect special police protection, especially with the damage being fairly minor."

"So far. What if things get much worse?"

"Then," Piper said, heaving a sigh, "I'm in trouble, and so is my pickling shop. But I'll worry about that when I have to. For now, I'm going to focus on Nate and the trouble he's in. Did you get a chance to look into Ralph Farber's whereabouts when Dennis was killed?"

Tina looked at Piper for a moment, as though wanting to say more on the current subject, but then nodded. "Yes, I did."

Piper waited, and Tina dragged a stool closer and sat down with a tired sigh. "One of my customers—your neighbor, actually—helped out with that."

"My neighbor?"

"Mr. Williams. The bookshop owner."

"Oh, right." Piper had met Gilbert Williams, of course, and had been inside his new-and-used bookshop next door to Piper's Picklings. But the older man was generally so absorbed with his books, to the point of near-reclusiveness, that she tended to forget he was even there. "Mr. Williams goes out to lunch?"

Tina nodded. "Tuesdays and Thursdays, like clockwork. But he missed last Thursday, which is how I learned about Ralph Farber's whereabouts. Farber was at Gilbert Williams's bookshop, delivering and installing a new sink in the washroom. Mr. Williams wanted me to know he hadn't gone elsewhere for his lunch but had felt he should stay at his shop while Ralph was there, in case any questions came up."

"I see."

"He's so sweet—Mr. Williams, I mean—for not wanting me to feel offended. He orders the same thing almost every time. Corned beef on rye. But if I haven't been able to find good corned beef that week, he'll change it to grilled chicken with lettuce and tomato."

"So Ralph Farber was at the bookshop all Thursday afternoon?"

"That, I don't know. Things got too busy at the coffee shop for me to ask. But I could run over to the bookshop right now, if you like."

Piper took in the dark circles under Tina's eyes and shook her head. "I can do that myself. If Mr. Williams gives Ralph Farber an alibi for the time Dennis was killed, then I'll cross him off my suspect list. If not, then we'll see."

"Is Charlotte on your list?"

"No, I didn't have any reason to connect her to Alan Rosemont's murder."

"Well, I don't know about Alan, though I wouldn't be surprised to find there was a grudge of some sort between them. But remember, she was the one who told Sheriff Carlyle about Nate going into the alley around the time Dennis was killed."

"Yes?"

"That means Charlotte was there, too. Who's to say she didn't go into that alley after Nate did and pull poor Dennis off that roof herself?"

Piper puffed out her cheeks, thinking. Tina was right. Who could say that hadn't happened? "And reported Nate to divert suspicion from herself?"

"Exactly!"

"It's possible," Piper said. "But I'll still need more to believe that actually happened."

Tina shook her head sadly, and Piper could guess what she was thinking: that Piper was being dangerously obtuse about a potential murderer in their midst. She certainly hoped not. Only time would tell which of them was right.

With traffic at her shop slowed to nonexistent near the end of the day, Piper closed up a few minutes early, then hurried over to Gilbert Williams's bookshop, hoping he would still be open. She brightened as she saw his lights on and spotted the sixtyish-looking man bent over his desk, examining one of his many books. Piper walked in, and Gilbert Williams lowered his reading glasses and looked up.

"Miss Lamb," he said, as a gentle smile lit up his thin face. "To what do I owe the honor of this visit?" Despite the warm day, he was wearing his usual brown, leather-elbow-patched cardigan. His white hair stuck out in a few places, as though he'd absently run a hand through it, and the plaid shirt beneath the cardigan looked clean but rumpled. Piper knew from Aunt Judy that there'd never been a Mrs. Williams.

"Gilbert never seemed able to pull his nose out of a book long enough to notice the women around him," Aunt Judy had said. "But he's a good soul and apparently quite content as he is."

"Mr. Williams," Piper began, her gaze involuntarily drawn to a group of cookbooks on a table nearby. "I understand Ralph Farber was here on Thursday afternoon. Is that right?"

Gilbert Williams thought back. "Thursday? I suppose that was the day. Yes," he said more firmly, probably remembering his missed lunch. "That's right. Why do you ask? I hope the noise wasn't disturbing you."

"Not at all. I wasn't even aware until today that he'd been here. No, I'm just trying to—" Piper stopped herself. Did she want to share her reason for checking up on the plumber, which was to decide if he would remain on her murder suspect list or not? Would that shock this quiet, bookish man? Then she spotted a selection of classic murder mysteries behind him. John D. MacDonald, Dashiell Hammett, Dorothy L. Sayers. The bindings looked original, though faded and worn.

"Have you read all those?" she asked.

Williams glanced over his shoulder, then nodded. "Those, and many more. There's nothing like a good mystery to keep—as Hercule Poirot would have said—the little gray cells active." He tapped his temple, smiling.

Hercule was right, Piper thought, although the Belgian detective could have added "as well as turn the little hairs on your head gray." "You must have been following our real, live mysteries, then. Alan Rosemont? Dennis Isley?"

Williams nodded. "With great interest. I intended to stop in and offer my sympathies over the unfortunate involvement of your pickling booth, but anytime I had a moment you appeared to be quite busy in your shop, so I put it off. Please let me do that right now, Miss Lamb."

"Thank you. And please call me Piper."

Williams nodded. "If you'll call me Gil. Now, what

does Ralph Farber have to do with Alan Rosemont and Dennis Isley?"

"That's what I'm trying to determine." Piper explained about Nate Purdy being under suspicion for both murders, partly from incriminating circumstances and partly, she feared, for simply being who he was: an unknown personage. "A few of us who believe in Nate's innocence are hoping to turn up enough real evidence to pull the sheriff's attention away from Nate and toward the actual murderer."

"And you think my plumber might be the murderer?"

"I don't think anything, right now. All I know is that Ralph Farber had a few run-ins with Alan Rosemont over his persistent bagpipe playing, living, as he did, next door to him. Plus, Farber was at the fairgrounds the night Alan was murdered. I think Dennis Isley's murder is connected to Alan's. Which is why I want to pinpoint Ralph Farber's whereabouts at the time of Dennis's fall from the roof."

An odd look passed over Williams's face, and he opened his mouth as if to speak. But the shop door burst open at that moment, and a large man blustered in.

"Good! You're still here," the man boomed. "That replacement faucet just came in. Thought I'd install it right away. That work for you?"

Gilbert Williams stood up and, with a glance at Piper, said, "Of course, Mr. Farber. That would be perfectly fine."

21

P iper stood face-to-face—or rather, face-to-chest—for the first time with the man she'd just been discussing as a possible murderer. Though tall and burly, Ralph Farber's physical size was far less intimidating than his manner. Nate had said he wouldn't have wanted to cross the man, and Piper understood. She could only imagine what the confrontations between Alan Rosemont and Ralph Farber had been like and wouldn't have wanted to be in the middle of them. On those grounds alone, Farber had currently risen to the number one spot on her list.

"Have you met my neighbor?" Gilbert asked and introduced Piper.

"Nice to meetcha," Farber said, lightening the deep scowl on his face a degree. "You got the pickle place over there?"

"I do," Piper said.

Farber whipped out a business card and handed it to her. "I did the plumbing there way back when it was a flower shop. Basic stuff. Give me a call when you're ready to upgrade."

Piper nodded and pocketed the card, and Farber proceeded to the back of the bookshop with his replacement faucet and bag of tools, knocking a book or two from their shelves in the process. Rescuing the first, Gilbert turned to Piper.

"Please continue your browsing, Piper. I'm sure you'll find that recipe you were looking for tucked away in one of these cookbooks. If not, there's a few more on a shelf near the back." With that, he followed Farber to the washroom, having thus given Piper leave to listen in to whatever might come up in his conversation with the plumber.

Piper lingered near the counter for a while, Farber's loud voice carrying clearly as he explained why the new faucet would be worth every penny of its cost and apparently improve Gilbert Williams's life tenfold by its very presence. She heard several clanks as he spread out his tools, then things quieted. Piper moved toward the back where she could see Gil near the doorway of the small restroom. How Ralph Farber fit into the rest of it, she didn't know, but she could hear him talking again as he worked, mainly complaints. She listened as he railed at some length against the rise in gas prices, the rotten service of his cable company, and the "stinkin'-hot" weather, among other things.

Gil Williams made noncommittal noises that could be taken for agreement if one were so inclined. There were a few loud grunts, presumably from the plumber's efforts with the faucet, and more clinks from his tools.

"Mr. Farber," Gil said, "I really appreciate your coming here late on a Saturday to install this."

"Yeah, well, I'd promised to have it done by the weekend, and I'm a man likes to keep his promises."

"Indeed you are, Mr. Farber. When you were here on Thursday, you seemed to have been convinced you'd be finished that day."

More clinks along with a grunt. "I woulda," Farber said, "but for that new girl I got in the office, now." *Clank!* "She ordered the wrong faucet. I didn't catch on to that until I had this sink in place and was ready to install the damn faucet. I had to go running back and see if by some miracle the right one came in along with the one I had. No such luck. She messed us both up."

"Oh, I see," Gil Williams said. "I'd wondered why you'd disappeared."

"Yeah. Well, I woulda called, but a lotta stuff came up. Lucky the right faucet came in today."

"Yes, it was." Gil Williams leaned back and caught Piper's eye.

"I tell you," Farber said, "ya can't get good help nowadays. I don't know what they're teaching kids in schools anymore. Junk like—"

Farber went off on a rant against the current educational system (using the less-than-perfect grammar he himself had managed to graduate with during the older system), and Piper set down the book on investment management she'd been holding in case the plumber happened to rush

out. She lifted a hand in silent good-bye to Gil, who nodded, and she left the store.

Well, Piper thought, all things considered, she just
might have her number one suspect.

Back at her apartment, Piper realized she had a message
from Will on her cell.

"I know this is last-minute, and I'm really sorry. I've
been out in the field all day, but I still should have called
earlier. Any chance you're free tonight? Maybe to grab a
pizza? I'll check back in a few minutes."

A last-minute date on a Saturday night? Ten years ago,
Piper might have hesitated, but she'd moved on from the
game playing since then. She called Will back.

"Sounds great. I can be ready in twenty minutes." With
that, Piper hopped into the shower, happy to wash away
the stresses of the day and hoping for a relaxing evening.

She met Will at her front door in capris and a cotton
top. Piper thought the navy tee Will wore over shorts made
his blue eyes look even bluer, something she wouldn't have
thought possible.

"It doesn't have to be pizza," Will said, "if you'd rather
have something else. It was just the first thing popped into
my head."

"Too late! I've been thinking of pizza since you called
and now I'm dying for it," Piper said.

"Then Carlo's it is."

Carlo's was a short ride from Piper's place, but by the
time they settled at a table at the modest but heavenly

smelling pizzeria, Piper felt she could devour an entire pie herself. They decided to share a large, fully loaded one, with the option of ordering a second if needed. The place was crowded and noisy enough to offer privacy, and Piper told Will what she'd learned about Ralph Farber, as well as Nate's unemployment predicament.

"That's a crying shame," Will said. "The management at A La Carte will be sorry. Their business will drop off."

"Maybe so. I wonder, though, if they might have had pressure to fire Nate."

"Pressure from who?"

Piper shrugged. "I couldn't say for sure. But not everyone looks at Nate the same way we do." She was thinking of Charlotte Hosch, but there might have been others. Their server brought the frosty beers they'd ordered, and Piper waited until he'd left before continuing. "Aunt Judy said she'd ask around for a job Nate could take until this all blows over."

Will took a swallow of his beer and wiped the foam from his lips. "If it blows over," he said, grimly.

"What do you mean?"

"I haven't been able to determine if the sheriff has been hauling anyone else in for questioning. That doesn't guarantee he hasn't, since he doesn't exactly call me to report his every move. But I'm not picking up talk of there being any other 'persons of interest.'"

Piper frowned at that, but the arrival of their pizza eased it, at least for the moment. Finding it impossible to remain somber while sinking their teeth into thick mozzarella cheese, spicy tomato sauce, and layers of pepperoni, mushrooms, sausage, peppers, and more, their conversation, when they could manage it, switched to lighter topics—such as Christmas trees.

Will was in the middle of describing the new signs he'd ordered for his tree farm when Piper spotted a tall man heading determinedly toward their table. She hastily wiped a paper napkin over her grease- and sauce-stained mouth and gulped down her latest bite of pizza.

"Hello, Mr. Yeager," she greeted the Realtor.

"Saw you sitting here," Yeager said cheerily. "Stan Yeager," he said, holding out his hand to Will, who took it with a slightly puzzled air. "Just wanted to tell you Dorothy Taylor's place will be open to look at anytime you two want to take the tour."

"Huh?" Will said.

"Just give me a call. I'll set it all up."

"Mr. Yeager, I—" Piper began, but the sight of a dark-haired, muscular man in formfitting jeans and a black tee coming up behind Yeager stopped her.

Yeager turned. "Ah, there you are, Robby. This is the couple I told you about who's interested in your mother's place. Robby Taylor meet Piper Lamb and Will Burchett."

"Glad to meet you," Robby said, nearly crumpling Piper's hand with his grip before turning it on Will. Will looked stunned, and Piper didn't think it was from Robby's bone-crushing handshake.

"Mr. Yeager," Piper said, "I didn't mean—" She stopped. How could she explain her true interest in Robby Taylor with the man standing right there? "That is, I'm not sure I'm ready to buy just yet."

"Don't worry about it!" Yeager said. "We can work that

all out further down the line. Just come by and we'll talk. I know you'll love the house once you see it." He winked at Will. "Lots of room for the little—"

"Yes!" Piper chirped. "Thank you, Mr. Yeager. Nice to meet you, Robby."

The two men moved off at that, and Piper kept her gaze on them to avoid Will's. Finally, she turned to him and offered a weak smile. He grinned in return.

"Lots of room for the little what?" he asked.

Piper groaned.

"So you think Robby Taylor might have murdered Alan Rosemont in a fit of fury over Rosemont's fleecing of his mother's antiques," Will said, rehashing Piper's earlier explanation as they walked to his van. To Piper's relief, he'd dropped any further comment on Stan Yeager's assumption that he and Piper were house hunting as a couple. Yeager and Robby, she'd noticed, had taken a table across the room and were deep in discussion when she and Will slipped out.

"That's my theory," Piper said. "It's based on what I've learned about Robby as well as his presence in Cloverdale at the time of both Alan Rosemont's and Dennis Isley's murders. And now that I've seen him in person, it's clear he's definitely strong enough to have tipped Alan's body into my pickle barrel."

"Yes, I'd have to agree with that." Will rubbed at the hand Robby had recently gripped.

"The problem is," Piper said as they reached the van and climbed in, "I also think Ralph Farber is a very good possibility. From what I saw of his aggressive personality, I can totally picture him coming across Alan Rosemont, marching along and playing his bagpipes that night at the fairgrounds, and going ballistic after all their previous arguments. But I have no proof that actually happened. Nothing whatsoever to take to the sheriff."

Piper sighed. "Then there's Gordon Pfiefle, of course, but the same for him. No evidence, just theory."

"Don't worry too much about it," Will said. "Something may come up."

"Maybe, but in the meantime Nate has lost his job and might be out on the street if he can't pay his rent. I highly doubt he has a hidden cache of money, as Ben Schaeffer wants to believe, to tide him over. And what will he do about food?"

Will looked over at Piper with a small smile, one eyebrow cocked. "I wouldn't worry about the food part. Your Aunt Judy and all the kindhearted ladies of the town like her will probably take care of that."

Piper smiled. "You're probably right on that count. But he'll still need a roof over his head and at least a minimal-paying job to keep his spirits and self-respect intact."

Piper continued to worry about that last part after Will dropped her off, and in fits and starts for most of the night. But the solution showed itself fairly soon and from a very unexpected quarter.

22

"Do you think Nate Purdy would find that agreeable?" Gilbert Williams asked.

He'd knocked on Piper's back door the next afternoon, having seen her light on. It was Sunday afternoon, when Piper's Picklings was closed, but Piper had been working on her store's books. Finding the bookshop owner standing in her alley was a mild surprise, but his proposal bowled her over.

"I think Nate would be very happy to live above your shop as well as work for you, Mr. Wi—ah, Gil."

"The living quarters haven't been used in quite a while—since my last tenant moved out at least two years ago, actually, when I decided I preferred the quiet to the income. So I'm afraid it'll need a bit of dusting up."

"Nate and his friends can take care of that."

"There's a few pieces of basic furniture, though again, not in the best condition."

"I'm sure he'll love it," Piper declared, "just as he'll love working for you."

"He'll be welcome to stay as long as he likes, though I understand working in a bookstore isn't exactly on his career path. I can really use his help, though. Books are quite heavy to move around, you know, and I'm not as young as I look." Gil Williams's eyes twinkled at this, and Piper grinned.

"I'll get on the phone and have Nate come talk it over with you. This is really great of you, Gil."

"Not at all. My dusty old shop has been in need of perking up for some time. Nate will be doing me a favor."

Gil Williams turned back to his shop, and Piper called Amy, pulling the phone away from her ear at the joyful squeal that flew out at her news.

"I'll call Nate right away," Amy said.

"I thought he'd prefer hearing it from you. It won't be luxury accommodations by any means, but Gilbert Williams will be a very considerate landlord and employer."

"And we'd be working right next door to each other!"

That should cause Sheriff Carlyle a bit of indigestion, Piper thought with a wince. As well as Charlotte Hosch, Ben Schaeffer, and who knows who else. But Piper would let Amy handle her father, and the others could just—

"Thanks, Piper. Talk to you later!" Amy hung up, eager to reach Nate, and Piper smiled, glad that one problem was taken care of for the time being. Then she thought of Aunt Judy, who might be still working busily on behalf of Nate, and dialed her number.

"Aunt Judy," Piper said when her aunt picked up, "I have good news, for a change." She explained the situation, hearing a pleased "ah" as she did so.

"Gil Williams surprises me, now and then," Aunt Judy said. "He'll keep to himself so long that you think he's become totally out of touch. Then he does something like this that shows it's just the opposite. That's very good of Gil. And fortunate for Nate. I wasn't having much luck with my efforts to find something for him, though if worse came to worst, your uncle and I would have brought him here. I don't know how Nate would have taken to farmwork, though."

"I'm sure he would have been fine and grateful," Piper said. "But the bookshop will put him much closer to Amy when she's on the job here."

Aunt Judy chuckled. "A definite plus. Thanks for calling, dear. I'd better make one or two calls and take people off the search."

Piper went back to her account books but found it difficult to refocus on numbers, bills, and payments. Her thoughts kept going back to Nate, whose reprieve from unemployment and homelessness, she knew, was only a temporary fix. They moved on to her discussion of the murders with Will the previous evening, then settled on Will himself. She was liking him more and more and found herself getting less unsettled by the assumptions of townspeople like Stan Yeager that she and Will were a couple. A long way from wanting to march down the aisle with him, but not totally appalled at the suggestion, either.

Piper was smiling at the memory of one of Will's comments when she heard a second knock on her door.

Thinking it might be Gil Williams again, she was surprised to instead find Roger Atwater, husband of Mindy Atwater who ran the knitting shop down the street. At least Piper thought it was Roger. With the large box he was holding covering his face, all she could see was the top of the man's bald head and the round edges of his body on each side of it. His telltale, often worn, plaid golfing pants, however, gave him away.

Roger tilted his head and one eye peered around the box. "This was delivered to Mindy's shop by mistake, yesterday. She gets so many that she didn't get around to checking it right away. I took a chance you might be here."

"That was very kind of you," Piper said, reaching out.

"I'll carry it in," Roger said. "Just tell me where you want it." Piper stepped back, indicating an empty spot on her floor, and Roger gently set the box down.

"I wasn't expecting an order," Piper said. "I can't imagine what—" She leaned over the slightly battered box to read the labels and winced.

"Came all the way from Thailand," Roger said, pulling out a handkerchief to wipe at his bald head."

"Yes, it certainly did." Piper could see that Roger was hoping she'd open it in front of him. But Piper wasn't sure she wanted to open it at all. "It's probably those specialty canning tools I ordered," she fibbed and saw his eyes instantly glaze over.

"Okay," he said, pocketing his handkerchief. "I'll leave you to it, then. Mindy said to say hello."

"My best to Mindy, too, and thanks, Roger," Piper said, ushering him out. She waved good-bye, then shut the door and turned toward her package.

What had Scott sent her this time? She circled the box a few times, nudging it cautiously with her toe as though fearing it might suddenly come alive. Finally she found a box cutter and cut through the taped edges. She knelt down and pulled out mounds of packing material, little by little revealing the item beneath. Piper tugged the Bubble-Wrapped piece out, judging it to be at least twenty by thirty inches, and carefully cut through the layers of plastic, intrigued despite her strong reservations.

When she peeled off the last layer and was able to fully behold it, Piper sighed. It was beautiful. A delicately carved wooden wall plaque, obviously teak. She gazed at it, gradually taking in all the fine details. Slender wooden branches interlaced with one another holding a myriad of vegetables and fruits: pineapples, squashes, beans, peppers, and more. The craftsmanship was exquisite. A card had been tucked in with the packing materials, and Piper reached for it.

Thought of you when I saw this and knew it would be perfect for your pickling store—Love, Scott

Piper let the card flop down. *Oh, Scott*, she thought, *why do you do this?* She'd sent him a clearly worded e-mail—finally—about the inappropriateness of the bouquet he'd ordered for her. Apparently it wasn't clear enough for Scott. Except—

Piper reached over to check the delivery markings on the package. The plaque had been dispatched days before he sent the bouquet. That figured, since there were plenty of travel miles to cover between Thailand and Cloverdale.

Even so, Scott shouldn't be sending her gifts. Especially thoughtful, lovely, probably expensive gifts. And there was no way she could send it back to a former fiancé who was constantly on the move.

She'd have to hold on to the beautiful piece. But as soon as Scott came back home she'd hand it to him and wish him good luck with his life. In the meantime, she'd store it away safely in its box.

Piper ran a finger over the plaque. What a shame, though, to hide such a beautiful thing away. Somebody, thousands of miles away, had poured all his artistic talents and skills into creating the piece. It deserved to be out to be admired instead of hidden away. She knew the perfect place for it on her shop wall, where it would be the first thing—Piper stopped herself, seeing what was happening.

"Scott?" she asked with exasperation, gazing at the ceiling as though his image floated there. "Why, why, why do you do this to me?"

"It's very nice," Aunt Judy said cautiously, as Piper propped up the wooden wall plaque to show her aunt.

"It's more than nice," Piper said. "It's absolutely beautiful. Which makes me furious." She had let Aunt Judy in at the back door where her aunt quickly spotted the box from Thailand and its disgorged contents.

"Furious?" Aunt Judy asked. "Why?"

"Because Scott shouldn't be sending me things like this. And because I really love this plaque, and I kind of like that he was thoughtful enough to know that I'd love it.

When we were together, I highly doubt that that would have been the case. But these travels seem to be changing him, or bringing something out in him that he kept hidden before. But if so, what does that mean for our relationship? I thought we were over. Done with. Kaput! Now I'm starting to have second thoughts, and that makes me furious!"

Piper realized her voice had risen and she'd been rocking Scott's plaque back and forth for emphasis. She grinned ruefully, saying, "Sorry," and carefully lowered the carving down.

"Don't worry about it," Aunt Judy said, patting Piper's arm. "You have plenty of time before you'll see Scott again. Where is he going next? Japan?"

"China."

"Well, there you are. Half a world away and no need for any decisions to be made for quite a while." Her aunt smiled wickedly. "And I hear they have perfectly lovely gift items in China."

"Aunt Judy!" But Piper smiled, too. Her aunt was right. She shouldn't let herself get worked up over something that might never need to be addressed. Hopefully Scott would see her latest e-mail and view their relationship more clearly.

Piper grabbed her purse. "Ready to tour the Taylor mansion?"

Aunt Judy had called Piper about Dorothy Taylor's open house that afternoon and suggested they go to it together, saying, "It could be an opportunity to talk to Dorothy about Robby."

Piper thought that was a fine idea, and going with her

aunt instead of Will or even alone was much better as far as the town gossip mill was concerned.

"It's not exactly a mansion," Aunt Judy said, "but yes, I'm ready."

Piper locked up, and Aunt Judy gave directions to Dorothy Taylor's home as they climbed into Piper's hatchback, whose tires had thankfully been repaired and plumped. "She grew up in that house," she explained as Piper drove off, "and her father, who'd been widowed by then, turned it over to Dorothy when she and Henry married. Her father was born in the house, but he decided to move to Arizona for his arthritis."

"So the house has been in her family for quite a while?" Piper asked.

"Oh yes, ever since her grandfather built it nearly a hundred years ago. Plenty of furniture was passed down as well, though Dorothy wasn't fond of most of it and gradually moved pieces up to the attic. Those were the things Alan Rosemont got from her at a real bargain price. He sewed up the deal in a flash before any of her friends, or Robby, knew what was going on. Dorothy, as you know, thought she was simply getting paid to have someone clean out her attic for her."

"So the pieces were pretty valuable?"

"A few were. I'm sure there was plenty of junk like most of us have mixed in. But Alan obviously had a sharp eye and spotted the good stuff."

"What a shame. I wouldn't blame Robby for being furious."

"There's the house, dear." Aunt Judy pointed out a gray

clapboard-sided house with white trim. The large railing-edged front porch added plenty of charm to the two-story structure, but Piper could already see signs of age and lack of maintenance in the peeling paint and scrubby front lawn. She pulled up behind a black Audi.

"That looks like Stan Yeager's car," Aunt Judy said. "We're going to have to find a way to talk to Dorothy without him around." She opened her door as Piper climbed out from her own side.

"I'm surprised she's having this open house so soon," Piper said. "Mr. Yeager gave me the impression the decision to sell had just been made."

"It does seem a rush," Aunt Judy agreed. "It reminds me a little too much of Alan Rosemont's dealings, except Stan Yeager would never behave so unethically. It wouldn't be up to him, anyway. The push must be coming from Robby."

As they walked up to the porch steps, the front door opened. Stan Yeager stepped out.

"Welcome! Welcome! Glad to see you got the word, Miss Lamb. I was about to give you a call to let you know."

"No need," Piper said. "The news reached us through the grapevine. We were surprised, though, at the suddenness."

"Once Mrs. Taylor made up her mind, she saw no reason to dawdle," Yeager said. His expression sobered. "It's often hard for the older clients to make the change. Some look at it as pulling off a Band-Aid. You know—painful, but best to do it fast." His smile reappeared. "I know you'll love the place. It's loaded with character."

He waved them in, and Piper stepped into an entry

hallway with a living room to the left. A bay window over-looked the porch, and an old-fashioned radiator lined the inner wall.

"They used to call this the 'front room,'" Yeager said. He pointed out the abundant natural light coming from the large window as well as its hardwood floors as positive features, though the floors looked uneven to Piper and the window frames leaky. She also thought the room looked seldom used, with its 1970s furniture nearing museum-level preservation even though no seat cushions were covered in plastic.

"Dorothy mostly entertained in the sunroom at the back," Aunt Judy said. "She and Henry added that on some years ago, and it was much more spacious."

"Right," Yeager said, nodding. "We'll get to the sunroom in a minute. In the meantime, across the way, here, is the dining room." He led them into another hardwood-floored room that should have been as bright as the front room but instead was darkened with heavy draperies and a massive dining table, chairs, a buffet, and china cabinet.

Yeager gave them a moment to scan it, then said, "And at the back of the house is the kitchen." Piper and her aunt dutifully followed the Realtor. Piper's first thought on entering the kitchen was that if she were actually buying, she'd have a huge amount of renovation to do. The appliances were years old, the cabinets dated and too few, and the counter space severely limited. This was definitely not a kitchen in which she'd want to do pickling and canning. Which was a moot point, of course, since she had no intention of becoming its owner.

The sound of footsteps drew Piper's attention to a back

hallway connected to the kitchen. There, an older woman gradually materialized out of the dimness, a stiff smile on her face. Feeling instant guilt from her critical thoughts as well as the false pretenses under which she was there, Piper pulled up a smile that certainly must have matched the woman's for stiffness until Aunt Judy cheerily cried, "Dorothy! There you are!"

23

Dorothy Taylor's expression softened on seeing Piper's aunt in her kitchen.

"I've brought my niece to see your lovely place," Aunt Judy said. She introduced the two, adding, to Piper's surprise, that they had actually met years ago at a church picnic. Dorothy, from her doubtful look, was just as clueless as Piper on that point. But after a minuscule pause, both heads bobbed as each said, "Oh yes, that's right," along with, "How nice to see you again."

Piper thought she could see a slight facial resemblance to Robby, but unlike her son, Dorothy Taylor was plump and far from fit. She also sported bright red hair rather than Robby's dark waves, but considering her age as well as the shade, the color hadn't risen from her genes. Dorothy, in addition, seemed more reserved than her son. That last might have come from negative feelings over selling her house. Piper hoped to learn more about that.

"Are we the first ones here?" Aunt Judy asked.

Dorothy shook her head and pursed her lips. "The Satterfield couple is upstairs with their baby. I don't think she likes the house. She thought the bathroom was old-fashioned."

"Maybe I'll just run up and point out a few of the finer features," Stan Yeager said, and as he hurried off, Aunt Judy caught Piper's eye. Piper knew what she was thinking. *Here's our chance.*

"We don't mind waiting till the other couple is done," Aunt Judy said. "Would you like to sit for a bit, Dorothy? Maybe in the backyard with a glass of something nice and cool?"

Dorothy Taylor smiled—her first genuine smile so far, Piper thought. "I'd love that, Judy. I have a pitcher of iced tea chilling."

"I'll get it," Aunt Judy said. "Why don't you show Piper your lovely garden, and I'll be right out."

Dorothy Taylor agreeably beckoned Piper toward the hallway and out through a screen door that led to a small patio with an aged umbrella table and chairs. To their right was the sunroom Aunt Judy had mentioned. That attachment, though nicely spacious, looked to Piper out of sync with the rest of the house, as though it had been sliced off of a much more modern structure and glued onto this nearly century-old one.

"I'll miss my garden," Dorothy said, walking on with some effort across her uneven lawn toward a grouping of faded, end-of-summer perennials. "It's so full of memories since many of my plants came from good friends as they divided up their own gardens." She pointed to a drooping clump of daylilies. "Those were from Ellie Peterson. The hostas over there came from your aunt years ago. And I have scads of daffodils and irises that were given to me by dear friends who are no longer with us." She heaved a sigh, and Piper was about to express sympathy until Dorothy added, "Patty Hendrickson and Enid Bates moved down to Florida some time ago."

They turned at the sound of the screen door banging. Aunt Judy had stepped onto the patio with a tray of iced tea, so they made their way back to join her.

"Thank you, Judy," Dorothy said, taking one of the glasses from her and settling heavily in a chair. She looked about her somewhat morosely. "This might be the last time we'll sit here together."

"We'll still see each other, Dorothy," Aunt Judy said, sitting next to her friend. "It won't matter exactly where that will be. What are your plans? Will you stay in Cloverdale? Or are you thinking of moving closer to Robby?"

Dorothy looked away from Aunt Judy. "I haven't exactly had time to make plans, at least not anything definite. First things first!" She switched on a bright, but not terribly convincing, smile. "So!" she said, turning to Piper. "You've seen at least half of my house. What do you think so far?"

Piper scrambled to come up with a proper answer. "It's quite an interesting place," she said, hoping that sounded positive. "There's obviously a lot of history attached to your house."

Dorothy nodded. "There is that." To Piper's surprise, she then chuckled and rolled her eyes. "Not all of it wonderful, though, right Judy? Remember the incident with Pop?"

Aunt Judy grinned but said, "That's all water under the bridge, Dorothy."

Dorothy said to Piper, "You'll probably hear about it eventually, so you might as well get it from the horse's mouth. When Henry and I were first married, my father turned the house over to us before moving to Arizona. My mother had passed away—bless her soul—years before, and as far as I knew Pop had lived the quiet life of a retired widower after that.

"Well! One day, my doorbell rings, and I answer it to find this strange woman on my doorstep, baggage at her feet, demanding to see my father. At least, that's what I eventually figured out she wanted, since her accent—from someplace like Romania or Lithuania, I couldn't tell you exactly where—was so thick I could barely understand her.

"Come to find out the regular visits Pop was making to Rochester, which I thought were simply to meet with an amateur astronomy group he'd got interested in, were for another interest as well, which he never happened to mention." Dorothy turned an amused, head-shaking glance to Aunt Judy before going on. "Turned out Pop had set up this woman—Nadia was her name—in a little apartment and was having a much better time in Rochester than any astronomy club ever offered."

"Dorothy!" Aunt Judy protested, but her shoulders were shaking and she pressed her fingers to her lips.

"Now, my father was a single man and free to do what he wanted as far as I was concerned. I was certainly surprised, but I wasn't about to judge him. The only thing was, he apparently decided this little arrangement had run its course, and when he left for Arizona he neglected to say anything about it to this woman. She, obviously, was not pleased to be left hanging and had tracked him down to here. When I informed her he had given the house to me and moved on, she was furious and screamed that he had promised to take care of her. He'd stopped paying her rent in Rochester, so she was going to stay here. At that she picked up her bags and marched upstairs!

"I didn't know what to do. But I certainly didn't want a strange woman moving into my house. I threatened to call the police. That's when she said she would sue to take our house altogether if we didn't let her stay."

Dorothy took a sip of her tea before going on. "Henry and I were horrified, of course. We didn't think there was any way she'd win her suit, but we didn't have the money at that time to hire a lawyer to defend ourselves. We were young and naïve and felt pretty helpless. So there she stayed, in our spare bedroom, smoking up a storm, coming down and messing up my kitchen and bad-mouthing Pop with every other word that came out of her mouth.

"It got really bad when she started doing the same around town—complaining about Pop to anyone who would listen. Finally, Henry and I scraped together a bit of money. We offered her travel fare to Arizona along with my father's address if she would leave and never come back. She snapped up the cash and took off."

Dorothy swatted at a fly circling the table. "The last I heard," she said, "she showed up at my father's, stayed awhile, then decided to move on to Las Vegas. I learned all this from a neighbor of my father's. Pop never mentioned

Nadia to me, and I never mentioned her to him." Dorothy took another sip of her tea, looking over the top of her glass at Piper and waiting for her reaction.

"Well," Piper said. "That wasn't exactly the kind of history I had in mind, but it does make a good story."

Dorothy cackled and reached over to pat Piper's hand. "You were hoping for something like 'George Washington slept here,' I suppose. The house is old, but not that old. I like you, Piper. I'd like to think of you living in my house." At that, Dorothy's smile faded. She blinked and looked away.

Stan Yeager popped his head out the screen door. "The Satterfields have left. I can show you the upstairs if you like."

They heard the front doorbell ring. "Take care of whoever just arrived, Stan," Aunt Judy said. "We'll sit awhile longer with Dorothy."

"Lord, I hope that's not Shirley Pettit," Dorothy said. "She hinted she wanted a place with room enough to raise more Siamese cats!"

"Dorothy," Aunt Judy said, "are you sure you're ready to sell your house? I mean, this all seems such a rush. Have you thought it all through carefully?"

Dorothy shook her head. "I have to sell. I can't expect Robby to help me keep the place up."

"But you could afford to pay for help, couldn't you, Dorothy? I mean, not to be too nosy, but it did sound like Henry left you well enough off to pay for repairs and upkeep on the house."

"He did," Dorothy agreed. "At least enough for a while. That got to be so expensive, though, and other things," she said, vaguely, "came up. Then, too, hiring people doesn't always work out, you know. Just last spring I hired that Dennis Isley to replace my old toilet. He offered me the lowest price, so I went with it. But the new toilet kept leaking and Robby ended up having to do it over himself as well as patch up my kitchen ceiling from the water damage. He was furious!"

"Yes, I can imagine he would be," Piper said. "I'd sure want my money back from anyone who did such a shoddy job. Did Robby talk to Dennis about that?"

"Well, ah, he might have. Yes, actually, I think he did. They worked it out, I'm sure. More tea, Judy?"

"No, I'm fine, Dorothy, thank you. That is a shame about the leaky toilet. I hate to speak ill of the dead, but Dennis wasn't the most capable handyman. He was definitely cheaper, though, which might be why Alan Rosemont employed him now and then."

"Oh! Alan!" Dorothy's face darkened at mention of the swindling antique dealer's name. "That snake! Yes, Alan was always on the lookout to make or save a buck, wasn't he? He and Dennis must have got along just fine."

"Actually," Piper said, "I don't believe they did. Cheap as Dennis's services may have been, I think Alan still tried his best to underpay him. I understand why you feel that way about Alan. It sounds like he acted very unethically regarding your family antiques."

"Oh, Robby was so upset," Dorothy said, shaking her head. "And it wasn't just from the money I lost. There were things that had belonged to my father—the old telescopes from that astronomy hobby I mentioned, for one. I never realized, but Robby said later he always intended to take up the hobby himself when he had time."

"Really?" Aunt Judy said.

Dorothy nodded. "Robby never knew my father that well, Pop living so far away until he died. But he still grew to be very like Pop in some ways." She frowned. "Well, I mean, with their interests in astronomy, of course, and . . . and . . ." She paused, searching, then brightened. "And physical fitness! Pop always rode a bike if you remember, Judy. He had energy to spare, just like Robby."

"That's right, he did," Aunt Judy said. "He had a quick temper, too, didn't he?"

"That he did," Dorothy agreed. "Which is probably why he and Nadia didn't get along for very long. If they'd spent too much time around each other, they'd have been at each other's throats, would be my guess."

Aunt Judy cast Piper a glance, and Piper thought she might be wondering, as she was, if this was another similarity between grandfather and grandson. At that moment, Stan Yeager reappeared.

"All clear. Who wants to see the upstairs?"

Nobody within hearing distance, was Piper's first thought, but since that was supposedly the reason she was there, she gamely stood up. "Back in a minute," she said, leaving Aunt Judy to see what more could be learned about Dorothy Taylor's son.

As she reentered the house, she heard her aunt ask, "More tea, Dorothy dear?"

24

Early Monday morning, Piper looked out her apartment window and saw Amy's orange Toyota pull up in front of Gilbert Williams's bookshop. She spotted Nate sitting in the passenger seat, so Piper put down her just-filled coffee mug to run out and say hi. As Nate climbed out, she called, "Moving in?"

Nate looked up and grinned. "Right." He swept his arm toward the small-sized car. "And this is my moving van. Took us close to ten—maybe fifteen!—minutes to load it up."

Amy climbed out from her side. "Good thing Mr. Williams has a bed up there. Otherwise Nate would be sleeping in the bathtub."

"This is all I really need," Nate said, pulling out his guitar. But he then reached back for a well-filled duffel.

"Need any help?" Piper asked.

Amy grinned. "Not with carrying things in, that's for sure. Erin and Megan are coming in a minute to help with the dusting up. We'll be fine."

Gil Williams opened his bookshop door and called, "Welcome!"

"Hey, Mr. Williams," Nate said, moving forward. "I really appreciate this."

"The benefits, I'm sure, will be even greater for me," Gil responded genially. He held the door for Nate and Amy as they carried in their loads, then asked Piper, "Coming in? I have a fresh pot of coffee."

Piper thought of the cooling mug left behind and nodded. "Just for a minute." She joined the others, then followed all three up the stairs to Nate's new living quarters.

The building that Gil Williams's shop occupied was similar to Piper's, and she had pictured Nate's new apartment to be like her own. The space above the bookshop, however, was cut up differently. Much of the area toward the back had been partitioned off and was being used, Gil explained, for book storage. Nate's living area turned out to be an efficiency, with a tiny kitchen alcove next to the small living room and a bedroom separated from both with an accordion-style folding door. Piper assumed a second door led to a bathroom. The air was stuffy and a layer of dust covered most surfaces.

"As I said, it's modest to the extreme," Gil said.

"No," Nate said, setting down his guitar. "This is great. Perfect!"

They heard a car horn beep, and Amy ran to the window. "Megan and Erin are here." She raised the sash, letting in welcome fresh air. "Come on up!" she called. "Bring the mops and buckets."

"Let's leave them to their work," Gil said to Piper. "My coffee is downstairs."

Piper followed him down and greeted Amy's two friends as they bustled their way into the shop full of energy as well as cleaning supplies.

"I wish I could have had the place professionally cleaned for him," Gil said, pouring out a mug of coffee for Piper. "That expense, I'm afraid, wasn't worked into my budget this month."

"You're doing more than enough as it is," Piper assured him. She took the mug gratefully and sipped from it. "They'll probably have a ball up there doing it themselves."

"Yes, the enthusiasm of youth. Any progress," he asked, "on the situation that brought this young man to such dire straits?"

Piper was about to update Gil when she spotted a UPS truck pulling up to her shop. "That must be my latest spice order," she said. "I'm sorry. I'd better go check it."

She started to set down her still-full coffee mug, but Gil said, "Take it with you. I'll pick the mug up a little later, and we can continue this conversation."

"Come anytime," Piper said, then dashed out to meet the UPS man.

An hour or so later, Amy bustled into Piper's Picklings, ready to begin her shift there. "Nate's all settled," she announced, grabbing a clean apron and tying it on. "Mr. Williams is so sweet. He kept apologizing for the state of the apartment, but the four of us cleaned it up in a flash. It's not that large, you saw."

Amy took a step into the back room and stopped. "Oh! Where did that come from?"

Piper knew she'd spotted Scott's wall plaque, which Piper had left leaning against the wall next to its box. "From Thailand," Piper answered, "with a brief stop at Mindy Atwater's knitting shop." At Amy's questioning look she explained further. "My ex-fiancé sent it."

"It's beautiful!" Seeing Piper's dour expression, Amy asked, "You don't like it?"

"I love the plaque," Piper said. "I don't like the strings that came along with it."

"Ah. From your ex. What'll you do with it?"

"I'm still debating."

"Going to let Will see it?"

Piper grinned. "I'll think about all that later." Piper picked up the plaque and started rewrapping it. "For now, I'm going to concentrate on more immediate problems. Like turning this batch of red bell peppers that Uncle Frank dropped off into sweet red pepper relish while they're still fresh."

"Yes, ma'am! Just let me at them."

Amy got to work washing and chopping the peppers while Piper dealt with the customers who had popped in. When she returned to the work area, Amy was ready to stir in the kosher salt that would draw water out of the vegetables. Piper helped her do that, saying, "I became very fond of this relish because of Aunt Judy. She always spread it over the top of her meat loaf, along with catsup. I loved the sweet-tart crusty glaze that made." As they set aside the bowls to sit for a couple of hours, Gil Williams walked in the front door, and Piper grabbed his washed coffee mug and carried it out to him.

"It's such a treat," Gil said, "to be able to leave the shop for a few minutes without having to close up. Nate is unpacking a box of books for me right now."

"I know he really appreciates your taking him in, Mr. Williams," Amy said, joining the two and wiping her hands on her apron.

"It's really nothing," Gil said, waving it away. "What I wish I could do is clear up this mystery that has people treating Nate with such suspicion." He turned to Piper. "To repeat my question of this morning, has there been any progress made in that direction?"

Piper puffed out her cheeks and blew out. "I've acquired more information. Unfortunately, it's nothing definitive." She first caught Amy up on what she and Gil had learned about the actions of the plumber, Ralph Farber, on the day Dennis Isley died. Then she told both what she'd picked up about Robby Taylor.

Amy listened solemnly. "So both of them had the possibility of doing it—I mean, killing Alan Rosemont and Dennis Isley—and both had enough to be plenty mad about to want to do it."

Gil nodded. "It appears that way. So which one is our man?"

"I sure wish I had the answer to that," Piper said.

Amy plopped down on a stool, looking dejected. "I wish Alan Rosemont had never come to Cloverdale. Hardly anyone liked him, although a lot of people pretended to because of the power he grabbed on the town council. He was nothing but trouble for Nate when he was alive and worse now that he's dead."

She looked up at Piper with anguished eyes. "Poor Nate.

I've been trying to be upbeat for him, and he puts on a brave front. But I know he hates being under suspicion like this. What if we never find out who killed Alan and Dennis? People will go on thinking Nate did it."

Piper had had those same fears herself, so patting Amy on the back and saying everything would work out was not an option. Instead she pulled out her suspect notebook.

"Let's run over what we have so far," she said. "Maybe if the three of us put our heads together we'll see something we've missed." She flipped the notebook open to a fresh page. "First, we have Lyella and Gordon Pfiefle," she said, writing down their names, then writing "Motive" on the line below.

"Lyella was furious with Alan Rosemont," she explained to Gil, "for turning her library into a pink horror."

"And Mr. Pfiefle," Amy said, "is furious with anyone who upsets his wife."

"Gordon Pfiefle," Piper said, "had scratches around his face and neck the day after Alan was killed—"

"Which could have come from a scuffle between the two," Amy said.

"Neither Pfiefle has an alibi for the time Alan was murdered," Piper said. "Plus, they both behaved suspiciously around the time Dennis Isley was murdered. Lyella stayed home and Gordon left work with a phony flat tire excuse. They could have slipped out of their house without being seen by their neighborhood watch-woman, Martha Smidley."

"So," Amy asked, "would a librarian and a supermarket manager be capable of murder?"

"A very good question," Gil said. "I'm sure you've pondered it, Piper. What did you conclude?"

"Only that Lyella is a very strong-minded woman, and she may have considered Alan Rosemont an enemy to all she held dear. If Gordon met with Alan that night at the fair, he might not have had murder on his mind, but an argument could have escalated to that point, especially if Alan said anything derogatory about Lyella."

"What about Dennis Isley?" Gil asked.

"Dennis's murder was, I think, not a crime of passion but one of necessity. If he was blackmailing the Pfiefles, he was a danger that needed to be removed."

Amy shivered. "That sounds so coldhearted."

"It does," Gil agreed. "But from what I know about murderers—which is limited to books, I admit—once a first murder is committed, carrying out a second one for self-protection becomes much easier."

Piper filled in the information on the Pfiefles' opportunities, then turned the page and wrote down "Ralph Farber." Beneath that, she wrote "Motive."

"Ralph Farber lived next door to Alan Rosemont," she said. "He'd argued with Alan often about the bagpipe practice at all hours. From what I saw of Farber, he's not someone who's willing to put up with aggravations. I've heard of fights between neighbors over lesser things like a tree hanging over the fence that ended up in murder."

Amy nodded vigorously. "I can imagine Alan purposely playing his bagpipes in the middle of the night, knowing it would drive Mr. Farber crazy."

"We know Farber was called to the fairgrounds that night for a plumbing problem," Piper said. "And we know Alan had his bagpipes with him, because they were found next to my pickle barrel." Piper ground her teeth briefly at the memory of her cherished pickle barrel's involvement in the crime.

"I can really see Mr. Farber going bonkers," Amy said, "if he heard those bagpipes again."

"And, by his own account," Gil added, "he could have ducked into the alley the day Dennis was working on the Perkins' roof and pulled at Dennis's rope."

"I think he did it," Amy said. "I think he was furious enough to whack Alan, strong enough to drag him into your pickle barrel, and went on later to deal with Dennis."

"Maybe," Piper said, cautiously. "But if nobody saw him do it, except possibly Dennis, how do we prove it?"

"Ah, there's the rub," Gil agreed. "But we're not finished with your list of suspects, are we? What about Robby Taylor?"

"Robby," Piper said, "was furious with Alan for cheating his mother out of her antiques. We know he was in Cloverdale for the fair, and he was in town talking to Stan Yeager the day Dennis was killed. As a fitness trainer, he's in great shape, which means he could physically have handled Alan's murder. Plus there's the probability that he's pressuring his mother to sell her house, which might come from his having to pay blackmail to Dennis."

"But with Dennis dead," Gil pointed out, "the presumed blackmail has ended. Yet Dorothy Taylor is still selling her house."

"That's true," Piper said. "The payments to Dennis totaled six thousand. Seems like he could have covered that amount somehow and called off the house sale once the blackmailer was done away with." Piper chewed at the end of her pen. "Does that eliminate Robby?" she asked.

"Not necessarily," Gil said. "But it's something to keep in mind. Perhaps there's another reason his mother is selling her house?"

"She's clearly not happy with the idea," Piper said. "She's doing it for Robby. Maybe it started with the need for blackmail money—which I doubt Dorothy would be aware of—but continues for another reason. I'd say Robby is still a good contender on our list."

"I'm still not seeing anything that points to one more than the other," Gil said, shaking his head.

The phone rang, and Amy picked it up. After a moment she said, "Mr. Williams, Nate says there's a customer who's asking for your expert help."

Gil Williams chuckled gently. "That probably means someone who can't remember if they already bought *Five Red Herrings* or if they still need it to complete their Dorothy L. Sayers set. I'll have to show Nate where I keep my records on regular customers. Ladies, we'll need to continue this another time. In the meantime, I'll think hard about all we've discussed."

"And so will we," Piper said.

As Gil pushed out the door, Tina approached, and he paused to hold the door for her, wishing her a good day and looking as though he'd tip his hat if only he happened to be wearing one.

"Gil is such a gentleman," Tina said, looking back at his departing form.

"He is," Amy agreed. "Did you know he's letting Nate stay in the apartment above his shop?"

"What do you mean 'letting'? Why did Nate have to move?"

Amy explained about Nate losing his job at A La Carte and therefore his ability to pay the rent at his last place. Piper silently wondered if Amy had been told of Ben Schaeffer's theory that Nate could have been paying Dennis's blackmail from a secret cache of funds. Obviously, if there'd been such a cache, Nate would be living a lot more comfortably, but Ben's bias against Nate apparently kept him from reasoning that far.

"That's terrible!" Tina cried. "Nate shouldn't be getting that kind of treatment when he didn't do anything whatsoever to deserve it. Which is exactly why I'm here. I've known all along who does deserve such treatment and now I can prove it."

"You can?" Amy cried. Piper was interested, too, though she thought she knew who Tina was going to name.

"Charlotte Hosch has finally tipped her hand!" Tina stated firmly.

Piper wasn't at all sure that would be the case. But she waited to hear what Tina would say.

25

~~~~~

"What did Charlotte Hosch do that convinces you she's a murderer?" Piper asked, dearly hoping no customer would walk into the pickling shop in the midst of Tina's explanation. Tina looked agitated, her movements and breathing rapid, and Piper could foresee a dramatic tale coming. Whether or not it would be something to share with Sheriff Carlyle was yet to be determined.

"I saw it! I saw it this morning!" Tina said.

"Saw what?" Piper asked.

"The white paint can! It was in Charlotte's trash. The can for the white paint she threw on your front brick."

"You searched through Charlotte's trash?"

Tina shook her head. "I was in her alley early this morning. I couldn't sleep, so I got up early and went for a walk. I went farther than I meant to, so I took the shortcut through her alley to get back to my place. The recycling truck had just pulled in there, and I saw them dumping out Charlotte's bin. The paint can tumbled out along with all the newspapers and bottles. I saw it clear as day!"

"A white paint can?" Piper asked.

Tina must have heard the uncertainty in Piper's voice, since her "Yes!" came out at least half an octave higher. "Don't you see? This proves Charlotte is the vandal! She's been trying to scare you away from looking into the murders. She's petrified that you'll find her out, and this is her way of stopping you!"

"That could be true," Piper said cautiously. "Or it could also be that Charlotte was doing a little touch-up work at her shop."

"Did you get hold of it?" Amy asked. "Maybe there's a way of matching the paint. They do that kind of thing on *CSI* all the time. Your splotch hasn't been cleaned off yet, Piper."

"No, it hasn't," Piper agreed, grimacing, since that had been a matter of increasing annoyance for her.

"The recycling truck drove off before I could think fast enough to stop them," Tina said. "Who knows where that can is now? So I guess I can't prove anything, huh?" She looked crestfallen.

"I'm afraid not," Piper said. "But it's definitely information to keep in mind."

"I'm just so sure Charlotte is behind all this," Tina continued. "You may not believe that yet, but I'll find a way to convince you. And the sheriff. Why oh why didn't I grab at that paint can the minute I saw it?"

Tina looked so wretched that Piper rushed to reassure

her. "We have three other strong suspects, Tina. They all have stronger motives than Charlotte, miserable a person though she may be."

"Right!" Amy added. "And Mr. Williams has started working with us. He knows his way around an investigation, what with all the detective novels he's read. With all of us putting our heads together, I know we'll clear Nate in no time."

"Gil Williams is helping?" Tina looked surprised.

"He's been great," Piper said. "Once he realized what a predicament Nate was caught in, he was completely willing to get involved."

"I just never thought of Gil doing anything like that," Tina said. "He always seemed so reclusive and absorbed in his books. But . . . that's great! As you said, the more people working on the case, the better."

Tina looked somewhat encouraged, so Piper gave her an update on what she'd learned about Ralph Farber and Robby Taylor since they last talked. Tina nodded and appeared at least marginally willing to expand her suspicions beyond Charlotte Hosch. By the time she was ready to leave, Tina seemed less hell-bent on dragging the candy maker off to the sheriff's office, which was a relief to Piper. When Piper first asked for Tina's help, she had hoped only for the odd tidbit the coffee shop owner might pick up in the course of her day. She never envisioned bringing on stress and sleeplessness for anyone. At the door, Piper grabbed a jar of tea jelly from a nearby table and handed it to Tina.

"It's something I've never tried before," she said. "It's

made with chamomile citron tea and green apple pectin stock. Let me know how you like it."

As Piper watched the coffee shop owner trudge back to her place, Amy commented from behind, "That was nice of you."

Piper turned. "If I can picture the chamomile working its soothing magic on Tina, at least a little, I'll feel better for causing the stress in the first place."

"The best stress relief for all of us," Amy said, "will be coming to the end of this investigation and putting the real murderer in jail."

"Amen to that." Piper saw Amy's face brighten as her eyes shifted over Piper's shoulder. Piper turned. Nate was heading their way from the bookshop.

"Hi!" he said as he pushed through Piper's Picklings' door. "Gil sent me off on a lunch break. Mind if I pick up something and bring it back here?"

"Darn!" Amy said, stamping her foot. "I meant to bring along the leftover beef bourguignon that we all took home from the restaurant last night. With your move into the new apartment on my mind this morning, I walked off without it."

Piper remembered Amy calling Nate over to the A La Carte kitchen after his performance the other night and knew Nate's food budget must be stretched pretty thin now that he was no longer working at the restaurant. A bookshop offered food for the soul but did nothing for the stomach.

"I still have a bunch of Aunt Judy's tomatoes upstairs that I'll never finish. And I have some nice bread in the freezer. Why don't you two run up and make sandwiches for us all?"

"Really?" Both Amy's and Nate's faces lit up. "That'd be great." Amy led the way as they trotted up to Piper's apartment, and Piper's mouth began to water at the very thought of the gourmet sandwiches Amy would likely throw together. No mere sliced tomato and mayo would suffice for her.

Within minutes all three were seated in Piper's workroom, munching on tasty concoctions of crusty bread, mozzarella, tomato, basil, and Piper didn't know what else. All she knew was that it was delicious. She remembered Will's comment about the ladies of Cloverdale likely to look after Nate's care and feeding and made a mental note to put a bee in Aunt Judy's bonnet in case it wasn't buzzing around in there already.

As they ate, Amy brought up their earlier discussion with Gil Williams on possible suspects.

"Yeah," Nate said, taking a swig from one of three bottles of green tea Piper had pulled from her workroom refrigerator. He brushed his dark blond hair—in definite need of a trim, Piper noticed—away from his face. "Gil was telling me about that. It's weird how many people had a reason to knock off Alan Rosemont." He scowled. "And I was one of them, I guess. But I never acted on it."

"That's what I keep trying to tell Daddy," Amy said. "He should be looking at these other people."

"We don't know that he isn't," Piper said.

"And we don't know that he is," Amy said, her lips pressing into a thin line.

"Amy," Nate said, "I don't want to cause trouble between you and your dad. I really appreciate what you guys are doing on my behalf. But why don't I take it over from here?"

"Nate!" Amy cried.

"I mean it. For one thing, I don't like that stuff that's been happening to you, Piper. It could be fallout from all the questions you've been asking about this case."

"What's happened is more annoying than worrying," Piper said.

"For now," Nate said. "What if it escalates? I wouldn't be able to live with myself if you—or anyone else"—he glanced at Amy—"got hurt because of me."

"It wouldn't be because of you," Amy insisted. "If anything happened—which it won't—it would be because of someone who should be in jail for what they've done!"

"It's too late to call us off, anyway," Piper said with a smile. "It's just too darned interesting. I'm learning things about the people of Cloverdale I never would have known otherwise." She told them the story of Robby Taylor's grandfather and the gypsy woman from Rochester, which had them chortling.

"Why don't I see what I can dig up about Taylor's financial situation," Nate said. "I think Gil will let me use his computer off-hours."

"That'd be great," Piper said. "But what can you expect to find? Isn't most credit info off limits without a person's permission?"

"It is, but I may know one or two ways of getting around that. I'll give them a try and see if they still work."

"One or two ways?" Amy asked. "Where would you have picked up anything like that?"

Nate flushed slightly. "Oh, just from people I used to

know. No big thing. Hey, thanks for these great sandwiches, both of you. I'd better be getting back. Gotta make a good impression my first day on the job." Nate picked up his plate, but Amy took it from him.

"I'll clean these up. You go on. Sell a lot of books. And dig up a lot of dirt on Robby Taylor!"

"I'll do my best," Nate said, grinning, but then he sobered. "And be careful, both of you." With that, he took off, leaving Piper and Amy to their own, unspoken thoughts.

Later that afternoon and shortly before Amy would leave for her second job at A La Carte, Ben Schaeffer walked into Piper's Picklings. He had on a white shirt and striped tie rather than his auxiliary officer uniform, which told Piper he'd come from his insurance office. But he still managed to project an officer-on-duty attitude, nonofficial though that was. At least until Amy stepped out from the back room. Then his sternness melted to mush.

"Hi, Ben," Amy said cheerily. "What's up?"

"Hi! Oh, um, not much." Ben shifted from one foot to the other, fidgeted with his tie, and slipped his hands in and out of his pockets, suddenly looking, Piper thought, more like a middle-school adolescent than the competent businessman he was.

She took pity on him and asked, "How's the insurance business going?"

Ben matured several years at the question. "Not too bad," he said, straightening. "We have a new small business policy that covers things you might not have thought of if you'd like to look it over."

"I think I'm fine for now, Ben, thanks."

He nodded. "But that's not what I'm here for. I wanted to offer a word of warning to you both."

"Oh?"

Piper saw Amy's cheeriness dim, though Ben seemed oblivious.

"I've just become aware that that musician has moved in next door." Ben jerked his chin toward the bookshop.

"That musician has a name," Amy said, her smile grown stiff. "It's Nate Purdy."

"Yes, yes, of course," Ben said with a brushing away gesture as though Nate's name had no importance. That bothered Piper as much as anything, erasing much of the pity she'd felt earlier for the man.

"And I know," Ben continued, digging himself in deeper, "that you tend to see only the good side of people, Amy, but I think you should be very cautious about any dealings with this, uh, with Purdy. We have reason to believe—"

"You have no reason WHAT-SO-EVER to believe anything bad about Nate!" Amy blurted.

Her vehemence caught Ben off guard, and he rocked backward.

"That's not exactly—" he began, but Amy would have none of it.

Her eyes flashed. "I don't know what you and my father have against Nate that you can be so eager to convict him of something he would never, ever do. But I'm telling you, Ben Schaeffer, that you'd better stop it right now or you'll have me to answer to."

"Amy," Ben pleaded, "it's nothing personal. You only have to look at the facts."

"Facts?" Amy cried. "What facts?"

Ben stiffened, standing his ground. "He was seen in a vicious argument with Rosemont only hours before he was murdered. It nearly came to blows."

"But it didn't, did it?" Amy countered. Her face flushed, and Piper wondered if Amy was thinking how close that fight at the fair had actually come to getting physical. If Amy hadn't been there and called out to Nate, would he have walked away from the confrontation?

"He has no alibi for the night of the murder," Ben went on, still blindly trying to bring Amy around to his own way of thinking. "And even worse, he was actually seen entering the alley at the very time Dennis Isley was killed."

"Ben Schaeffer, you're horrible!" Amy cried. "You've been putting terrible thoughts in my father's ear. It's all because of *you* that Nate is being persecuted. Go!" she said, pointing at the door. "Get out of here! I never want to see you again."

Ben's face showed the complete shock he must have been feeling. "But I was only trying to protect—"

"Out!" Amy's face was florid as she continued to jab her finger at the exit.

Ben backed away, still obviously confused over Amy's reaction. Hadn't he been doing all he did for her own good? Why didn't she see that? "I'm, ah, that is, okay, I'll go. But—"

Amy shook her outstretched hand again toward the door. Ben turned and stumbled out onto the sidewalk, venturing a single look back to see if the creature who'd somehow taken over Amy's body had returned it to the sweet, lovable young woman he knew. Then he dashed off, disappearing quickly.

Amy sank onto one of Piper's stools and crumbled into tears. "I'm sorry. I shouldn't have done that. It's your store. I shouldn't have done that."

"Completely understandable," Piper said, wrapping her arms around her assistant's shoulders and leaning a cheek on the top of her head. "You've been under a lot of stress. Ben was the last straw."

"I just couldn't stand listening to what he was saying. And he's probably not the only one saying it. The awful thing is that he almost had me doubting Nate for a second. What does that mean, then, for all the people who don't know Nate as well as I do?" Amy wiped her eyes and pulled herself together. "We really have to do something, Piper. And we have to do it fast."

Piper nodded. "I know." But how were they going to figure out what that something would be?

26

～～～

Piper strolled alongside Will. She had called that evening and asked him to come by. "I just need someone to talk to," she explained, and he'd shown up without questions, which she liked. They headed out on foot toward the Cloverdale Park playground after Will pointed out that it would be vacant in the approaching dusk.

They walked past the small shops and businesses with darkened interiors, including, thankfully, Charlotte's Chocolate's and Confections. Tina's coffee shop showed some light in the rear, indicating that Tina might be doing cleanup or prep for the next day's breakfast menu. Piper hadn't noticed when she and Will began holding hands. Had she reached for his or was it the other way around? Whichever, it felt natural and comforting.

"I'm not sure what I've gotten myself into," Piper said,

getting to what was weighing on her mind. "I thought I was making progress for a while, but now I don't know. I'm afraid I've only been running in circles, maybe making things worse. Nate's livelihood is hanging by a thread, and Amy's nerves are stretched thin. I wanted to help them both, but I haven't done any good whatsoever."

"Don't sell yourself short. Just knowing you're on their side must make a world of difference to Nate and Amy. And you were Nate's link to Gil Williams—don't forget that. Where would he have ended up otherwise?"

Piper smiled at the thought of Gil, her reclusive neighbor who'd certainly shown he could pull his nose out of a book in a hurry when needed. They arrived at the playground, and Piper wandered over to one of the empty swings and sat down.

"The trouble is, I feel like I've reached a dead end. What I found out isn't enough, not nearly enough, to convince the sheriff to search for someone beyond Nate."

As Piper set the swing into motion, Will leaned against one of the support poles. "He may be focusing on Nate, but at least he hasn't charged him with anything yet."

"Only because he doesn't have solid evidence against him. What if the real murderer found some way to incriminate Nate? That's all it would take to get him arrested."

"Incriminate? How?"

"I don't know." Piper pushed the swing with one foot. "The murderer might have something with Alan's blood on it. Or a blackmail note from Dennis Isley. All he'd have to do is plant it on Nate."

"You say 'he.' You've decided, then, that the killer's a man?"

"It seems logical, doesn't it? Alan's murder required plenty of strength to lift his body into the pickle barrel." Piper's lips twitched at another thought. "Though Tina sees Charlotte Hosch as the murderer."

Will smiled. "Well, Charlotte's probably got some muscle on her from stirring all that fudge. Plus, she's never been one to back down from an argument, has she? I know I wouldn't like to run into that woman in a dark alley if I'd ever crossed her."

Piper grinned. "If she attacked you with her big metal candy spoon, you could always fight her off with your pruning saw."

"Which I keep handy in my back pocket, of course. Just in case."

"Or you could simply avoid dark alleys."

"Better to avoid ever crossing Charlotte Hosch."

"Probably the wisest course, if not the easiest." Piper turned her swing, twisting the chains. "You know, the more I think of it, the more Tina's claim makes a certain kind of sense. Except I don't know that Charlotte had any particular reason to kill Alan Rosemont. I'm sure she didn't like him. Nobody seemed to. But that doesn't necessarily lead to murder."

Piper let the chains unwind, spinning her in circles. When the swing stopped, she sighed. "There I go, down another dead end." She stood up, swaying dizzily, and Will reached out to steady her.

"Don't worry about it too much. You're doing what you can. You've done great, actually. As a matter of fact," he said, pulling her closer, "I think *you're* pretty great."

"Really?"

Piper looked up at Will, ready for what was coming next. Will tightened his hold on her and kissed her, and Piper kissed back. Then she leaned her cheek on his shoulder and gave him a hug. "You really know how to cheer a girl up," she said against his shirt.

As an answer, Will tilted her chin up and offered more encouragement, which was, Piper decided, exactly what she needed.

Piper woke. She'd been dreaming, something about fixing waffles—with cucumbers?—and the waffles had started burning—and—she sniffed and smelled smoke. Real smoke. At the same time she heard loud pounding on her door.

"Piper!" a voice shouted. "Wake up, Piper! Fire!"

Piper sat up like a shot. A look to her back window showed a horrifying sight: black smoke and flashes of light. She froze for a moment, her brain not willing to believe what her senses were telling it. Then it kicked in, telling her to get out! Get out now!

Her first confused, panicky thought was to look around and grab what she could save, but the pounding and shouting at her front door escalated, urging her not to waste time. Barefoot and in flimsy cotton pajamas, Piper ran out of her bedroom, spotted her laptop glittering on a tabletop in the terrible glow from the windows and grabbed hold of it, then ran down the front stairway, fumbling blindly at the lock before flinging open the door.

Nate Purdy stood at her doorstep, hair spiked in every direction but dressed in jeans, T-shirt, and sneakers.

"Thank God! I was ready to break in. I called for help." As he said it, Piper heard the shriek of sirens. In moments a fire truck roared onto her street, lights flashing.

The rest of the action became a blur. Firefighters spilling from the truck, unwinding a hose, shouting. Someone pulling her away from the building. The hiss of water on flames, more smoke rising from behind her building. Piper clutching the blanket someone had wrapped around her and watching numbly, trying to comprehend all that was going on. What had happened? How could her building have caught fire? What if she hadn't gotten out in time?

That last thought made her shiver despite the blanket that warmed her. She looked around for Nate. He stood several feet away, talking to a uniformed man next to the fire truck. That man left him to meet Sheriff Carlyle, who had just driven up. Nate spotted Piper and came over.

"Thank you," she said. "I think you saved my life."

Nate looked as shaken as Piper knew she would feel as soon as reality sank in. "I saw the flash from my window," he said. "It overlooks the alley. I called you, but all I have is your shop number. You didn't answer."

"I turn the shop phone off when I close up. Apparently not such a good idea." What *was* a good idea, Piper realized, was having decided no longer to leave her car in the dark, unprotected alley after the damage that was done to her tires. She glanced down the block to see her trusty hatchback parked on the street and out of harm's way.

"When I couldn't get you I ran out and pounded on your front door. The flames were at the back."

"And closest to my bedroom." Piper shuddered. "What caused the fire?"

Nate shook his head, shrugging.

Piper noticed that spectators had gathered beyond the rescue vehicles. Most looked disheveled, dressed in hastily thrown-on clothes after being roused from bed in the middle of the night by sirens. Though they might have been conversing with each other, none of that carried Piper's way above the noise and activity surrounding her. Their seemingly silent gazes projected an air of eeriness intensified by the flashing lights. She scanned the faces, hoping to find a familiar and friendly one.

The first recognizable, though not particularly friendly, face she spotted was Charlotte Hosch's. Piper's gaze quickly moved on. It passed over several people she'd seen around the neighborhood or who'd stopped into her shop. She wished she would see Gil Williams, but the bookstore owner, she knew, lived several miles from his shop.

Piper's search stopped at sight of a tall man at the rear of a clump of spectators. Gordon Pfiefle. What was he doing here? Gordon and Lyella's house, while within walking distance, was still too far away to have heard the commotion. Or was it? Piper suddenly had a frightening thought, and she examined the crowd more carefully.

There! She spotted Ralph Farber, standing at the far edge. Did she imagine it, or did the plumber see her looking at him and turn away? What was going on? Was Robby Taylor there as well? Or his mother, Dorothy?

Piper heard her name called and turned.

"Piper!" Aunt Judy was pushing through the crowd toward her, followed closely by Uncle Frank. "Piper, are you all right?"

Piper rushed toward her aunt. Uncle Frank caught up,

and both hugged her tightly. The relief Piper felt over-whelmed her, and she found herself choking back tears.

"Are you hurt?" Aunt Judy asked, stepping back and scrutinizing her niece worriedly.

Piper shook her head. "I'm fine," she said, managing a shaky smile. "And the shop might not have been damaged too badly. At least that's what I've been overhearing."

Aunt Judy clucked and fussed, and Uncle Frank patted Piper's shoulder, both asking questions she had no answers for yet, though she immediately credited Nate with having quickly gotten her out of danger.

"Where is that young man?" Aunt Judy asked.

Piper looked around, unsure.

"There he is," Uncle Frank said, pointing to the sheriff's cruiser where Nate stood talking with Sheriff Carlyle. Giving a report on his actions?

Piper looked beyond them to the crowd she'd been scanning moments before. Gordon Pfiefle, Charlotte Hosch, and Ralph Farber had disappeared.

27

M ost of the fire vehicles had cleared off and spectators dispersed when Will suddenly drove up. Piper was about to climb into Uncle Frank's truck, having been convinced to spend the night at the farm.

"Are you all right?" Will called out, cutting his motor and jumping out.

Piper dropped the small bag she'd been allowed by the rescue team to run up and pack and was glad she'd been able to exchange the Cloverdale FD blanket for her light coat as well as slip on a pair of sandals. Aware of the many eyes currently on them, Piper and Will simply grasped hands as he explained, "I didn't know about your fire until your aunt called me," sounding frustrated that he hadn't been on hand to rescue Piper.

"I'm fine, and I think my place is fine. A little smoky, but that'll be taken care of."

She gave him the short version of what had happened, secretly pleased all the same at the distress evident on his face. "I'd better go, though," she said, glancing back at the truck. "My aunt and uncle could probably use a little more sleep tonight."

Will nodded and promised to check back with her the following day.

Piper rode off with Aunt Judy and Uncle Frank, feeling extreme fatigue set in as her adrenaline spike faded. At the farmhouse, she staggered into the guest bedroom and collapsed onto the bed, not even aware that Gracie, her aunt's plump gray cat, had slipped in to curl up beside her until Piper woke the next morning to the smell of coffee and bacon.

Much pleasanter than the smell of smoke, she thought as she stretched stiffly and gave Gracie a quick rub. Piper climbed out of bed and hopped into the shower, appearing in the kitchen a few minutes later dressed in fresh shorts and a tee and feeling ravenously hungry.

"Good morning!" Aunt Judy said, immediately pouring out orange juice for Piper. "I heard you in the shower and fried up more pancakes. We let you sleep in a bit. You looked so tired last night."

"I was," Piper said, taking a grateful swallow of the juice and helping herself to two of the pancakes that her aunt had stacked in the center of the table. Uncle Frank had already worked his way through his own helping and was leaning back in his chair, holding his half-filled coffee mug.

"I hope you two managed to grab a few winks?" Piper asked.

"Frank was out like a light," Aunt Judy said with a laugh, looking over fondly at her husband. "I was a little keyed up, but I managed to doze off."

Piper saw dark shadows under her aunt's eyes and felt terrible to have been the cause, however unintentionally. Aunt Judy still bustled about the kitchen with her usual energy, however, urging Piper to eat before bringing over coffee and sitting down herself. Gracie immediately jumped onto her lap.

Uncle Frank sipped at his mug silently, letting Piper enjoy her breakfast and Aunt Judy enjoy fussing over her for a while, then said, "Sheriff Carlyle called earlier."

"Oh?" Piper grabbed her napkin to wipe her fingers of grease after nibbling at a crispy strip of bacon.

"Chief Branson says the cause of your fire was arson."

"Arson!" Aunt Judy cried, startling Gracie, who leaped to the floor.

"They found evidence of an accelerant. They think it was gasoline. Nate Purdy also told them he'd happened to look out his window last night because he heard a noise. He thought he saw a dark figure running away as the fire flared up."

"Oh my Lord," Aunt Judy said.

Piper was silent. She was thinking of the trash dump, the paint splash, and her tire damage, three vandalisms that were more aggravating inconveniences. If the fire had been started by the same person, he'd taken things to a frightening level.

"Did they find any other evidence?" she asked.

Uncle Frank shook his head. "Didn't say. You might get more out of him later. Chief Branson said there's no reason you can't be back in there and start cleaning up. They doused the fire before there was any structural damage."

"Thank God for that," Aunt Judy said. She reached down for Gracie and lifted her back onto her lap, and Piper thought the soft stroking that followed was likely as soothing to her aunt as it was to Gracie. She noticed a lingering worried look on her uncle's face as though he had more bad news.

"What else?" she asked.

Uncle Frank cleared his throat. "Well, seems like Russell Johnson told Sheriff Carlyle he happened to turn into your alley around the time of the fire, and the only person he saw there was Nate Purdy."

"The whole town's out to get Nate!" Amy paced around Piper's Picklings, her arms crossed tightly across her chest.

"Russell Johnson only told your father what he saw."

"What was Russell Johnson doing in your alley in the first place!"

"Well, it's not only my alley, of course, since it runs behind several shops and a few houses. He said he was walking his dog."

"In the middle of the night?"

"The dog's old, according to Aunt Judy. He has to go out a lot."

"So Johnson saw Nate from which end?"

"His house is near Mindy Atwater's yarn shop, so I suppose he entered on the south end."

"The person Nate saw could have run north and disappeared by the time Nate came down from his place."

"I think that's entirely possible," Piper agreed. "And I'm sure your father will see that."

"I'm not so sure," Amy said grumpily, though she'd slowed her pacing. "I wouldn't be surprised if Ben Schaeffer is currently pushing a theory on how Nate managed to dispose of a huge can of gasoline before anyone arrived. Oh, and miscalculated the ignition time of the fire before calling 911.

Piper wouldn't have been surprised, either, but she said nothing.

Amy looked around. "Thank goodness they put it all out before you had any real damage."

"I have Nate to thank for that, absolutely. The fire only scorched the bricks and siding. Plenty of smoke got in, of course, but the fans are getting rid of it. I've already called someone to come check the outside and clean or repair what's needed." She paused a moment. "Maybe they can take care of the paint on the front of the building while they're at it. I might as well give up on Max Noland, who keeps promising to do it but never shows up."

Amy smiled ruefully. "I'm so sorry, Piper. What did Nate and I get you into when we asked for your help?"

Piper was saved from having to answer when her phone rang. She picked up with a crisp, "Piper's Picklings."

"Miss Lamb?" a woman inquired softly.

"This is Piper Lamb. How can I help you?"

"This is Brenda Franklin. I heard about your latest troubles, as well as your interest in Alan Rosemont's murder."

"Yes?" Franklin's name rang a bell but not loud enough for Piper to place it.

"I was a good friend of Alan's. I was so distressed over his murder and wasn't able to speak to anyone about it for days." *Alan Rosemont's girlfriend!* "But," Franklin continued, "hearing about your fire last night on the heels of your other occurrences has shaken me. You've been trying to do the right thing. I think I have something to share that might help you."

Piper's heart jumped. "Really? What is it?"

"It's much too complicated to explain over the phone. Would you be able to come here at four thirty?"

"Yes, of course." That meant finding someone to watch the shop or closing it, since Amy would be gone. But Piper would do that. This appointment sounded much too important to haggle over the time. She wrote down Brenda's address.

After hanging up, Piper turned to Amy, excited. "We just might be getting the break we've been hoping for."

28

~~~~~

"What can you tell me about Brenda Franklin?" Piper asked Aunt Judy, who'd been more than happy to come watch the shop so Piper could keep her appointment with Brenda. She'd brought along the fixings for a casserole for Nate, intending to put it together in Piper's kitchen while she was there.

"Well," Aunt Judy said, picking up a jar of mustard seed from the shelf and checking its label before setting it back in place. "Brenda has been a widow for several years, although she's only in her early fifties. No children, and apparently well-off enough not to need to work, which is a shame in a way."

"How so?"

"Brenda is shy. Keeping to herself is probably much easier than going out and getting to know people. If she'd needed to earn a living, it would have forced her to get out more and might have been good for her."

"Then how did she get involved with Alan Rosemont?"

"Probably through his antique shop. From what I've heard, she enjoys collecting things—china dolls, glass animals, things like that. She's an attractive woman, but between you and me, I suspect her bank account attracted Alan as much as anything."

"Meaning?" Piper asked, one eyebrow raised.

"Oh, not that. I didn't mean he would have fleeced her out of her money. But she has a lovely house that he would have shared if they'd married, and a very nice car, and she probably can afford to travel extensively, though she never does. But Alan might at least have encouraged that and expanded her horizons a bit."

"But at what cost, I wonder? From what I've learned about the man, he would have taken over and run her life."

"Very possibly," Aunt Judy agreed. "It's hard to know what makes a workable marriage for other people, though, isn't it? Maybe Brenda would have been just fine with having someone make all the major decisions for her."

The idea made Piper cringe. Even her younger, more naïve self had never considered turning over control of her life to any man. Compromise, yes, but control? No way.

Piper's musings were interrupted by Tina's brisk entry into the shop. "I couldn't come by before this," she said, strands of hair escaping and flying loose from the several barrettes that were meant to tame it. "But I've been hearing about your fire from customers all day and had to see for myself."

"It wasn't too bad," Piper assured her. "Though waking

up to fire in the middle of the night was a definite scare." Piper didn't like to admit exactly how bad a scare it had been. Just talking about it made her feel edgy, but she managed a smile. "As you see, I'm still able to open my shop. Except for the lingering smell of smoke that I'm gradually blowing out, all the damage is on the exterior."

"Thank heavens for that! I couldn't believe it when I first heard about it. I didn't hear a thing myself last night. But that might have been because I took something to help me sleep. I've been having a little trouble with that, as you know."

"What a shame," Aunt Judy said. "Have you tried warm milk? Or maybe yoga to help you relax?"

Tina nodded, smiling. "Been there, done that. Last night I needed something stronger, just to get me over the hump, you know?"

Piper thought Tina did look rather ragged and was sorry. Obviously the chamomile tea jelly hadn't been much help. "I had a call today that definitely perked me up," she said, hoping it would do the same for Tina. "Brenda Franklin says she has something to tell me that could help with our investigation."

"Brenda Franklin?" Tina's face went blank.

"She had been seeing Alan Rosemont before he died," Aunt Judy explained.

"She had? I never heard that. So what does she know?"

"I'll find out at four thirty," Piper said. "That's when I'm heading over to her place."

Tina eyes lit up. "This might be just what you need."

"That's what I'm hoping. I'll let you know."

"Yes, call me tonight. I'll be anxious to hear. I'll bet it

has something to do with Charlotte Hosch. Well," she said, glancing at her watch, "I'd better be off. Got to fix some pasta salads for tomorrow."

"I hope you get a good night's sleep tonight," Aunt Judy said. "I've found taking a little walk before bedtime can be very relaxing."

Tina nodded. "I might try that. Thanks."

"She might be working herself too hard," Aunt Judy said, as she watched Tina head down the street. "You'd think getting good and tired from such a busy job would make sleeping easy, but it can also wind a person up too much."

Aunt Judy glanced at the wall clock. "Well, you'll be leaving for Brenda's in about an hour. Why don't I run upstairs and get my chicken breasts cooking for Nate's casserole?"

"Sure. Give a holler if you need anything."

A customer stepped in as Aunt Judy left, and Piper waited on her, answering, in the process, more questions about her fire, something she'd been doing since she opened up. The excitement of the night before had definitely stepped up business at the shop. But she'd trade slow and safe for brisk but dangerous any day.

Soon after that customer took off, Piper was surprised to get a second call from Brenda Franklin.

"Miss Lamb, would you mind if we postponed your visit to six thirty?" she asked. "I'm afraid working in my garden has given me a slight headache. I'll need to rest for a while."

"Six thirty is fine," Piper assured her and wished her speedy relief. After hanging up, she called out the change of plans to her aunt. "I'm sorry," she said. "Seems I dragged you here for nothing."

"Not at all, dear," Aunt Judy answered. "I'm getting my casserole for Nate made, which is all I was going to do at home anyway. I'll go ahead and finish, plus fix a little extra that the two of us can share before you leave for Brenda's. How does that sound? Uncle Frank will be fine. There's leftovers at the farm he can warm up."

Piper heard her aunt bustling about the kitchen overhead as she handled a few more sales until about five forty-five. By that time she could pick up tasty aromas coming from her apartment, and with no approaching customers in sight she decided to lock up a few minutes early. She pulled her shades, dealt with her cash box, and ran up the stairs, eager to dig into Aunt Judy's chicken casserole.

"Go freshen up if you like," her aunt said as Piper appeared at the top of the stairs. "This can cool for a bit. Do you want iced tea?"

"Yes, please," Piper called and dashed off to her bedroom and bathroom. When she returned to the kitchen, Aunt Judy had dished out two servings onto plates, and she joined Piper at the table to enjoy the creamy chicken, noodle, and vegetable mixture that had long been a favorite of Piper's.

"I thought about Brenda the whole time I was cooking," Aunt Judy said, "wondering what she can have to tell you. Do you suppose Alan told her something that nobody else knows that will lead us to his killer?"

Piper paused, holding a forkful of noodles over her plate. "Since she seems to have been the person closest to Alan, that certainly seems possible." She chewed the noodles, then stabbed at a chunk of chicken, taking a quick glance at the kitchen clock. "I just hope she doesn't have a change of heart by the time I get there. Her calling to postpone the appointment may have been because of her headache or may have been an uneasiness over sharing private information. I hope it's not the latter."

Aunt Judy nodded. "As I said, Brenda is a very shy person. This might be difficult for her."

They finished their meal in companionable silence until Piper hurriedly scraped up her last morsel of celery. "I'd better get moving. Leave the dishes, Aunt Judy. I'll clean up after I get back."

"Don't even think about it. I plan to wait right here to hear every word of what Brenda tells you, assuming it's not confidential, of course. We can have a nice dish of ice cream over it." Aunt Judy stood, picking up both plates. "While you're getting your things, I'll give Nate a call and tell him I'm bringing over a casserole."

Piper left to gather up her purse and car keys. When she returned from her bedroom, Aunt Judy had just replaced the phone, a small frown puckering her brow.

"Nate didn't answer. I'll try again a little later."

"I'm off," Piper said. "Thanks a bunch for dinner." She gave her aunt a quick peck on her cheek, then trotted down the front stairs and out to her car.

Aunt Judy hadn't exaggerated when she'd described Brenda Franklin's house as lovely. The white siding of the two-story colonial looked freshly painted, as did the black shutters that framed sparkling windows. A low stone wall edged a front garden filled with end-of-summer blooms with not a single weed mixed in that Piper could see.

Piper walked up to the wood front door with its stained glass insert and checked her watch. Six thirty on the dot. She smiled and pressed the doorbell, hearing the chime echo inside. She waited but heard no approaching footsteps or turn of lock. After a minute or so, she pressed the bell again, shifting her purse to the other side and listening. There was no response.

Piper frowned, not sure what to do. Had Brenda changed her mind? But why not call and cancel? Perhaps she'd simply fallen asleep, resting from her headache. But wouldn't the doorbell rouse her?

Piper pressed the bell one more time, then decided to walk around the back, hoping to find Brenda there, out of earshot of her doorbell. She followed a flagstone path that led around the side of the house to the rear, ending at a thick, green lawn and a second garden, both dotted with bird feeders. A screen porch was attached to the house, affording a perfect place to sit and enjoy the view. Which was where Piper spotted Brenda. Except she wasn't sitting on any of the pretty white wicker furniture. She lay sprawled on the floor.

"Mrs. Franklin!" Piper cried, thinking the woman had fainted. She ran to the screen door and flung it open but instantly pulled up short.

The trim, middle-aged woman stared sightlessly upward from the porch floor. Blood pooled around her head, matting the long brown hair that spread like a fan on the concrete. Scattered about were dozens of broken glass animals apparently knocked from a shelf that had been pulled down and now lay among overturned end tables.

Piper gaped, frozen in place. Then she spotted something that made her gasp. In the middle of all the shattered glass lay a bloodied, broken canning jar. The label could be seen clearly.

It was a jar of Piper's honeyed bread-and-butter pickles.

29

"Okay, let me get this straight." Sheriff Carlyle lifted his hat briefly to wipe the sweat off his brow with the edge of his sleeve and studied his notes. "You arrived at Mrs. Franklin's house at approximately six thirty—"

"Exactly six thirty," Piper said. "I looked at my watch before I rang her bell, and I know my watch is right." They were standing beside the sheriff's car in front of Brenda Franklin's house in the fading light. The place was a beehive of activity as crime scene personnel swarmed over the house and yard, doing their jobs. Piper had calmed from her initial shock of finding Brenda Franklin dead, though the scene before her brought uncomfortable flashbacks of discovering Alan Rosemont's body the morning of the fair.

She had related what she knew more than once already,

to various officers along the chain of command, but she understood the need for repetition and expected to describe her actions many times more. After all, she was a potential suspect, wasn't she?

The thought was grim but, Piper felt sure, accurate. She was, after all, the one who reported having discovered the body. How best to explain any possible blood on one's clothing, or having left fingerprints and footprints, than by claiming to have innocently stumbled on the scene. And this time there'd been no Ben Schaeffer beside her to verify her statements as he'd done at the fair. Then there was the fact of her pickle jar lying there. Had it been the murder weapon? Piper dreaded to find out.

"And your reason for coming?" the sheriff asked.

"Brenda Franklin called and said she wanted to talk. She was upset over the fire at my place as well as the other things that have happened to me and said she understood I was only trying to help find Alan Rosemont's real murderer."

The sheriff coughed and cleared his throat at that but simply said, "Uh-huh. And you first arranged to arrive earlier?"

"Yes, she suggested four thirty. I agreed and called my aunt to watch the shop for me because Amy would be gone. Aunt Judy arrived around three or three fifteen. But then Brenda called and changed our appointment to six thirty."

"When did she call that second time?"

"I think it was around three thirty or three forty-five. I can't be a hundred percent sure of that, but Aunt Judy might remember."

The sheriff nodded. "So you didn't leave your place until what time?"

258

"Around six twenty, maybe six twenty-five. I knew it'd be a short drive. Aunt Judy and I had a quick dinner after I closed up a few minutes before six."

"And your aunt was with you from the time of her arrival until you left around six twenty?"

"Uh-huh. That is, she was upstairs in my apartment most of the time, cooking, and I was dealing with customers in the shop, but, yes, she stayed with me."

"And those customers were?"

Piper rattled off the names once again, not having to think as hard as she did the first time. She also knew she could back up her memory with the receipts at the shop. She had wondered, at first, why the sheriff needed that information. Then it occurred to her. He was checking her whereabouts minute by minute.

Piper knew now how Nate must feel to be under suspicion, and it wasn't a pleasant feeling. Every word she said and every expression on her face was probably being scrutinized, and though she was telling the simple truth, she began to worry that the way she said it might be misconstrued or that she would leave out a detail that could be pounced upon later on.

Except, this was Amy's father talking to her, a man who was highly regarded by townspeople, including her aunt and uncle. But Sheriff Carlyle had acted unfairly, she believed, toward Nate. Would that now be turned on her?

The sheriff thanked her and headed over to Aunt Judy, probably to verify Piper's story. Aunt Judy had rushed over to Brenda Franklin's once Piper called with the terrible news but hadn't been able to do more than give a worried wave to Piper, who'd been kept occupied answering questions. Uncle Frank, thankfully, had also arrived soon, and he stood with one arm around his wife while tossing concerned glances Piper's way.

The usual gathering of the curious formed, and as Piper waited beside the sheriff's car with a young deputy, she wondered what they all might be saying. She'd been at the center of several "incidents" in her short time in Cloverdale. So far, they'd provoked only sympathy—along with plenty of questions. Would things start to tip the other way and would townspeople begin looking at her with suspicion as many already did with Nate?

Piper remembered that her cell phone had rung at one point but she'd let it go to voice mail. She checked it, finding a message from Will.

"I'm in Rochester," he said, sounding super-frustrated. "One of my tractors needed a part. I just heard what happened. Give me a call. I'll get back as soon as I can."

Poor Will, Piper thought. How tired he must be of getting bad news. If she were Will, she'd start spending a lot more time in Rochester. Piper saw the sheriff walking toward her and sighed, wondering if more questions and double checking lay ahead. To her surprise, however, Sheriff Carlyle said, "You can go on home, Miss Lamb, if you like."

Really?

Aunt Judy and Uncle Frank were close on his heels. "Let's go on back to your place," Aunt Judy said. "I'll fix a pot of tea and we can talk."

Once Piper got over her shock she didn't waste time. She made her way to her car and nudged it away from the official vehicles and standing crowd as quickly as she dared. Uncle Frank was soon behind her, with Aunt Judy behind him, and all three arrived at Piper's Picklings—which seemed strangely dark and quiet after what she'd been in the midst of—within minutes.

Inside her apartment, Aunt Judy set a kettle of water to boil as Piper, still puzzled, asked, "What happened back there? Why didn't they take me back to the station for more questioning?"

"You told them everything you could, didn't you?" Aunt Judy asked.

"Many times." Piper pulled down a box of tea leaves. "But I was sure they'd still want more."

"If you're thinking they might have suspected you," Uncle Frank said, "they probably did, at least routinely, for a while."

"Oh, that's ridiculous, Frank!" Aunt Judy said. "Suspect Piper? Why would anyone in their right mind think our Piper could have murdered poor Brenda Franklin."

Uncle Frank held his hands up defensively. "I'm just saying they had to rule her out, Judy. It's strictly procedure, as they say on TV."

"He's right," Piper said. "And I admit I was plenty worried about that bloodied jar of my pickles that was lying next to Mrs. Franklin."

"Oh!" Aunt Judy cried. "I didn't know about that."

"Me neither," Uncle Frank said. He lifted the kettle of boiling water from the stove at that point and emptied it into Piper's teapot himself. "Sit," he said to both women, then found mugs, spoons, and sugar to bring over to the small table.

"I did happen, however," he said, "by some strategic

maneuvering, to overhear the doc giving his estimate of the time of death. Brenda Franklin was dead at least two hours by the time you found her, Piper. Maybe more."

"Thank God!" Aunt Judy said. "I mean, I'm very sorry Brenda was killed, of course, but that rules Piper out, doesn't it?"

"It does," Piper said, pouring her aunt a cup of the steeped tea, then some for her uncle and herself. "That must be why Sheriff Carlyle was asking for so many details about my afternoon. I had a verifiable alibi for every minute up until the moment I went to Brenda's house." She stirred sugar into her tea, thinking. "And that would have still been the case if I'd gone over at the original time of four thirty. But Brenda wouldn't have been dead as long, would she? It wouldn't have mattered what sort of alibi I had before I got to her house if Brenda had been killed just before I found her."

"Piper," Aunt Judy said, "if you'd gone over at four thirty you might have run into the murderer! You might have been killed yourself!"

"No, I don't think so." Piper reached out to squeeze her aunt's hand. "I don't think I would have surprised anyone. I think the murderer may have expected me to arrive at the original time."

Piper paused, looking back and forth from her aunt to her uncle.

"I think someone tried to set me up."

30

Aunt Judy and Uncle Frank left at Piper's urging, though they were both obviously torn between wanting to stay and keep watch over Piper and carrying her back with them to the farm where they could protect her.

"I'll be fine," Piper assured the two as she eased them out. "I'll double-lock my doors, check all my windows, and promise to stay inside until the light of day." *Unless another fire breaks out*, she thought but kept to herself. When she heard Uncle Frank's truck and Aunt Judy's Explorer start up then fade away, Piper opened her laptop and clicked it on. Though she'd implied she would immediately fall into bed—and heaven knew she was exhausted enough—there was something she needed to do to settle a niggling thought at the back of her mind.

Timing. The timing of Piper's arrival at Brenda Franklin's had made a huge difference. Timing, as the saying goes—and it was so true—was everything. But there was another instance where, looking back, the timing hadn't been quite right. She didn't realize it when it happened, what with all the stress and distraction going on at the moment. But now the particular incident took on much greater importance. Or seemed to. She could be totally wrong about what it meant. But if she could find anything that backed up her suspicion, the sheriff would be very interested.

Piper typed Alan Rosemont's name into her search engine. It had sounded like a good idea when Tina offered to handle the chore of checking out Alan's background. The investigation and the mounting vandalisms had been stretching Piper thin. It was time, however, to take that job over.

Unfortunately, Alan Rosemont's name was not an unusual one. Several thousand results popped up, including Facebook pages that were obviously not his. How many "friends" would Alan have had, Piper wondered, if he'd actually set up a page? Piper sighed at the enormous sifting job ahead of her and went to her kitchen for coffee. The tea she'd drunk a few minutes ago wasn't going to do it for her.

Back at her laptop, Piper clicked through website after website—some having Rosemont's full name, some only "Rosemont" or "Alan." Car dealerships, dental offices, high school reunions. She checked them all on the chance there would be a real connection to the right Rosemont. She found newspaper articles mentioning Alan Rosemont but only in connection with his town council work. Most articles appeared in the *Cloverdale Chronicle*, but a few made it into Poughkeepsie and Rochester newspapers. None were particularly useful.

After a couple of hours, the tedium on top of the fatigue Piper had started with was beginning to take its toll. What were the chances she'd find anything the sheriff or his staff had overlooked? But perhaps she'd been working from the wrong angle? One that the sheriff surely wouldn't have considered? Piper typed in a new name and moaned as a matching high number of results popped up. Where to start? At the beginning, she sensibly answered herself and began clicking. Within a few minutes, though, she realized she was reading words but her foggy brain wasn't translating them into anything that made sense. Perhaps if she just closed her eyes for a few minutes?

Piper laid her head on her arms and was aware of thick blackness quickly descending. In seconds she was dead to the world. However long she slept, she woke suddenly to the sound of loud cracking noises from outside. Gunshots! She waited, tense, then heard them again, this time farther away and accompanied by faint laughter. She relaxed. Teenagers with firecrackers, by the sound of it, and out much too late.

Though they'd caused her heart rate to triple, she didn't begrudge them their fun. Without their noise who knows how long she might have slept? She stretched stiffly out of her awkward position, padded to the bathroom to splash water on her face, then veered over to the kitchen for a shot of orange juice. All helped chase some of the grogginess out of her brain. She hoped a large mug of strong coffee would take care of the rest, and popped the mug into her microwave to heat before heading back to her work.

Piper returned to the search engine results she'd pulled up earlier and began clicking once again. Alan Rosemont's name had yielded nothing, but Piper had higher hopes with her new search. She clicked and read, clicked and moved on, site after site, stopping only to stretch occasionally to keep herself alert. As the night hours slipped by, the sun slowly peeked through her windows, brightening her living room until the lamp she'd had on became unnecessary.

The clock inched closer toward opening time for the shop, but Piper's focus remained on the job in front of her: closing in on a murderer. She was getting there; she knew it. She could almost taste it. Maybe the next website. Or the next newspaper story. One link led to another in a seemingly endless trail, but she was sure she'd find her pot of gold before much longer.

Then she opened a website page that was filled with photos, pictures of well-dressed people at fund-raising dinners that spanned over twenty years. These events had apparently supported an athletic complex in Scranton, Pennsylvania. Piper scanned the photos carefully, stopping finally at one. She stared, not quite believing what she was seeing. But the more she studied the photo, the clearer it became. Even though she'd never been sure exactly what she was looking for, she was convinced she'd finally found it.

Piper leaned back, still gazing at the screen, feeling at first triumph but changing soon to sadness. But, she told herself, at least it was over. The murders would end.

After sitting immobile for several moments, wrapping her head around the significance of what she'd found, Piper shook herself. It was time to get moving. She printed out the photo and the accompanying article, which she would take to Sheriff Carlyle immediately. A glance down at her disheveled self changed "immediately" to "very soon." No use frightening the populace, but she could tidy up in a flash. And a little food might also be a good thing.

Piper grabbed a bagel in her kitchen, not caring that it was three days old, and ate as she pulled out fresh clothes. *What was proper attire for presenting evidence of guilt?* she wondered, then grabbed whatever looked clean. She hopped into her shower and scrubbed, dried, and dressed. Somewhat refreshed, though still feeling on the edge of exhaustion, she slipped her printed material into a nine-by-twelve envelope and grabbed her purse and keys.

As Piper stepped out of her front door and headed to her car, her thoughts were on what she would say to Sheriff Carlyle when she found him. It took a moment, therefore, for her to notice she wouldn't have far to go. There, parked in front of Gil Williams's bookstore, sat the sheriff's patrol car.

31

~~~~~~~

Piper's first concern when she saw the sheriff's car in front of the bookstore was for Nate. Was he in for another grilling? If so, she was holding the perfect antidote. She hurried on over.

"Sheriff Carlyle," Piper said as she pushed into the bookshop. "You can forget about Nate!"

The sheriff, who had been conversing with Gil Williams at his front counter, looked over, eyebrows raised.

"Would you like to explain that, Miss Lamb?"

"I mean you can stop questioning Nate because Nate didn't murder anyone. I know who did."

The sheriff looked as skeptical as he had when Piper first mentioned her suspicions about Gordon Pfiefle to him. She didn't blame him, since she'd been wrong—so wrong—about Gordon. And, of course, Lyella.

"It came to me when I thought about how important timing is. It really has to make sense, doesn't it?"

The sheriff nodded cautiously. Gil was looking at Piper as though he hoped she would start to make sense very soon.

"I'm sorry," she said. "I'm babbling, I know. It's because I've been up all night looking for this." She held up the envelope containing her printouts. "When I realized how close I came to being set up for murder, dodging it only because I showed up at Brenda Franklin's two hours later than planned, I started thinking back to something that had bothered me before but I'd shrugged it off."

"And what was that?" Gil asked

"Tina fainted at the wrong time."

The two men stared at Piper, the unspoken "huh?" hanging in the air.

"At the fair," Piper explained. "After I found Alan's body in my pickle barrel. The crime scene crew had cordoned off the area around my booth, and crowds of people gathered around to stare. Tina pushed through to ask what had happened. When I told her that Alan Rosemont had been murdered, she looked shocked, but no more so than anyone else. But when a bystander told her that Alan's body had been found in my pickle barrel, Tina turned white and fainted!"

Piper looked with frustration at the two. "Don't you see? The timing was all wrong! Tina didn't faint when she heard about the murder. She fainted when she heard where the body was found. Because she didn't leave it there. Tina must have murdered Alan in another spot, and someone moved his body into the pickle barrel after she left."

"Someone like Dennis Isley?" Gil offered. The sheriff looked sharply at him but didn't say anything.

"Very possibly," Piper said. "But if the timing of Tina's reaction isn't enough for you, Sheriff, look at what I found on the Internet." Piper pulled out the photo. "Tina claimed never to have met Alan until she moved to Cloverdale. She acted puzzled over why he gave her such a hard time about setting up her coffee shop. When she offered to do a background search on him for me, she definitely implied that she knew nothing about him to begin with. But here she is on his arm at a charity dinner. They're both nineteen years younger, but still very recognizable."

The sheriff took the photo and studied it, then read the printed material Piper handed him. He looked at Piper through his bushy brows, which were tightly knit at the moment.

"Tina Carson is the reason I'm here this morning," he said. "She called to tell me she'd seen Nate breaking into Dennis Isley's truck the day before Dennis died, but that she'd struggled with saying anything that would get him into more trouble. Brenda Franklin's murder, she said, convinced her she shouldn't hold back such information, and that I might want to search Nate's premises in case there was incriminating evidence that would—as she put it—end this madness."

"Oh dear," Gil said. "Nate told me that Tina was here the other day when I was out. She had him searching fruitlessly through my back room stock for a book she claimed she'd ordered. She could easily have slipped up to his apartment and planted something while Nate was busy back there."

"I don't have a search warrant that would allow me to

run up there and take a look," the sheriff said. "Thought I'd talk to the boy first and see if this claim held any water. It sounded fairly dicey to me."

Piper was surprised but pleased to hear that. "Where is Nate now?" she asked.

"I worried that he didn't seem to be eating in the morning," Gil said, his expression concerned. "So I said I'd buy him breakfast if he'd bring back a Danish for me. I sent him to Tina's."

The sheriff met Piper's eyes. "I think it would be a good idea," he said, "to get on over there."

The early-morning breakfast rush had apparently ended as Piper and Sheriff Carlyle arrived at Tina's coffee shop. Through the window, Piper could see Nate sitting alone at the counter. Tina was clearing a table of dirty dishes nearby, and the rest of the shop appeared empty. *Good*, Piper thought. The sheriff demonstrated the same preference for privacy as they walked in by flipping the "Closed" sign on Tina's door outward.

"Miss Carson," he said, nodding to her and then to Nate, who'd turned around in some surprise. "We need to have a little chat."

Tina looked at the sheriff, then at Piper, an expression of apologetic concern crossing her face. "I'm sorry, Piper. I had to tell the truth of what I saw. Believe me, it broke my heart. But I'm afraid we were wrong about Nate."

"Were we?" Piper asked.

"What? What are you talking about?" Nate slid off his counter seat to face the three.

"I'm sorry for you, too, Nate," Tina said. "But not as sorry as I was for poor Brenda Franklin. I couldn't deny what you were anymore." Tina had moved behind the counter with her tray of dirty dishes where she set them down. "Not after you killed Brenda."

"I didn't kill anybody! Sheriff, I don't know why she's saying that. It's not true!"

The sheriff raised his hand in a calming gesture, and Piper shook her head silently at Nate, wanting to say more but willing to let the sheriff take the lead.

"Miss Carson," the sheriff said, "you said you saw Mr. Purdy break into Dennis Isley's truck?"

"I did," Tina said solemnly.

"So, the item we found in Mr. Purdy's apartment came from Dennis Isley's glove compartment?"

"I never—" Nate began, but was again cut off by the sheriff with a swift gesture. Piper, who knew the sheriff had never set foot into Nate's apartment, thought she knew where he was heading.

"I'm afraid so," Tina said.

"That's pretty incriminating, son," the sheriff said to Nate, who'd given up protesting, seeming to realize, as his eyes darted from face to face, that something was going on that would be best served by his silence.

"I'm sorry, Nate," Tina said. "I wish it weren't so. But photos don't lie, do they, Sheriff?"

"No, they generally don't, Miss Carson. Unfortunately, people do."

Tina nodded and shook her head sadly.

"I'm curious, Miss Carson," the sheriff said, his tone deceivingly casual, "how you knew the item was a photo?"

Tina's head, which had been bent down to her cluttered work counter, snapped up. "Why, I . . . you just said so, didn't you, Sheriff?"

"No, I didn't identify the item at all. But you seemed to know that I would find a photo in Mr. Purdy's apartment. Could that possibly be because you put it there?"

"What?" Tina cried. "How could you say such a thing?" She looked to Piper for support. "Tell him that's totally ridiculous, Piper! Why would I do such a thing? All I've done is try to help."

"That's what I once thought, Tina. But now I believe the person you wanted to help was yourself."

"You also," the sheriff said, "seemed awfully comfortable just now having Nate here with you, alone, in your shop, Miss Carson. Someone you believed was a murderer."

"I, I—" Tina sputtered. "The place just cleared out a minute before you got here. Besides, I knew you'd be here soon."

"Did you?" The sheriff slipped out Piper's Internet photo. "You've claimed to have no relationship with Mr. Rosemont prior to your arrival in Cloverdale. You also just stated that photos don't lie. Would you like to explain this to us?"

Tina looked at the photo showing her younger self on the arm of a smiling Alan Rosemont. Her hands started shaking. "Where did you get this? That's not me! What are you trying to do to me?"

"According to the website that displays this photo, that is you, Miss Carson. You are identified by name, though Alan Rosemont—and it's clearly him—is misidentified as Alan Carson, not Rosemont. A reporter's mistake?

Possibly. But the two of you are listed as co-owners of the Swing 'n Bounce Miniature Golf and Trampoline Center in Scranton. I'd say you must have known Alan Rosemont pretty well, wouldn't you?"

Piper watched Tina's face slowly crumble. Nobody spoke for what seemed an eternity as tears filled Tina's eyes.

"Alan treated me very badly," she said, her voice trembling. "I was in love with him, silly fool that I was. I believed in romance and fairy tales back then, and I convinced myself he was perfect and wonderful. My Prince Charming," she said with a pained laugh.

Piper remembered Tina, that night at A La Carte, requesting that Nate sing a particular song from *The Student Prince* and tearing up when he did. Had that been a remnant of her naïve and idealistic self?

"Yes, Sheriff," Tina said, "we co-owned the Swing 'n Bounce—at least I saw it as co-ownership. Alan talked me into believing it would be an amazing investment that would make our fortune. And as soon as that happened we would get married. The thing is, I was the only one who had money to invest and credit for a loan, so it had to be in my name. But Alan had management and business know-how—or so he said. That made it an even balance in my mind."

Tina exhaled loudly. "The business flopped. We had a few good weeks at the beginning, but then problems cropped up and public interest waned, and we began bleeding money. I didn't realize it at the time, of course, since I'd let Alan handle all the finances." She shook her head. "I was so trusting! But Alan saw where things were heading and made plans to save his own skin. One day I woke up and he was gone, along with all the money in our shared bank account. I was left with a pile of bills and no way to pay them. Plus, I'd recently found out I was pregnant."

"Oh, Tina," Piper said softly. "Did Alan know?"

Tina nodded. "That probably was one more reason he took off. I could tell he wasn't thrilled with the news, though he tried his best to cover that." She grimaced. "Not the greatest way to start off a pregnancy—finding yourself abandoned, penniless, and besieged on all sides by creditors. The doctors wouldn't say for sure, but I'm convinced that's what caused my miscarriage." Piper winced, but Tina drew a deep breath and went on.

"It took me years to recover from it all, but I finally got back on my feet and managed to actually build up savings. That's when I discovered where Alan was. It was totally accidental. An acquaintance of mine showed off an antique doll she'd bought at his shop while passing through Cloverdale."

"And you came here to confront him?" the sheriff asked.

Tina shook her head. "I didn't expect any compensation by then. He'd made sure the Swing 'n Bounce was all in my name, so the debts were all mine. Our bank account? As I said, it was shared. He could claim it had been mostly his money, I suppose. It was too long ago. I didn't want to haggle over it with him. What I wanted to do was to make him uncomfortable."

Tina looked at the three skeptical faces and insisted, "Yes! I wanted to remind him daily of his horrible behavior. I wanted him to worry that at any moment I could ruin the reputation he'd built up so carefully in Cloverdale, the reputation that got him elected to the town council and found him a well-to-do, trusting girlfriend. I wanted him to be forever on edge that I might tell Brenda Franklin what he was really like."

"So you did know he was seeing Brenda?" Piper asked.

Tina turned to Piper, her expression pained. "Oh yes, I knew. And when you said Brenda had something to tell you, I worried that Alan had in fact shared his past with her— probably a whitewashed version that put all the blame on me, but still enough to get the sheriff asking questions."

"Was Dennis Isley blackmailing you?" the sheriff asked.

Tina began pacing behind her counter. "That's where the photo came from that I slipped into Nate's guitar case. Dennis snapped it after I fled from the fairgrounds. I didn't mean to kill Alan that night! I didn't! I only wanted to insist he stop harassing me with those endless restaurant regulations and hoops he had me jumping through that he thought would discourage me from settling in Cloverdale. But our argument got nasty, really nasty, and all the anger I thought I'd been rid of came bubbling up so that I couldn't even think straight!

"The last straw was when Alan laughed at me. He turned his back on me and walked away and started blowing on that damned bagpipe! I couldn't stand it. So I picked up a tent stake that was lying nearby and swung it at him. Twice! I didn't intend to kill him. I was just so mad that I needed to hurt him for all he'd done to me. When I realized he was dead, I panicked and ran off."

Tina had been picking up and setting down things on her

work counter as she talked—salt shakers, salad tongs, catsup bottles. She grabbed a striped dish towel and rubbed at her face. "Dennis must have seen the whole thing. He took that cell phone photo of Alan, and another of me standing over Alan holding that stake." She laughed startlingly. "I couldn't very well plant that one at Nate's, could I?" she said, then sobered. "Dennis showed up with his photos later that night and said I'd have to pay him to keep him quiet."

"Did Dennis move Alan's body into my pickle barrel?" Piper asked.

"He did, though I didn't know that right away. That was his surprise for me to find out on my own." She grimaced. "He thought it was a great joke. Remember that 'pickled pink' comment of his? Alan always treated him like scum, and Dennis hated him. He might have wanted to kill him, but he didn't have to. I took care of that. Dennis simply added his own touch of revenge."

"And you pulled Dennis off that roof?" Nate, who'd stayed quiet up until then, spoke up.

"He wanted so much money! I could see it was never going to end. I'd be living in fear as I worked my fingers to the bone to pay him off. When I saw my chance to end that, I knew I had to take it. I didn't try to pin it on you, Nate. Charlotte Hosch did that." Tina's lips twisted with disgust. "I wish I could have pinned it on Charlotte. But not you, Nate." She looked pleadingly at him. "It was driving me crazy to think that you might go to prison for what I'd done."

"But you were willing to send me to prison for Brenda's murder?" Piper asked.

Tina slapped down her towel. "You wouldn't stop

digging! No matter what I tried to do to throw you off or to make you think it wasn't worth it, you kept on poking around!"

"Paint on my storefront or damage to my car wasn't anywhere near as important as clearing Nate's name. But you were willing to burn my place down—and me with it—to save yourself?"

"Don't you dare judge me! Do you think you wouldn't have done the same if you were in my shoes?"

Piper highly doubted that but kept silent. The sheriff, though, had heard enough. He stepped forward.

"Miss Carson, I'm arresting you for the murder of—"

"No!" Tina suddenly grabbed a huge knife from the nearby butcher block. "No, you're NOT arresting me!" She held the knife in front of her.

"Now, Miss Carson, there's no need—"

"I'm not going to prison. I've suffered too much already! Alan deserved exactly what he got. Dennis was as bad as Alan, and when I got rid of him I did the world a favor. You're not going to put me in prison for that. Nobody is!" She waved her knife menacingly.

The sheriff had eased himself in front of Piper. "Just calm down, now, Miss Carson. We can talk about this—"

"I'm done talking! Alan could disappear for nineteen years. I'll do it, too!" Tina stepped out from behind her counter holding the large knife in front of her with both hands. "All of you, move back there." Tina jerked her head toward her storeroom.

Did Tina really believe she could simply lock them up and make an escape? It was insane, Piper thought. But then hadn't Tina been acting irrationally for days? Unfortunately, Piper had kept making allowances, putting it down to stress and lack of sleep.

The sheriff obviously saw he was dealing with madness as he kept his voice even and calm. "No one wants to hurt you, Miss Carson."

"Just move!" Tina swished her knife—which looked dangerously sharp—through the air. "Or else!" She took a step forward.

The sheriff pushed Piper back hard before grabbing a chrome-legged chair. He held it out in front of him. "Miss Carson, put that knife down now!"

"No!" Tina screeched. She reached back with one hand for a glass carafe, half full of hot coffee, and flung it at the sheriff. It didn't have far to go and her aim was spot-on, catching the sheriff full in the face and stunning him, causing him to drop the chair. Tina took that instant to lunge at him with her knife. Before she could stab him, Nate threw himself at her. Tina turned and slashed.

Piper saw blood burst from Nate's arm. She grabbed the closest thing at hand—a chrome napkin dispenser—and threw it at Tina, striking her head hard. Tina faltered, and the sheriff, back in the game, kicked at Tina's legs, sweeping them out from under her. The knife flew from her hands as she fell and Piper ran to stomp on it. The sheriff had Tina's hands behind her in an instant and locked in handcuffs.

As he held her down and radioed for help, Tina wailed and thrashed, finally sobbing uncontrollably. Piper spared her little sympathy as she stepped widely around the two to get to Nate with a clean towel. He had staggered back against a wall and slid down, his face pale as blood flowed between the fingers he held against his wound. Piper pushed his hand off and wrapped the towel around his arm. As she pressed down firmly, he smiled weakly.

"Thanks."

Piper nodded but glanced toward the sheriff. "Actually, I think you're the one who deserves to be thanked."

32

~~~~~~

Piper spotted Will from the picnic table where she sat
with Nate, Amy, and Megan and waved him over. He'd
been flipping burgers for the crowd and finally took a break
to load up his own plate from the huge spread of potluck
dishes being overseen by Aunt Judy and her friends. The
gathering had been planned originally as a modestly sized
celebration of Nate's release from the hospital but had rapidly grown to include most of Cloverdale and was moved
out of necessity from Amy's backyard to the large park
just off the town square.

Nate sat at the head of the rectangular table in a well-
cushioned lawn chair that Uncle Frank had brought specially for him. His left arm rested in a sling on a small
pillow. As Will stepped over the picnic table bench to join
the group, he asked, "How's the arm doing?"

"Pretty well. Doc said I'll be playing guitar again before too long."

"And thank goodness for that," Amy said, taking the glass of lemonade from his right hand and setting it on the table for him. Piper suspected she would have happily spooned bites of food into Nate's mouth if he'd allowed it.

"Hey, Nate! Welcome back!" two people called out on their way to the food tables.

"Everyone's been great," Nate said, after acknowledging the pair. He looked bewildered by the attention that had started when he'd first arrived and been fairly mobbed by townspeople patting him on the back and wishing him well. "But they're acting as if I were some kind of hero, which I'm not."

"My father would have been stabbed—who knows how badly—if it weren't for you," Amy said. "He told me so himself."

"That crazy woman," Megan said, shaking her head as she scraped up the final crumbs of her cherry cheesecake. "But the scary thing is that nobody spotted that about her until you figured it out, Piper."

"I kick myself for not recognizing it sooner and for letting myself be too distracted by the others on our 'possibles' list."

"But Gordon and Lyella Pfiefle seemed so likely!" Amy protested, then looked around and lowered her voice. "Remember those scratches on his neck the day after Alan Rosemont's murder?"

Piper smiled to herself. Aunt Judy had whispered an explanation for that after Piper had confided her earlier suspicions of the couple. But Piper wasn't about to pass it on.

"Lyella and Gordon are said to have a very . . ." Aunt Judy had paused, searching for a delicate way to put it. ". . . an extremely loving and active married life." She'd looked at Piper meaningfully. "I got this on good authority from Millie Tildenbocker. She lived next door to them in the apartment they rented before they bought their house, and the apartments apparently had very thin walls. Poor Millie Tildenbocker took to wearing earplugs in order to sleep."

Which might also explain why Gordon had rushed home with the cover excuse of fixing a flat tire for Lyella the afternoon that Dennis Isley was killed. Lyella had demonstrated to Piper very clearly that she held her husband in high regard and brooked no improper interest from other women. But murder, it appeared, was never considered as a deterrent.

"And then Robby Taylor," Megan pointed out. "He seemed to need a lot of money in such a hurry, pushing his mother to sell her house. We were sure he'd been paying blackmail to Dennis."

"Well, it turns out there were other, legitimate reasons for Robby needing money in a hurry," Piper said. "It will all come out soon anyway, so I can tell you what Dorothy Taylor explained just yesterday to Aunt Judy and me. It seems Robby has behaved fairly unprofessionally by having relationships with female clients at the gym and now finds himself in the middle of two separate paternity suits."

Megan gasped and Will's eyebrows shot up, but Amy and Nate looked amused, possibly remembering the story that Piper had shared with them of Dorothy Taylor's father and the woman who'd shown up on her doorstep. They might have been thinking, as Piper did, that Robby had much more in common with his grandfather than an interest in astronomy.

Megan looked on the verge of a comment when Erin walked up. Erin had left the table earlier with the explanation that there was someone she wanted to speak to.

"Megan," she asked, "didn't you say Ben was going to be here?"

Megan rolled her eyes at mention of her brother. "Oh, some bigwig in his insurance company is making a surprise visit to his office. Ben was beside himself all morning getting ready for it."

"Insurance company?" Nate asked. "Which insurance company is that?"

Megan looked at Nate with surprise. "USIA. Why?"

Nate suddenly looked highly uncomfortable, and Piper somehow didn't think it had anything to do with his injury. "You don't happen to know the name of this bigwig, do you?" he asked.

Megan stared at Nate, a strange expression crossing her face. "Now that you mention it, it was Purdy, the same as yours. Randall Purdy. I thought at the time what a funny coincidence, but I'm thinking now that maybe it's not a coincidence. Do you know him, Nate?"

Nate squirmed in his chair and looked over his shoulder before he answered. "Yeah, kind of." He looked at Amy apologetically. "He's my father, and also the CEO of USIA."

"What!" Amy cried along with most of those at the table. "Why didn't you tell me?"

"That I had a father? I thought—"

"That your father is the CEO of Ben's insurance company!"

Nate winced. "We're not exactly on speaking terms."

"Why don't we let you two talk about this," Piper suggested, half rising. Will was barely a split second behind her. Megan, however, looked glued to her chair.

"No," Nate said, waving them down with his good hand. "It's okay. I owe you all the explanation, though it's probably pretty boring."

Piper doubted that, but sat down quietly and waited.

"Dad," Nate started, "can be pretty bullheaded. I probably take after him to some degree, though I went along with a lot of what he wanted as I was growing up—just because I was a kid, I suppose, and, well, he turned out to be right most of the time.

"But one thing he was definitely wrong on was what to do with my life after school. Dad made a pretty good living in the insurance business, and he thought I should do the same. I tried it for a while, just to be fair, I guess, but I could see it wasn't for me. I loved my music, but Dad always pooh-poohed music as something you do only in your spare time—if you had spare time. That was always frustrating, that he couldn't see how important it was to me. But, as I said, I tried to see things his way, even though as time went on I hated the insurance business more and more."

Amy's eyes suddenly lit up. "Was that what you meant when you said you knew of a way to search out Robby Taylor's credit rating?"

"Uh, yeah. We're not supposed to let that get around, but there are ways of finding those things out if we want."

"Oh, I'm so glad. I was worried it might have been something worse! Though not *really* worried," she amended.

"Well, anyway," Nate went on, "the final straw came

when Dad began pushing me hard to start seeing the daughter of one of his big-deal insurance buddies. I mean, browbeating me into a career he wanted was bad enough, but to call the shots on my love life? I mean, first of all this girl came on all sweetness and light to Dad and her own father, but believe me, she was a Leona Helmsley in the making. When Dad couldn't see that, I packed up and told him I was out of there."

Piper saw that that last boundary cross had won over Amy's approval of Nate's action. Megan and Erin looked pretty sympathetic, too.

Erin suddenly piped up. "Oh, there's Ben! And there's a man in a suit with him. Is that your father, Nate?"

Nate jerked around to see, then swiveled in several directions as though deciding which way to run first. But Randall Purdy, since that's who Piper figured it was, caught sight of his son, and Nate froze as the two locked eyes. Nobody at the table spoke until Amy patted Nate on his good arm.

"Go to him, Nate," she said.

Nate turned to her, then nodded, launching himself out of his chair and heading over to his father. Piper watched as Randall Purdy met Nate halfway, hesitated, then enveloped his son in a great bear hug, a hug that Nate returned as best he could with one usable arm.

"Oooh," Megan and Erin said simultaneously, and Piper saw Amy's eyes blink rapidly. Piper felt Will's hand cover hers, and she turned to smile, blinking once or twice herself.

Nate and his father obviously had a lot of catching up

to do, though standing in the middle of a gathering of most of Cloverdale wasn't the best place to do it. Nate made a start, though, by bringing his father over to the table to meet his friends.

"This is Amy," he said, beginning with her. "A very special person in my life."

Amy stood to shake hands, but Randall Purdy, showing a strong, outgoing personality that went with his tall, barrel-chested frame, would have none of it, giving her an enthusiastic hug instead. "I'm very happy to meet you, young lady," he said as Nate beamed beside him.

Nate introduced the others, ending with Piper. "You might have found me in very different circumstances—like, maybe in jail—if it weren't for Piper," he said.

Randall Purdy nodded. "I got the gist of the story from Ben Schaeffer on the way over here. I owe you a debt of gratitude, Miss Lamb."

"It was a team effort," Piper said. "And we were all happy to do it. You have a great son, Mr. Purdy."

Purdy put his arm around Nate's shoulders, careful to avoid pressing the bandaged arm, and said, "That I do, ma'am," his voice suddenly husky.

With that, Will popped up. "Have a seat, here, sir. Piper and I will get you something to eat."

Piper rose quickly, signaling Megan and Erin with a look to do the same, then left Nate to begin his long-overdue talk with his father. As they headed toward the food tables, Piper spotted Ben Schaeffer talking rapidly to Sheriff Carlyle, who was glancing in Nate's direction, eyebrows raised. She thought the sheriff might be fairly pleased to hear what Ben was telling him and expected to see him make his way over to the table where his daughter still sat before too long.

Will started loading up a plate for Randall Purdy, and Piper filled a tall paper cup with iced tea, having no idea what the man's preferences were but figuring what he ate or drank were the least of his concerns at the moment.

"Let me take them over," Erin offered, taking the plate and cup from Will and Piper. They watched as she carried them to the table and slipped both in front of Mr. Purdy as unobtrusively as a butterfly lighting on a leaf. She then turned to her left, where Ben now stood by himself looking just a bit lost, and walked in his direction with a warm smile.

Good for her, Piper thought, and said to Will, "I think Ben just might have a chance at getting over Amy before too long."

Will replied, "Huh?" and Piper simply smiled.

She and Will strolled off, greeting others and pausing to chat here and there, and Piper enjoyed the calm contentment that gradually settled on her. Cloverdale had given her a few stressful moments—okay, a lot of stressful moments—but things had definitely taken a turn for the better. There was healing to do, but Piper felt that all in all, coming to Cloverdale and opening Piper's Picklings had been a good decision. Walking along with her hand in Will's added greatly to that feeling until Will suddenly released hers.

"Jim Reilly is waving me over. Probably something to do with the grill. I'll just be a minute."

Piper nodded, and as she watched him go off, her cell phone rang. *Who in the world would be calling her when everyone in town is right here?* she wondered. But as she reached into her pocket she had an uneasy thought, which a glance at the display proved right.

"Yes, Scott?"

"Hey, Piper! Glad I caught you. How's it going?"

"Fine, Scott. What's up?"

"Good news! I'm coming home."

"Ah! Well, that's nice to know, Scott," Piper hedged. "You mean you're heading back to Albany?"

"Oh, I'll probably get over there, eventually. But first I want to see you! I'll be back in the States by Monday, and I'm heading straight for Cloverdale!"

Piper knew her mouth had dropped open because she suddenly had to spit out a gnat. Scott was coming to Cloverdale? And he expected she'd be waiting for him with open arms?

"Didn't you get my e-mail? I thought I explained everything very clearly. We're not a couple anymore."

"Oh, sure, I know I haven't been the greatest fiancé. But travel has been so great for me, Piper. I've learned to appreciate the simpler things in life. Which is why I'm also thinking I might settle in Cloverdale myself. Nothing definite, you understand, but it sounds like the perfect place for the person I've become. Just you wait till I get there. We'll have so much—" The connection began breaking up. Piper heard one or two more words before it was lost altogether. She looked at her phone, then turned it off and stood staring blankly into space.

Scott coming to Cloverdale? Maybe settling in Cloverdale?

"Piper, you look like you just bit into a sour pickle," Mrs. Peterson teased as she walked by.

A sour pickle? Piper shook her head, disagreeing. Nothing about pickles ever made her feel this disturbed. Pickles were wonderful, dependable, predictable. What Piper really felt was that this sudden change in her *It's a Wonderful Life* picture was as unsettling as discovering a bug in the middle of a jelly jar.

But she reminded herself that Scott was free to live anywhere he chose. If he picked Cloverdale, she would deal with it. Life, after all, was all about adjusting, wasn't it? If you lived in the mountains, you boiled your canning jars a bit longer. If you suddenly had more pounds of tomatoes than anyone could possibly eat, you made catsup. And if a man you were once in love with came to town and started knocking on your door while your new boyfriend was calling on the phone, you—Piper stopped to think. You did what? Then she grinned.

You enjoyed it!

At that, Piper turned toward the dessert table and grabbed one of Aunt Judy's homemade cookies topped with mango jam. Before she bit into it, she paused, then reached back to pick up a second one. That one was for Will.

Recipes

WATERMELON RIND PICKLES

YIELD: 3 PINTS

8 cups prepared watermelon rind cubes (1 large
   watermelon)
½ cup pickling salt
2 quarts water
2 cups white vinegar
3 cups white or brown sugar
1 thinly sliced lemon
2 cinnamon sticks
1 teaspoon allspice berries
1 teaspoon whole cloves

Trim off the skin and pink flesh from the watermelon rind and cut into 1-inch squares. Put into a large bowl with a mixture of ½ cup salt and 2 quarts of water, cover, and soak overnight at room temperature. Drain in a colander and rinse and soak in fresh water, then drain again. Cover again with fresh water, then simmer until the cubes are tender. Drain.

Mix together vinegar, sugar, lemon, and spices tied in a cheesecloth bag and simmer for 5 minutes. Add the rind cubes and cook until the syrup is clear.

Ladle the hot rind and syrup into clean, hot pint jars, leaving ½ inch headspace. Use a damp paper towel to wipe the rims of the jars, then put a flat lid and ring on each, turning to finger tight. Process in a boiling water bath canner for 10 minutes.

SWEET-AND-SOUR ZUCCHINI PICKLES

YIELD: 4 PINTS

8 cups sliced small zucchini
2 onions, quartered and thinly sliced
¼ cup pickling salt
Cold water
2½ cups cider vinegar
1½ cups sugar
1 tablespoon mixed pickling spices

2 teaspoons mustard seeds
4 sprigs fresh dill

Scrub zucchini and cut into ¼-inch rounds. Add to sliced onions in a large bowl and sprinkle with salt, tossing, then cover with water and let stand for 2 hours. Drain and rinse well.

In a nonreactive pot (stainless steel or ceramic), mix vinegar, sugar, pickling spices, and mustard seeds, bring to a boil, and simmer for 2 minutes. Remove from heat and stir in zucchini and onions. Let stand for 1½ hours, then bring to a boil and cook for 1 minute.

Put a sprig of dill in each of 4 clean, hot jars. Ladle zucchini and liquid into jars leaving ½-inch headspace. Use a chopstick or knife to remove air bubbles, then wipe the rims with a damp paper towel. Seal each jar with a flat lid and ring, turning to finger tight. Process in a boiling water canner for 10 minutes.

Pickling Tips

- Use only fresh, high-quality, unbruised produce.

- Process produce as soon as possible or refrigerate immediately.

- Use a vinegar with 4–6 percent acetic acid or a 40–60 grain strength.

- Use pickling salt, which does not contain the additives of table salt.

- Avoid hard water, which will cause dark, discolored pickles.

- Use fresh herbs and spices, stored in glass jars, within a year of opening.